CHRONOS ONE

CHRONOS ONE

Dean Palmer

ELITE

Xulon Press Elite
2301 Lucien Way #415
Maitland, FL 32751
407.339.4217
www.xulonpress.com

Unless otherwise indicated, Scripture quotations taken from the Holy Bible, New International Version (NIV). Copyright © 1973, 1978, 1984, 2011 by Biblica, Inc.™. Used by permission. All rights reserved.

Edited by Xulon Press.

Printed in the United States of America.

ISBN-13: 978-1-54563-831-6

Prologue
August, 1987

The wind cut like daggers across his face. Commander Joshua Stark's throat tensed with every breath. His toes throbbed. He held his MP5-ST3 rifle in ready position, his gloved finger extended next to the trigger. Grateful for the snug cap over his ears, he pulled the hood of his parka back and squinted through protective goggles at the frozen wasteland. Several meters ahead, an icy slope emptied onto a solid white sea. Barely visible through blowing snow, the dark metal sail of a Los Angeles-class submarine stabbed through the ice in the distance.

He forced a deep breath to ease the heaviness in his chest. *Lord, get me home from this one. Just one more chance.*

He checked his watch for the umpteenth time, grimaced, and examined the rest of his white-camouflaged SEAL team. They knelt in a broad circle and scanned the horizon. He stood and slung his rifle over his shoulder. The snow crunched beneath his boots as he made his way to the team of scientists at the center of the circle.

He shouted over the whistling wind. "Dr. Sekulow, we're out of time."

A short man in his twenties with round glasses knelt beside a stretcher as another man mounted a snowmobile to tow it away. He checked the frozen corpse one last time and reached for the zipper on the cadaver pouch. "Just finishing up, Commander Stark."

Stark saw the corpse and furrowed his brow. Its head was tilted up and to one side, its disfigured face contorted in an expression of pain, its tightfisted right arm clenched over its abdomen. "It looks like your 'ice man' was holding something."

Dr. Sekulow closed the bag and gestured to the driver, who sped away in the snowmobile, body bag in tow. "He was, Commander."

He opened a pouch, retrieved a gold cylinder with pointed ends and held it with careful reverence. The device stretched just over a foot long, with what looked like two rows of large, square-cut crystals set near each end.

"What is it?"

"No idea, but it's ancient."

Stark wanted to hit something. He closed his eyes and turned away. "So we've risked our lives for some museum piece?"

"Not just any museum piece, Commander. This one's been transmitting a complex code for three days."

Stark stared back at the device. "Transmitting. Is it Russian?"

"It isn't like any Soviet technology I've ever seen, and I'm certain our—*ice man* predates the Cold War by thousands of years."

"So why did it start now?"

"I'm guessing it activated when enough of the permafrost melted for it to surface. I doubt if the Soviets even know it exists."

Stark scanned the horizon. "Yeah, speaking of the Soviets, Doctor, we've gotta leave. They can never know we were here."

"The snowmobile will come back for me shortly."

"We can't wait. The president won't be happy if we demolish *glasnost* by being discovered."

Sekulow drew his shoulders back. "President Reagan personally authorized this mission, Commander. It was my technology for his Strategic Defense Initiative that detected the signal in the first place."

"Talk and walk, Doctor."

Sekulow pinched his lips together and opened the pouch to reinsert the device. An amber stone at one end glowed brightly. "Wait a minute."

A bright flash and a crack drew their attention behind them. About ten meters away, blue bursts of light and bolts of energy emanated from a single point just above the ground. Then a brilliant, blue field opened and stretched high above them. A massive shadow grew within the opening.

Stark pulled Sekulow away. "Run, Doctor."

The other SEALs looked up, eyes wide. A deafening roar pierced the air and the ground shook. Stark ran with Sekulow as cracks of gunfire erupted behind them. One of the SEALS grunted and fell. A gargantuan spear whizzed by Stark's head and plunged into the snow. Another man's yell ended with a gruesome *crunch*.

Stark reached the top of the slope with Sekulow. "Run, Doctor, and don't look back. We'll give you time to escape." He helped the doctor over and watched him slide down.

The gunfire and shouts continued. Stark wheeled around and squinted through the blowing snow. The last three of his team stood a few meters ahead, firing at a freakishly large form, at least ten meters tall. Its angry roars had become desperate screams. Stark stepped forward, aimed, then opened fire. After a few seconds the giant fell, silent.

Stark's heart pounded. *What was that?* Blood-curdling shrieks ripped through the air. Dozens of shadows appeared in the snow, and an arrow whistled past Stark's head. He aimed, fired, and downed his target, then another. His men followed suit.

A massive volley of arrows whistled by. Stark's men grunted and fell. He stepped back to dive down the slope for cover, but an impact pushed him back hard. He tripped and slid down on his back. Searing pain tore through his chest. He struggled to stop and pull himself up but couldn't move. Only then did he notice the arrow protruding from his chest.

Stark hit the slope's bottom and gasped for air. *This is it, isn't it?* He tried to raise his weapon but couldn't feel his arm. Blood filled his throat. He coughed and spattered the snow red.

He watched Sekulow's shadow disappear into the snow in the distance and scanned the top of the slope. The enemy didn't follow.

His vision tunneled, and each breath was more difficult than the last. Then it hit him. *No going home. No more chances.*

He clenched his teeth, and bitter tears filled his eyes. He squeezed them shut, and the tears streamed down his temples. "Son... Will... I'm so sorry." He opened his eyes and gasped. "Lord... *please* help him."

Conflicting voices swarmed his ears. *Just relax, Joshua Stark. It'll be over soon.*

No, Joshua. Don't do it. Don't give up.

A cold rush swirled through his head. He squinted through his narrowing circle of vision.

Breathe out and relax. You're almost there.

No! Fight! Don't give up! Fight!

He gasped a heavy, labored breath, forced it out, and drew again. A blue light shone down on him, and a dark silhouette appeared.

Searing pain tore through his chest. He grunted and struggled to draw breath, but his chest seized in a painful spasm. He heaved for air and got none. He heaved again.

Fight!

The world went black.

wwwwwwwwww

The basketball swooshed through the net and bounced on the pavement with a hollow ping. Twelve-year-old Will Stark snatched it out of the air with both hands, spun, dribbled away from the driveway-mounted hoop, spun, and shot. *Swoosh.* He leapt forward, snatched the ball again after only one bounce, and executed a perfect layup. *Swoosh.*

Tires rubbed the pavement. A car rounded the corner near his house and crushed the layer of dry, brown leaves. Will's heart leapt, and he shouted with a wide-eyed grin, "Dad." He let the ball bounce away and sprinted to the end of the drive. The car passed slowly and pulled into a drive, two doors down.

Will slumped, looked to one side, and puffed a frustrated burst of air. He heard that a team from his father's unit had gotten back. *Come on, today* has *to be the day.* He drew a crisp breath and his face brightened. He dove into the garage, retrieved his football, and dashed around the house. Leaves crunched with each step. He cupped a hand over his eyes to ward off the cloudy glare and gazed down the street. *Yeah, better. I'll see them coming sooner.*

He grasped the football, stepped back, and passed it through a wooden target his father had built. He ran to retrieve the ball, squinted to scan the road, ran back, paused, and passed it again.

He grinned. His father was going to be proud. His gaze fell. *Please Dad, be proud this time.*

The clouds drifted lower. Cold mist dampened the leaves and brown grass. Will shivered, zipped his jacket, and flipped his collar. He stared at the target, stepped back, and raised the football. The faint rush of an approaching car pierced the fog. Will squinted hard and just made out the car's fuzzy silhouette. *Finally!* He dropped the ball and sprinted around the house. The car rounded the corner. It wasn't his father's. Will blinked and drew back beside the house.

Maybe it's someone visiting the neighbors. He swallowed, stayed hidden and stared through wide eyes. The car crept into his drive and squeaked to a stop. Will's heart pounded. Both front doors opened, and a man and woman in Navy dress blues stepped out. Will's chest nearly pulled him to the ground. He forced his tense muscles to draw breath.

The two officers stopped at the front door, swept the mist off their uniforms, and rang the doorbell.

Will blew a quivering puff of steam through his tense throat and reached out to lean on the house. He choked down the lump in his throat and struggled to keep from throwing up. He peered around the corner.

The front door opened. Will drew back around the corner and strained to hear.

"Mrs. Stark, we regret to inform you..."

Will doubled over and covered his ears.

CHAPTER 1

Present Day

The voice from the loudspeaker echoed across the hot, desert sand. "Test sequence in two minutes and counting. All non-essential personnel clear the test site. All non-essential personnel clear the test site."

Lieutenant Colonel Will Stark stood atop an elevated platform with his arms folded and a pair of binoculars draped over his chest. An array of mobile labs, support vehicles, and heavily armed military vehicles stretched in either direction.

He tugged at his flight suit, and his muscles complained about their last workout while his mind reviewed every facet of their mission. But deep beneath his rugged exterior, a thousand questions nagged his heart. *Should we have done this test airborne? What if something goes wrong? What if I do something wrong? Am I up to this?*

Will pushed the thoughts down hard. He hated fear, and he hated the insecure boy inside him even more than his father had. *There's no room for fear, Will. No room for failure.*

He took a deep breath. *Just don't* let *anything go wrong. All according to plan.*

He lifted the binoculars and stared in the distance.

Dr. Sekulow, with a few more wrinkles and a lot less hair, tucked the tail of his white lab coat and sat at a nearby workstation. He adjusted his glasses and wiped sweat off his bald streak. "Good morning, Colonel Stark. So, do you think your engineer is ready?"

"Chris is ready, Dr. Sekulow." *If only I could be that certain.*

Thirty meters in front of the platform, Lieutenant Commander Nur "Chris" Saif-ad-Deen leaned over a workstation within a crude apparatus suspended above the desert floor by a combination of struts and cables. Two technicians sat on either side of him and a dozen others trotted away from the test site toward the row of labs and trailers.

Behind Chris and the other two men, the pointed cylindrical device, code-named *Snowman,* stood mounted in a solid support frame. A fine laser-emitting tool pointed precisely into one of the crystals, held by a robotic arm, awaiting the command to fire.

Will glanced around the platform. "Has anyone seen Major Dalton?"

Major Katherine "Kat" Dalton climbed the stairs behind the platform, grasped her green flight suit at the waist to pull it taut, and took a seat near Will. She stared at the apparatus in the distance. "I still wish you'd call me Kat, sir."

Will watched her sit but then forced his eyes away. *Still off limits, Will.* He refocused on Chris. "He seems off his game today."

"He didn't sleep well last night. Something down there keeps creeping him out."

"He said that?"

"No, our resident Barbie doll did."

"You mean Dr. Michaels?"

A slender, long-haired brunette with a sharp business skirt beneath her white lab coat, Dr. Jamie Michaels turned from her workstation next to Sekulow. When Kat didn't meet her gaze, she dropped hers and looked away.

Kat scrutinized her sneakers. "No heels today, Jamie?" Jamie didn't bother turning to Kat. "Even Barbies need to be able to walk in the sand, Kat."

The loudspeaker interrupted. "Test sequence in one minute, thirty seconds."

Jamie looked down at her terminal, and a frown crept over her flawless face. She spoke to Chris in her headset. "Good luck, Chris... and be careful, okay?" She bit her lip and glanced at the others before continuing in a lower voice. "I love you."

Will pretended like he wasn't paying attention. He had considered objecting to their relationship many times, but in truth he envied them. He stared through his binoculars and swallowed in a vain attempt to moisten his parched throat.

Chris's voice squawked from a speaker on Jamie's workstation with a humorous tinge of rebuke. "Thank you, *Deputy Director Michaels*."

Kat folded her arms. "We should be running the exercise airborne... and by his side."

Will felt a rush of heat. "Why didn't you say so before?"

Kat glared into the distance. "Would you have listened?"

Will massaged his temples with one hand. *Man, I get that command is lonely, but does every crew I command have to be so difficult? I miss flying... just flying.*

Will took a deep breath and touched a comm panel nearby. "Chris, what's your status?" On a nearby monitor he watched Chris reach to his own comm panel.

"Just fine, sir, but I really wish…"

"We already talked about it, Chris. Flying introduces too many variables right now." *Why can't everyone just get with the program?*

"Understood, sir."

Will deactivated the comm link and whispered. "Come on. There's no room for failure."

Kat heaved a bitter sigh and looked away.

Will's face flushed. He didn't mean to say that out loud.

"Test sequence in one minute and counting."

Will lifted his binoculars, watched Chris and his team, and furrowed his brow. He saw Chris shake his head, as if something was bothering him. One of the technicians gave Chris's shoulder a reassuring squeeze.

Come on, Chris, your intelligence is off-the-chart, so whatever it is, deal with it.

"Test sequence in thirty seconds…"

In the corner of his eye, Will saw Kat grasp the back of her neck. She shot to her feet and turned around, her hand still on her neck.

Will jerked his head back. "What?"

A gust of wind swept over the test site and snapped the shade canopy loose over Chris and the technicians. One of them hurried over to secure it.

"Test sequence in ten seconds… nine… eight…"

A support cable snapped, and the platform lurched. The technician working on the canopy lost his balance and fell.

4

A buzzer drew Will's attention to a warning light in front of Jamie. She focused on the display and shouted, "They never engaged the laser emitter clamps. It's out of alignment."

Will pounded the comm panel. "Chris, abort."

Chris didn't respond. Will realized the lights were out on his comm panel. He turned to Jamie. "We need comms now."

Jamie fell to her knees and frantically checked her systems. "Comms are down. Where's the bullhorn?"

Will watched through his binoculars as Chris looked at the technician on the platform floor, then back at the device. "Come on, Chris. Figure it out." He saw the urgency register on the engineer's face.

"...two... one..."

Chris snapped back around. "Abort the jump!"

The laser fired.

Will's gut wrenched. The blinding flash told everyone something was terribly wrong.

CHAPTER 2

Jamie jumped to her feet. "Chris!"

The men and part of the platform disappeared, but the field around them was too small. It left part of the surrounding apparatus behind, supported by hollowed-out remnants of the platform.

Cables now suddenly connected to nothing fell to the ground, and the remaining structure collapsed inward on the globe of empty space left behind.

Will's heart raced and his arms shook. *Chris! Please God let him be all right.* He bounded off the platform and barely touched the ground as he sprinted across the desert sand. The others scrambled behind him. *Control, Will. Control the situation.* He reached the site and heard Kat right on his heels. Jamie arrived soon after and covered her mouth, her eyes wide. On the ground amidst the debris, a shoe lay on its side on a growing pool of red sand.

She turned to Dr. Sekulow, who limped toward them, breathless. "It was supposed to be a one-hour jump, right?" She turned to Will.

Kat bored a hole through Will's forehead with a glance and turned away.

Will realized the whole team was staring at him. His chest was about to explode. *Do something, Will!* He put his hands on his hips and looked around the site. *Everyone's counting on me. I have to do something.*

He put his hand on his forehead as his greatest fear choked his breath away. *I don't know what to do.*

Dr. Sekulow's voice trembled. "We have to wait."

Will turned away from all the staring faces and looked up at the crude—and wrecked—replica of the spacecraft they were training to fly.

ⱱⱱⱱⱱⱱⱱⱱⱱⱱⱱⱱⱱ

Only a year earlier, he had stared up at the real thing for the first time in the hangar at Kennedy Space Center. A delta-winged vessel that more resembled a sleek, supersonic jet than a lumbering rocket or space shuttle, her long, narrow nosecone pointed directly over his head. He strolled around the ship, gazed up and down, and expertly noted every detail: the swept wings, the narrow, rectangular thruster cones, the small, maneuvering thrusters above and below, and the large, ventral thrusters under the fuselage and wings. *Chronos* was a vessel unlike any other, a vision of technological beauty.

He took a deep breath, returned to his position in front of her nose, and lifted his gaze again. The proud vessel seemed to meet his gaze, and for just a moment he was floating. But then he remembered his father's stare and settled firmly to the ground. His twelve-year-old voice cried out, "Don't go, Dad. What if something goes wrong? What will I do? I don't know what to do."

His father's angry words echoed over and over in his head. "Stop it, Will. I've told you over and over, my work is important, and it takes me away from home a lot. Now grow up and start taking care of your mother like a man."

"But Dad..."

Will's father silenced him with a stern look and an open hand in front of his face. "Will, you have responsibilities, and this attitude is unacceptable. We'll talk about this when I get back." The final point gashed his heart. His father's index finger pointed indignantly in Will's face had only made the moment worse. "Remember, Son, there's no room for failure."

It was the last time Will saw his father.

Will had lived by that mantra ever since. He made dead-level sure *always* to know what to do, and he left no room for failure. He served his country better than anyone else, even his father. Or so he hoped.

But now, standing in front of *Chronos,* that old and all-too-familiar sense of dread and doubt welled up in Will's heart, and he couldn't put his finger on the source. *What if something goes wrong? Why am I doing this? What if everything goes right, but no one knows about it?*

Will relaxed a little. *Yeah, maybe that's it. I've always hated classified missions, and this one's classified into oblivion. Yeah, that's definitely it.*

His mind did what it was told and calmed down, but his heart didn't buy it for one second.

He had been staring at the ship a long time when a loud, metallic bang echoed from across the hangar. The tall doors cracked open, and the sunset's blinding light streaked across the floor. Thunder from an approaching storm rumbled past, and a gust of wind swept in and cooled Will's face. A man and woman, each carrying a duffle bag, stepped in and paused, letting their eyes adjust to the dim light. They wore dress uniforms, hers Air Force blue, his that dark shade of navy blue that might as well be black. It was a rare formality reserved for specific occasions, like reporting in for new assignments. The pair approached Will with a determined pace. Their footsteps echoed across the hollow chamber, and he watched as they glanced at the beautiful spacecraft behind him. Will couldn't stop staring at the woman. He had never seen such deep, blue eyes.

Hands off, Will. You're her commander.

The hangar doors closed behind them and punctuated their arrival with another echoing bang. It shook Will from his trance.

The woman, senior to her counterpart only by date-of-rank, dutifully assumed the "position of honor" and walked to his right. As they stopped and rendered salutes, she reported in for both of them. "Sir, Major Katherine Dalton and Lieutenant Commander Nur..." She paused and cleared her throat. Her cheeks flushed red.

The man beside her held his salute, his face still frozen at attention, and turned his eyes toward her.

Will stifled his own smile. He knew that as a naval officer, the man named Nur wouldn't normally render a salute in this situation, but he appeared to be deferring to the Air Force tradition since the major was the senior member.

Mercifully, the naval officer broke the silence, "Saif-ad-Deen..." She sighed and continued, "...reporting as ordered."

Will straightened to attention, raised and dropped his own salute. They dropped their salutes as he extended his hand.

"Call me Kat." The woman shook Will's hand. She turned to her comrade and apologized. "Sorry about that."

Nur smiled. "No problem; I get that a lot." Then he added, "My call sign is Chris. Most of my friends seem to prefer it."

Will lifted his eyebrows and shook his crewman's hand. "Chris?"

Chris shrugged. "It's a long story."

A clap of thunder rolled by, this time louder than before. The hangar's metal roof rang with the strike of intermittent raindrops.

Pleasantries now finished, the three turned to the spacecraft. Chris was the first to reach up and caress the hull. "So here she is."

Kat shook her head. "Why do men always refer to aircraft as 'she'?"

"Oh, it isn't just aircraft," Chris said with mock seriousness. "It's nearly any machine that carries us around and makes us feel stronger."

Will nodded. "Sure. Planes, cars, ships..."

She chuckled. The rain outside grew in intensity, accompanied by louder claps of thunder. Kat narrowed her eyes. Will guessed she was trying to assess her new commander.

Silent and expressionless, Will stared back for a moment, then got straight to business. "I'm sure you're eager to be read into your new mission."

Kat's eyebrows rose. "Read in?"

"Yes, but not here. You came packed?"

Chris lifted a duffel in his left hand. "One bag each."

"Good, bring your bags and follow me."

They stepped from the hangar into the downpour to find a white, windowless C-38, the military version of a Gulfstream G100, its engines already whining, its hatch open, and an Air Force staff sergeant positioned outside the door. One by one they stepped in, shook off the rain, then made their way down the aisle. Will took a seat behind the others and watched as they handed their bags to the sergeant and sat. The hatch closed with a thud, muffling the engine noise. Kat turned back and asked the question Will was waiting for.

"So where are we going?"

"I don't know."

Her mouth fell open for an instant. "You don't know? You don't have a bag, so I thought you had been there."

"I have." He watched the staff sergeant step from the luggage compartment, unseat a nearby headset, and place it on his head. Will looked again at his curious comrades. "I'm sorry, but I can't answer your questions yet."

Kat furrowed her brow, tilted her head slightly, and stared at Will.

The aircraft took off and lurched violently in the wind and rain. Will folded his arms, leaned back, closed his eyes, and tried hard not to think about how much he wanted to be on the other side of the securely locked crew door, firmly in control of the aircraft.

The jet banked steep and pulled up in a tight turn to escape the storm. Fifteen minutes later, the jet reached an altitude above the storm, and the jarring ride settled into smooth flight. The cabin grew quiet, except for the dull roar of the engine. Without moving, Will turned his eyes to Chris, who was shifting around to find a comfortable sleeping position, then to Kat, who was staring at the sergeant removing and stowing equipment at the front of the aircraft. She looked at her watch, shifted in her seat with a heavy sigh, and stared where a window was supposed to be.

The staff sergeant startled Kat from nearby. "It'll be several hours before we arrive, ma'am. Would you like something to drink?"

"No, thank you."

"You're welcome to get some sleep. I promise to wake you before we land."

He returned forward, sat at his tight workstation, and turned a knob to dim the lights. Kat turned to say something to Chris only to see him fast asleep, breathing deeply, his mouth open and head turned to one side. Kat leaned back and folded her arms.

Will smiled a moment before his expression sobered. *If only we had met at another time, another place.*

CHAPTER 3

When Kat awoke, it was to the staff sergeant's voice. "Gentlemen, ma'am, we'll be on the ground in a few minutes." She and Chris stretched and looked back at Will. He gave them a nod. Soon after, the aircraft thudded onto the runway and taxied a short distance to a stop.

When the sergeant opened the aircraft door, Kat was surprised at how dark it was outside. She watched Will with interest as he led the way to the door. *He has fighter pilot written all over him. You know his type, Kat. Keep your distance. Besides, he's your commander.* She scratched her neck with one finger. *Then again, they can't all be that way.* She rolled her eyes and sighed. *Don't make this tough, Kat.*

She followed Will and Chris into cool, dry, night air and breathed in the familiar smell of dust and sand.

Apart from the aircraft, there were no lights visible—anywhere. The sky above the horizon in one direction betrayed the glow of a distant, medium-sized town, but apart from that, starlight reigned supreme, silhouetting small mountains that surrounded the desert valley.

They had only walked a dozen paces when the aircraft door shut behind them, and the whine of the jet's engines grew louder and higher in pitch as it taxied away. The engines blasted them with hot air and dust. She trotted with the others to a safer position and watched the aircraft abandon them.

Suddenly the desert floor ignited as brilliant lines of runway lights sprang to life and stretched across the valley floor. The jet turned, thrust hard down the runway, and soared into the night sky above. Then just as abruptly as before, the runway lights disappeared and left them in darkness. It took a moment for Kat's eyes to adjust again to the darkness.

The glow of Chris's watch drew her attention. Chris checked the time and surveyed the sky and the horizon. She wasn't sure, but it looked like he was noting the position of familiar stars and constellations. Her new commander was watching Chris, too.

He doesn't miss anything, does he?

She waited with interest to see his reaction, but he said nothing. Instead he turned and stared at a small building against a cliff wall across the tarmac.

He started for the building. "This way."

Kat and Chris followed Will around the potholes in the dark, World War II–era pavement. As they neared the lone building, she could just make out a metal door and, to its right, an arched, corrugated metal entry large enough to accommodate a bus or a medium-sized aircraft. The entry was sealed with a solid, metal gate. The building looked like a bunker extending from the mountainside.

What is this, Area 51?

The smaller door cracked open, and light streamed across the ground. Kat lowered her head and squinted at the glare as, one-by-one, they stepped in. A gray rug covered part of the tile floor and hid at least a few of the black scuff marks that littered the room. Black-and-white photos of old aircraft hung on the white, cinder-block walls, and two quiet, older men in grease-stained coveralls sat behind a black metal desk. They looked up from their card game and half-sipped cups of coffee and stared, silent. Behind them was a large, green glass window that obscured whatever lay behind it.

A tall, sharply dressed woman with long, dark hair and small, black-framed, rectangular glasses emerged from a vault door on the opposite side of the small, crude office.

Oh great. It's a human Barbie doll.

The woman's voice was bright and welcoming. "Good evening, Colonel Stark." She shook his hand and gave him a blue card with his photo. "Here's your badge, sir." Then she turned to the other two. "And you must be Major Dalton and Lieutenant Commander Saif-ad-Deen."

Chris looked pleased to hear his name pronounced correctly.

"Welcome to Facility Three-B-Four."

Kat noticed Will shaking his head with a slight grin as he affixed the badge to the collar of his flight suit.

Did I miss a joke?

The woman presented blue cards to Kat and Chris. "These are your temporary badges. You'll need them to get... well, everywhere." She shrugged with a sheepish grin and delicately shook each of their hands.

"I'm Jamie, by the way. Come with me, please." Jamie turned and placed her badge in front of a scanner hidden between books on a shelf. Then she pulled the handle of the large, metal vault door to her left. It didn't budge.

15

"O come on, Charlie, they're with me!" she yelled toward the green window to her right. "What, do you think they're stranded tourists, or something?"

A buzz and a click announced approval, and she pulled the door open. They followed her through a dimly lit, surprisingly large hangar. On one side of the space a row of Humvees painted in desert camouflage engaged in a face-off with three Blackhawk helicopters on the other.

Maybe this is Area 51.

Unlike the office behind them, the hangar floor was spotless. Jamie walked quickly ahead of them. The click of her high heels echoed fiercely off the distant walls. They reached a small, red light on the opposite wall, where she waved her badge in front of a scanner next to the light. The light turned green as a buzzer again announced permission to pass. She pulled another heavy, vault door open and led them through into an immaculate, well-furnished, well-lit, gray anteroom. A plush blue rug, tall potted plants, and several comfortable chairs adorned the comfortable chamber. To their left was another thick, green, imposing window. A few red and green lights from equipment panels were just visible from the other side, along with a few monitors flashing views of the hangar and the tarmac outside. In front of them, a thick, Plexiglas partition separated them from two elevators and a large, vehicle-sized freight elevator. Three cylindrical compartments served as entryways through the foreboding partition.

Jamie turned to the green window and hollered, "Our guests are with me, gentlemen. We'll process them inside."

A dark silhouette behind the green glass responded with a thumbs-up.

"Wait here, please," she said to Kat and Chris. She and Will both scanned their badges and punched codes into keypads to gain access to two of the cylindrical, "man trap" entryways. They followed a set of harsh, recorded instructions, recited their names, placed hands on scanners to each side, and finally bent over to look into a retinal scanner.

Kat was dumbstruck.

Just how many levels of security do they have?

She noticed as Chris tilted his head to get a better view of Jamie, her delicate frame slightly bent, her manicured hands innocently holding her glasses up, her eyes opened wide for the scanner.

Oh yeah. He's lost.

She thumped his shoulder with the back of her hand with a wry grin. He straightened and looked at the floor.

The opposite doors of the cylindrical mantraps opened for Will and Jamie. Jamie stepped to a wide door that appeared to be used for hauling large implements through to the freight elevator. With a flash of her badge, she opened it from inside and ushered them through to the opposite wall, where she flashed her badge against yet another panel. An elevator door obediently opened.

They rode the elevator down in silence. Kat soon felt pressure in her ears. Will and Jamie held their noses and blew a couple of times to equalize the pressure in their ears, so Kat followed their example. She wondered what lay ahead.

Probably some cramped, miserable Cold War-era launch control facility converted into a crude lab. What have I gotten myself into?

Then at last, the elevator slowed to a stop, and the doors opened to a frenzy of activity. She lowered her head and dropped her jaw. Dozens of people walked about or rode in electric carts. They wore an array of tidy, civilian clothes, variously colored coveralls or military working uniforms, all sporting green, red, and orange access badges. Kat noticed how few blue badges there were. Shrill voices, some male and some female, echoed from a PA system, "Dr. Bauer, please report to Lab Six. Chief Master Sergeant Kennedy, please report to the Command Section."

Kat stepped with the others from the elevator into a broad, glaringly lit corridor that stretched to both sides. Directly in front of them, a large, open atrium with high ceilings and soft, warm lighting stood in comfortable contrast to the bright, busy corridor. She scanned the atrium with wide eyes. It comprised a large, comfortable, carpeted lounge area with soft chairs, tables, a cafeteria, a commissary, and quiet lounges. Dozens of people slid trays along the cafeteria line, filled red tumblers at soda fountains, ate, visited, played games around tables, and lounged in easy chairs, reading books. In the middle of the atrium, a fountain sprayed a calming, constant whoosh of water, and on the far wall, a tall, broad waterfall rushed from the ceiling to a pool at the bottom. The air teemed with the rush of water, the murmur of conversations, and the clinking of silverware and dishes. Kat stared, speechless, until the rude "meep meep" of a passing electric cart demanded they clear the way.

Jamie gestured around. "We don't get out much, so they had to give us some amenities. Otherwise, we'd go stir crazy. People work odd shifts here, so the cafeteria is open round-the-clock."

A cart stopped nearby. Jamie smiled at the young driver and took a seat next to him. "Right on time."

On cue, Kat and Chris hefted their bags and followed Will aboard. A few minutes and a couple of turns later, they stopped in front of a set of vault doors.

Jamie exited the cart. "Your quarters are just past these doors. I think you'll find them comfy."

Kat and Chris followed Will and Jamie through the doors into a sizable, comfortable common room. Soft, brown sofas and easy chairs surrounded plush red and brown rugs. Warm lighting, beige wallpaper, and wood trim all contributed to the homey feeling. A large-screen television and green-topped mahogany pool table provided entertainment.

Jamie pointed behind them. "Your rooms are clearly marked. I know you're hungry, tired, and curious, but you need to stay here, sequestered, until you're fully briefed in the morning. The staff," she pointed to two young airmen in uniform at a reception desk to one side, "will see to your every need until then."

Kat broke her silence, "How long will we be here?"

"I'm afraid I have to leave now." Jamie ignored the question and looked at Will. "Sir, the director wants to see you right away." With that, she stepped out and closed the vault door behind her.

Will stepped into his own quarters to retrieve a folder and walked back through to the entry vault. "Be ready at oh-six for breakfast and in-processing."

Kat glared at Will as he badged out of the room, then exhaled hard.

Fighter jocks.

Chris broke the silence, smiled at the airmen behind the desk, and rubbed his hands together in anticipation. "So what can we get to eat around here?" Then he pointed toward the closed vault door with wide eyes. "Oh, and do any of you have her number?"

CHAPTER 4

Will looked down at the wrecked apparatus and wiped his brow with his sleeve. He threw an angry glance at the sun and turned away. *I hate the desert.*

The moment he turned, a dozen technicians looked at him with wide eyes as if expecting him to make everything better. He tightened his lips into thin, white lines, turned away, and ground some gravel into the ground with one boot. Then he pretended to wipe his brow again to dry his eyes.

Chris, Chris. You have to be okay. He took a deep breath and sighed. *Kat's right. We should have been with you.*

He glanced at Kat. She responded with a brief, steely stare.

I can't blame her. She needs someone to be angry at. Heck, I'd be furious.

She placed her hands on her hips, turned to one side, and muttered something. With that image a memory from months before swept over him.

wwwwwwwwwww

It was the day after Will met his crew for the first time. He sat back on his bed in his quarters and enjoyed a rare, quiet moment. He knew the morning had been a busy affair for Kat and Chris, with

21

biometric readings for their badges, a painfully redundant medical checkup, a fitting for their new, mission flight suits, and a long series of completely forgettable administrative headaches for what the military called "in-processing." He grasped a football, turned it in his hands, and remembered simpler days and past successes. He looked at his wall of trophies and awards, the desktop models of an F-22 and the space shuttle *Columbia,* and the sign over his door that read, "There's no room for failure." Dr. Sekulow had gone to great lengths to get as many of Will's personal effects there as possible.

It took a moment for him to notice Kat in the doorway.

She stepped in, glanced at him, then gestured toward the wall of monuments. "Do you mind?"

"Not at all." Will froze and studied her profile while she perused the plaques and trophies. He had been so lost in her deep, blue eyes—and her tough demeanor—the first time they met that he failed to notice much else. No longer in uniform, she had taken her hair from its tight bun and let the loose strands caress her shoulders. Her soft, deep red hair drew his eyes down to her athletic frame. His heart skipped a beat, maybe even two.

As she focused on a plaque's inscription, she moved her lips subtly with the words. The thought of kissing her swept over him. He took in a tense breath and froze. *Did she hear that?*

He was at war with himself. It was easier before when she was tough and guarded. Now she seemed open and relaxed, as if peering out from behind her shield.

Come on, Will, it's hopeless. Even if you leave the mission, she'll be here, and you'll never see her again. If you stay, she'll be your subordinate, and you know *commander–subordinate relationships are bad news.*

Will stood, the football still in his hands. She turned, swept her hair back over one ear, and then looked into his eyes. Her look pierced his soul.

Absolutely not, Will. He swallowed hard. "Can I help you with something, Major Dalton?"

She stepped back, cleared her throat, and looked down. "Sir, we're ready for lunch in the Executive Conference Room." She turned without looking up and hurried out.

Will took another deep breath, followed her out the door, and looked up at the sign as he walked through. *There's no room for failure.* It echoed in his thoughts along with all the cries of self-rebuke.

Lunch that day was a late-afternoon, sequestered event in a blue-carpeted, mahogany-furnished executive conference room. From Kat's demeanor, you'd never know they had just shared an awkward moment.

Not hungry, Will sat at the table, grasped his football just out of view, and turned it in his hands. It always seemed to make him feel better. He tried hard not to stare at Kat as she and Chris devoured their lunch on the opposite side of the table.

Chris swallowed and spoke with the next bite poised near his mouth. "I don't care what you say. It creeped me out."

Kat didn't turn from her food. "I can't believe a scientist of your stature believes in ghosts."

"I don't *believe* in them per se, but I'm telling you, I saw a shadowy figure in our common room last night, and it gave me the creeps."

Will furrowed his brow. *The last thing we need is for someone to go stir crazy.* "When did you see this... figure?"

Kat elbowed Chris with a wry grin. "He was on his way back from a romantic dinner."

Chris' face flushed. "I had dinner with Jamie Mi... Deputy Director Michaels." His eyes widened. "I hope you don't object, sir."

Will shook his head. "Not to the dinner or your company, but you were ordered to remain sequestered in our quarters."

"Well, I figured since I was with the deputy director, and since she was the one who told us to remain sequestered in the first place, it must be okay."

Will turned the football in his hands and pondered the other subject. "Be sure to let me know if you see anything else out of the ordinary. Both of you."

Kat's eyes were cold and hard. "You're not gonna question his competence over this are you?"

"No, but I need to know how you're both doing if we're gonna trust each other with our lives."

"Yeah, about that. Just when do we find out what our mission is?"

"Right after lunch."

The declaration brought the meal to a hasty end. Kat and Chris swallowed a few large, barely chewed bites and guzzled what remained of their drinks.

Kat wiped her mouth with a cloth napkin. "So let's get on with it."

A door at one end of the conference room opened and revealed a glimpse of Dr. Sekulow's opulent, executive-style office. Still wearing a gray suit and white lab coat, he stepped in, followed immediately by Jamie, who wore another sharp business skirt, her own white lab coat, and those killer high heels of hers.

Chris straightened in his seat.

Will stood, and Kat and Chris followed suit. Then a tall, distinguished man in a dark suit joined Dr. Sekulow and Jamie. Will glanced at the stranger's green badge. He didn't know him, and he didn't like surprises.

Will turned to Dr. Sekulow and gestured toward Kat and Chris. "Dr. Sekulow, may I present Major Katherine Dalton and Lieutenant Commander, Doctor," he added thoughtfully, "Nur Saif-ad-Deen."

Chris lowered his head and grimaced. Will had to admit combining military rank with academic credentials felt a little ostentatious.

Will turned to Kat and Chris. "Dr. Sekulow is the program director. You've already met the program's deputy director, Jamie."

The tall gentleman remained silent. Dr. Sekulow took a few broad steps toward the crew, secured his round, wire-framed glasses, then extended his hand up to Kat.

"Major Dalton," he said simply as he moved to Chris, "...and Dr. Saif-ad-Deen."

Chris returned the handshake and shuffled uncomfortably.

Will offered, "I think he prefers Chris, sir."

"Ah yes," Dr. Sekulow squeaked back, turning again to Chris. "Arab culture. Saif-ad-Deen was your father's name, right?"

"Yes, sir."

"Well we can't go around calling you by your father's name, can we? In Arab parlance, you'd normally be Dr. Nur, wouldn't you— Nur, son of Saif-ad-Deen?"

Will watched with interest to see how Chris reacted. Based on what he had observed so far, he wondered whether Chris might feel insulted or, on the other hand, whether he might try to find a humorous response that wouldn't insult the director's rank.

Chris avoided both extremes. "Yes, sir."

"Well then..." the director trailed off; then his voice brightened. "I'll call you Dr. Chris."

Chris blinked. Kat smirked.

Dr. Sekulow turned to his quiet comrade. "I'd like to introduce you all to Dr. Hans Aelter."

Dr. Aelter stepped forward quietly and extended his hand to Kat and Chris.

"Dr. Aelter joined us from Germany more than twenty years ago. He's the genius behind the *Chronos* spacecraft, but he's too modest to say so."

Dr. Aelter grinned. His German accent was subtle and just a bit aristocratic. "You're too kind, my friend." After shaking Chris's hand, he bent over and kissed Kat's. Her eyes widened for an instant, but she managed a gracious smile when he looked up. Then, after he gazed into her eyes long enough to make her feel uncomfortable, he pulled himself away. He stepped to Will, looked intently at him with narrowed eyes, and extended his hand. "I've been looking forward to meeting you."

Will returned the handshake. "Dr. Aelter." An awkward moment followed.

Dr. Aelter broke the silence. "But enough of that. I'm keeping you from the rest of your brief." He turned to Dr. Sekulow as he headed for the door. "Please excuse me, my friend." He stepped through and closed the door behind him.

Will watched the door close. Then Dr. Sekulow startled them with a clap of his hands and his high-pitched, "So. I guess you're ready to meet the Ice Man." The corners of his mouth lifted. "I have something to show you. Please follow me."

CHAPTER 5

Kat and the rest of the entourage followed Sekulow down the corridor, through another vault door, and through another security checkpoint to another elevator. This one took them down to the laboratory "clean rooms." Instead of going to the bottom, they stopped at the observation level and stepped onto a glass-enclosed bridge with slanted windows overlooking the labs below, a series of white rooms that contained an impressive array of equipment.

Dr. Sekulow shuffled along in the lead position and addressed Jamie. "Dr. Michaels, why don't you give them the lowdown?"

Kat smirked. *So the human Barbie doll has a PhD. Who knew?*

Dr. Jamie Michaels turned to face the group, but Kat knew this expedition was for her and Chris's benefit. Jamie walked backward slowly and ran her manicured hand along the handrail. "What you're seeing is all part of Project Ice Man. As you may know, frozen wooly mammoths have been surfacing in Siberia and Northern Canada for years, some so well preserved that we could identify their last meal. Over thirty years ago," she gestured to the lab below, "we found Ice Man."

Kat studied the lab. It was separated from the others by a secured entryway and a pair of doorways covered with hanging plastic. Two technicians mulled over a display panel on the far side, covered from head to toe with airtight, white lab suits and masks. The myriad of cabinets, computer workstations, and display panels all directed attention to the obvious focal point of the room: a metal forensics table on which lay the frozen corpse, still fully clothed, and still contorted in its final expression of pain.

Jamie continued. "He's the best preserved prehistoric animal found to date, and he's fully human. We found him in Northern Siberia in the late eighties. Apart from disfiguration of the surface flesh and skin, he's absolutely perfect." She gazed at the corpse as she spoke.

Kat didn't know what to think. She certainly didn't expect a lesson in archaeology—here of all places. "If he surfaced in Siberia, then why don't the Russians have him?"

Jamie turned her gaze to Kat. "Well, partly because they don't know about him. You have to understand; it was still the Cold War. We expended a lot of effort to get him here. We deployed a sub and a special ops team."

Dr. Sekulow cleared his throat, and Jamie looked at him for a moment. Then she turned to face the lab below and gestured enthusiastically. "I mean, he's perfect. His musculature is strong, his body fat low. We estimate his age to be well over eighty, and yet he shows no signs of heart disease, no arterial plaque buildup, not even a hint of organ degradation or the slightest indication of cancer."

Kat moved to Jamie's side, hands on the railing, and continued to look down at the body frozen in time.

"This is why you're here, by the way, Major Dalton," Jamie informed her.

Kat glanced at her. "This has to do with our mission?"

"Absolutely. We want to know what made him so healthy. Part of it may have been his diet. Your experience in botanical science and nutrition could be priceless to us. I mean..." She turned back to the view below, one hand cupped around her forehead. "This could be the end of heart disease, the cure for cancer!"

Kat might as well have been punched in the stomach. "My father has cancer."

Jamie spoke softly, apologetically. "I know.... I'm sorry. It was thoughtless of me to say that."

The obvious show of repentance changed Kat's mind about Jamie. *Maybe I was wrong about her.*

Kat tried to be merciful. "No, I didn't mean... I mean..." Kat took a breath and steeled herself. "It's all right, but I still don't see..."

Chris finished for her. "What this has to do with our mission." He raised his voice. "And why on earth did you send a Spec Ops team all the way to Siberia for a frozen corpse?"

Sekulow took this as his cue and pointed up with one finger. "Ah, that's the golden question, isn't it?" He walked farther along the bridge and spoke over his shoulder. "The secret to why we sent a team all the way to Siberia for a frozen corpse, Dr. Chris..." He continued in an energetic whisper. "...may be found in what he was holding."

Kat and Chris were right on his heels. Will and Jamie followed.

"You see, we had a new reconnaissance system in place... you're not read into that... but suffice it to say, we managed to pick up a faint signal accompanied by a mysterious heat signature. We might have ignored it, but..." He cleared his throat as if searching for the right words. "The signal carried a complex code."

Kat watched him intently. *He's hiding something.*

"We thought the Soviets were up to something. Well, as you can see, it wasn't the Soviets."

Chris jumped in. "And we had never picked up the signal earlier? Why?"

The short doctor shrugged as he continued to shuffle along the bridge, the end of which drew close. "Maybe because we didn't have the new recon system in place, maybe because the ice was blocking the signal, or maybe it started automatically when exposed to the sun."

"The sun?"

"When enough of the permafrost melted to allow our Ice Man to surface."

Chris blinked and shook his head. "So the Ice Man was sending the signal?"

Dr. Sekulow led them into an open elevator at the end of the bridge, turned, and pushed the button beside him to close the elevator door behind its last passengers. "Not exactly. What he was holding was sending the signal." When they reached the lab level below, the door opened to reveal the final, most secured lab: a small, austere, concrete and steel chamber that contained one small, sturdy metal table on which sat the gold cylinder with pointed ends.

Sekulow approached it slowly with wide-eyed awe and reverence. "Major Dalton, Dr. Chris, I'd like to introduce you to the star of the show, code named *Snowman*."

Kat and Chris approached and stared at the object.

Sekulow gazed on his prize. "*Snowman* was a persnickety fellow. It took us years to figure out what he was made for, and that only happened by accident." He took off his glasses and wiped his brow. "We were bombarding it with different types of energy and finally decided to try focusing a low-energy laser into one of its crystal settings."

Chris crouched and reached toward the device, apparently unwilling to actually touch it. "And what happened?"

A man in a lab coat entered from an adjacent office. His voice startled Kat. "It disappeared."

Dr. Sekulow grabbed Chris's arm to draw his attention away from the device. "Dr. Chris, this is Dr. Joseph Stephens. He leads the research team for *Snowman*. The two of you will be spending a lot of time together."

Dr. Stephens grinned broadly and shook Chris's hand. "It's a real honor to meet you at last. Call me Joe."

Chris looked puzzled. "Honor?"

"I knew we'd be friends the moment I read your dissertation. I liked the way you framed your thesis as a search for truth. I'd love to talk more about that."

Chris looked touched.

Kat was tired of the interruption. "This is all great, but you said it *disappeared?*"

Joe ended his enthusiastic handshake and gazed at the device. "Yes. As you can imagine we were devastated. Possibly the greatest discovery of the twentieth century, and we vaporized it, but then..."

Dr. Sekulow interrupted and leaned forward for emphasis. "It reappeared in the next room exactly twenty-four hours later."

"Well, of course we had to reproduce the effect several times to be sure, and then we got really courageous. We focused a laser into the corresponding setting on the other end."

Kat tried to hurry the conversation. "And it disappeared?"

"Yes. But unlike the other experiments, it didn't reappear. Another week of frustration, and we found it in the storage vault behind us..." Dr. Sekulow stood on his toes and whispered slowly and emphatically. "which was under constant video surveillance. When we checked the tapes, we found the device had appeared twenty-four hours *before* we initiated the experiment."

Kat was certain she had misunderstood. "Before?"

Chris sounded incredulous. "So you found a time machine."

"Yes, a time machine." Sekulow was practically jumping up and down. "Frozen in time for untold thousands of years, imagine the irony."

Jamie stepped in, "That's why *you're* here, Dr. Chris."

Chris raised a hand. "Please, it's just Chris."

She smiled warmly. "Okay, that's why you're here, Chris. Your dissertation got our attention. In fact, some of your theories helped us apply this technology more practically. It helped us figure out why it was rematerializing in different locations, for example."

Chris tilted his head and opened his eyes wide, clearly asking for more.

Joe moved in front of Chris. "Well, one clue was that it kept rematerializing the same distance from its point of origin."

Dr. Sekulow interrupted. "Yes, since our planet and, indeed, our solar system are in fact moving, then theoretically, the device reappears in the same *space,* but for us, in a different *place.*"

"And yet our knowledge of the motion of the solar system suggested it should be rematerializing much farther away. We struggled for years to understand it until we ran across your theories on sub-subatomic particle movement and applications for deep space travel. In particular, your notion of a sub-protonic fabric moving across space made the most sense."

Kat still wanted to get to the point. "So, this is the real mission for *Chronos One?*" She looked to Will, "And no one else will ever know what we really did?"

The room fell silent as her last words reverberated off the hard, concrete walls. Sekulow and Jamie looked at Will and then at each other.

Dr. Sekulow broke the silence. "Yes." He paused for a moment. "We've gotten pretty good at controlling it over the years. For instance, if we use a higher energy laser, it creates a larger field, carrying more with it through time. With the larger field, it can carry even the laser equipment with it, and the longer you continue firing the laser, the farther it moves through time."

Joe added, "The problem is the change in relative location. The farther we send it through time, the greater the physical distance it travels."

Chris nodded. "So you're going to do it in space?"

"Yes. It reduces the risk of rematerializing someplace dangerous..."

"Like inside a mountain?" Kat said.

"Yes," he answered simply. "Besides, we've also learned that if the device is *moving* in the right direction when we send it through time, it rematerializes closer to the point of origin."

Dr. Sekulow added, "It's as if it needs momentum to keep up with the sub-protonic movement you described in your theories, even in the near total vacuum of space. We just can't gain enough momentum on the ground."

Chris was fully engaged now. "Of course! With this, we can actually measure the speed of that fabric..."

Joe grinned broadly. "Already done."

Chris's eyes went wide. "Then we can match that speed before crossing time and try to arrive at the same point in the year, so we won't end up too far from the earth." His enthusiasm began to crescendo. "In fact, if we tried it the other way, we might be able to travel to other stars, using time to our advantage, and we could even theoretically create a caterpillar device that uses that fabric for thrust..."

Kat interrupted. "So everyone in this facility knows about this?"

Dr. Sekulow stepped toward her. "Goodness no. They're supporting your mission prep. As far as they know, the reason for the secrecy is the technology we developed for the spacecraft."

Will stood with his arms folded. "And Dr. Aelter developed the spacecraft. Does he know about *Snowman?*"

Sekulow faced Will. "He knows we have something capable of generating thrust, and he has been working to precise specifications we provide, but no, he doesn't know specifically about *Snowman.*"

"How did you find him?"

Dr. Sekulow stepped toward Will, his enthusiasm dampened. "We knew we'd need a platform unlike any other, so we started looking for the best. His company was trying to compete for a US defense contract, which was ludicrous, of course. Since neither he nor his company was American, he didn't get anywhere. To be honest, I don't know why he even tried, but it got our attention, and he has been a dream come true. When we offered him this job, he severed all ties to Germany and liquidated his interest in Aelter Aerospace. In return, he asked only for citizenship." Dr. Sekulow turned to the others. "Dr. Aelter developed the *Chronos* spacecraft to support this mission. It does more than most people know. It'll take off like a plane and then launch into space, but it's also capable of vertical takeoff and landing."

Kat gasped. "V-TOL?"

"Yes."

"Do you mean it can also take off like a rocket?"

"No, more like a helicopter."

She brightened. This was right up her alley. "It sounds like a Harrier jet."

"Yes, but much quieter."

"How?"

Dr. Sekulow pointed to the device. "By using this. We don't even fully understand it, but by energizing these crystals..." He pointed to additional settings along the reverse side of the device. "...we generate a field that physically moves whatever is contained within that field, including the device itself. We can't seem to change the direction of movement relative to the device, only the amount of force, so we simply use it the way one uses the vertical thrust of a helicopter. We designed *Chronos* with multiple maneuvering thrusters of its own to stabilize it and take advantage of this vertical thrust. Basically, *our* thrusters will control it in flight, but *this* device will lift the ship, enable it to hover, and propel it forward in the same way a helicopter moves. We've designed the controls on the ship to work much like those of a helicopter for this mode of flight, and the apparatus that houses the device will rotate forward to allow the ship to transition from hover flight to traditional, winged flight."

Kat smiled. "Like the V-22?"

Sekulow smiled and thrust his chest out. "The Osprey? Yes. That's where you come in, by the way. Colonel Stark will pilot the ship in aircraft mode and in space. You'll fly her in V-TOL mode."

"So, without Snowman, *Chronos* is incapable of hover-flight?"

"Not exactly. She is capable of hover-flight with conventional thrusters, but it wouldn't be wise. She wouldn't have the fuel to sustain it long."

"So how does Snowman's thrust work?"

Dr. Sekulow cradled the back of his head in one hand. "Like I said, we don't really understand it. We can't replicate the effect by any other means. I can't tell you what it *is,* but I can tell you what it *isn't.* It isn't like a jet's thrust, and it isn't magnetic."

Chris jumped back in. "Couldn't you disassemble it and study it further?"

Dr. Sekulow rubbed his forehead. "I suppose, but I've convinced our authorities to wait until after we've completed your mission. I'm afraid we might destroy it in the process, and the scientific potential of this mission is limitless."

Kat was unable to hide her sarcasm. "So what you're saying is that we're going into space to travel through *time.*" She emphasized the last word. "To when?"

Jamie was still enthusiastic. "Our best dating suggests our Ice Man has been frozen for 33,000 years. We want to send you there, or rather, *then,* to find out what made him so doggoned healthy."

"And to learn how they developed such technology," Dr. Sekulow added. "If we could replicate the thrust capability alone, why, it would be better than cold fusion!"

Kat had missed most of what was just said, still stuck on one phrase. "Did you say 33,000 years?" She looked to Will, then to Chris. Will remained stoic; Chris, however, looked ill. It was subtle, but she could see him slowly shaking his head. Even Joe was staring at the floor.

Dissension among the ranks?

CHAPTER 6

Will squinted in the desert sun. *How can we jump 33,000 years if we can't jump one hour without a crisis?* He checked his watch. Forty-five minutes had passed. He looked up and folded his arms. An hour should never last this long.

Solutions, Will. Think of solutions. How can we avoid this in the future?

He remembered what Kat had told him about Chris. Something kept "creeping him out." Will shook his head. It wasn't like he could replace Chris. The mission would be hamstrung without him. He glanced at the wrecked assembly nearby and closed his eyes. *There wouldn't be a mission without Chris.*

He might have quietly sought psychiatric help for the engineer if it hadn't been for that awful night. The night Will dreamed of his father and a very strange place.

wwwwwwwwwww

Will squinted from the harsh light and cold wind. Snow crunched beneath his feet with every step. The dark, metal sail of an attack sub stabbed through the ice in the distance. He heard voices and spun. Dr. Sekulow held an electronic device in one hand and walked a zig-zag, flanked by a dozen men in white parkas. They carried MP5-ST3 9mm rifles and scanned the horizon with careful discipline. One of the men stayed close to Sekulow.

The sight of him stole Will's breath away. He reached out. "Dad?"

Dr. Sekulow pointed and shouted. "There it is."

The men formed around a protrusion in the ice.

Will blinked, and suddenly Dr. Sekulow was dusting off the metallic cylinder they called *Snowman*. Just above the device, the frozen corpse looked as if it were struggling to pull itself from the ice. The unmistakable terror on its face sent a chill down Will's spine.

A freezing wind blew right through him. Every breath sent a puff of steam from his nostrils. He shivered and folded his arms tight across his chest.

It was worse, though. He felt sickly and pallid, like death. He shuddered and looked around. It was close. Something dark.

"Who's there?" He shouted again, this time louder. "I said who's there?"

He saw strange, blue sparks and a bright, blue glow nearby, and the men turned to look.

A muffled cry pulled Will away from the team. "Dad, no."

Then something massive cast a shadow from one side, and suddenly Will felt twelve years old again. His gut surged with adrenaline, and he froze. The soldiers shouted and opened fire. Will wanted to look but couldn't, frozen by terror. His father turned to him and shouted. "Will, look out!"

Will jumped from his bed, breathing hard, still shivering from the cold. Then he heard it again, a muffled cry for help. He pulled a sweatshirt on, grabbed his badge, and stepped into the dark common room. He rubbed his eyes and heard it again. It came from Kat's room. He stepped to her door and listened, his whole body still shaking.

Come on, Will. Get a grip. Chris's story about a shadowy figure nagged at him. Angry, he forced the fear down.

The mission, Will. Focus on the mission. There's no such thing as ghosts. He repeated that a few times until he thought he believed it again. He scanned the doorways that connected to the common room, including the heavy, secured vault door that led out to the corridor.

He heard Kat toss and turn again and weighed his options carefully. He didn't want to violate her privacy, but he was concerned for her. He decided to open her door and call out to see if she was awake. He slowly pushed it open and looked inside.

Just as he opened his mouth to speak, he saw it. A tall shadow leaned over Kat's head as if to smell her. Will blinked and shook his head, and then he could have sworn it turned to look at him.

A wave of sickly cold engulfed Will. Whatever it was, it felt unspeakably evil. The figure swept across the room as if a long cape trailed behind it and disappeared into the wall adjacent to the common room.

Will's whole body was tense, his feet stuck to the floor. *Move, Will. Move.* He mustered all his will and hurried to the common room. He searched for the apparition but lost it in the shadows. Then he saw something move next to the outer wall. He ran to the vault door, flashed his badge at the reader and plunged into the hall. It was a couple of hours past midnight, so the corridor lights were dim.

He looked both ways. Something moved around the corner in the distance. He walked quickly down the corridor and was about to round the corner when something made his gut wrench. He stopped and placed his hand on the wall.

Conflicting thoughts and emotions confused him. *Come on, Will. This isn't you. Since when are you paralyzed by fear?* He took a deep breath and stepped around the corner.

Then, just for an instant, an angry, terrifying face flashed in front of him. He gasped, backpedaled, lost his balance, and fell.

"Colonel Stark, is that you?"

Dr. Aelter came around the corner with a cup of coffee in his hand.

Will's heart pounded, but he knew how to overcome fear. He breathed steadily and slowed his heart rate. *It's over, Will. It's over.*

"Are you all right, sir?"

Will picked himself up from the floor and cautiously looked around him. "Yes, thank you. I just lost my balance."

"Is there anything I can do?"

Will put on his best poker face and looked down the hall in either direction. "No, thank you. I think I'll just go back to bed now." He pivoted and walked away. Will doubted he would be doing any more sleeping that night.

wwwwwwwwww

Dr. Sekulow's watch beeped loudly. Will spun to face him and raised a hand to shield his eyes from the blinding desert sun. "Is it time?" Before Sekulow could answer, a pair of blinding flashes fifty meters away preceded a thunderous crack. Part of the platform rematerialized in the air and fell with a loud crash. Two men fell with it and slumped to the ground. Will, Kat, and Jamie sprinted the remaining distance.

Chris sat up slowly amid the twisted remainder of the platform. He squinted, shook his head, and crawled to the moaning technician nearby. Will reached the technician at the same time. The man clenched his teeth, cradled his bloody left arm, and stared with watery eyes at the sharp bone sticking out just below his shoulder. Will supported his head and gestured to an approaching EMT.

Chris surveyed the rest of the damage around him. His eyes widened, and he went pale. He looked up at Will. "Joe! Joe! Where is he?" He gasped and jerked his head in every direction, scanning the wreckage.

Will closed his eyes and leaned his head back. *No way. It can't be.* If Chris's friend never rematerialized, then he either materialized somewhere else or worse—*he never would.* The thought of being lost outside of time itself made Will shudder.

Chris's eyes filled with furious tears. "Oh, Lord, no... please."

Several others arrived and rendered aid to the technician still on the ground. Will stood and stepped toward Chris.

Chris grabbed Will's collar. "Was he left behind? Was he left behind?" He looked at Jamie.

She covered her mouth and shook her head. Tears filled her eyes.

Chris trembled and his voice rose a full octave. "No!" He spun away from Will and looked back and forth, his hands on his head. "Joe, what have I done? My God, no—what have I done?"

Will grabbed him by the shoulders, steadied him, and looked squarely in his eyes. "Chris, this wasn't your fault."

Chris sobbed between labored gasps. "He's gone. He's gone."

Will threw his arms around him, pressed one tight fist into Chris's back, and held Chris's head against his shoulder with the other. Chris struggled against Will's grasp for a moment, then fell limp. "He's gone. He's gone."

Will looked at Kat, who wiped tears from her eyes. Gently, she put a hand on Chris's shoulder as he wept in Will's arms.

Will swallowed hard. He felt a sick, cold chill and heard his father's voice with a strategically added word: "Remember Will. There's no room for *a* failure."

CHAPTER 7

Will slammed the door to his quarters and clenched his fists against his temples. *Joe. Poor Joe. What have I done?* He squeezed his eyes shut and covered them with one arm. *Poor Chris.* He lowered his arm and found himself staring at his trophy wall through moist eyes. *Nineteen years of service, but no one prepared me for this.*

A knock on his not-quite-latched door pushed it open. Will wiped his face quickly and barked at the airman. "What?"

The young airman blinked and stepped back. "Sorry, sir. Uh, the director needs to see you sir." He dropped his gaze and hurried away.

Will shook his head and sighed.

A few minutes later he was walking down the corridor toward the atrium. His father's voice echoed in his head, "Remember Will. There's no room for *a* failure." He slumped and placed a hand on the wall. "When is it enough? Will I ever escape you?"

"From some things there is no escape, Colonel Stark." Dr. Aelter's voice surprised Will from behind.

Will straightened. "Dr. Aelter. I didn't know anyone was here."

"Yes, well there seems to be a lot of commotion today." He looked Will over for a moment. "I don't know what happened, but from all the frenzy, I'm guessing it wasn't good." He leaned in and spoke gently. "I don't suppose you can tell me, can you?"

Will's impulse to pour his heart out to a potential father figure surprised him. He swallowed hard and stared at the doctor's green badge, an indication of lower clearance.

He measured his words carefully. "Dr. Aelter, what do you think all this is for?"

The white-haired scientist straightened and curled his lips up. "What you really want to know is how much of your mission I know about." He took a deep breath. "I know you have something unique that will produce thrust, and I've designed your ship to take advantage of that. That's all they've told me."

"I see. How long have you been with the program?"

"Oh my, for decades. Since the beginning, I suppose."

"I heard you were a CEO."

"Yes, but I left that life behind to come here."

"Why? Why on earth did you do it?"

Aelter leaned forward and stared into Will's eyes. "To be part of something great, Colonel Stark." He let the words echo for a moment. "And you? Why are *you* here?"

Will didn't answer.

Aelter studied him for a moment, then turned away. "Well, if you'll excuse me, Colonel Stark."

Will felt like a rare opportunity had just slipped through his fingers. "Of course." *Screwed that one up, Will.*

He watched the doctor walk away, then straightened, wiped his face, and tugged at his flight suit. Then he realized Dr. Aelter's footsteps had paused. He looked up. Dr. Aelter stared at him while waiting for the elevator. The elevator chimed and opened. The doctor looked at the ground and stepped in.

Will rounded a corner and bumped into Kat. She stepped back and stared at the ground.

Don't screw this one up too, Will. He took a deep breath. "How's Chris?"

She looked up but to one side. "Pretty broken up. He and Joe were like brothers."

"I know." Guilt hung on him like a lead weight.

She met his gaze for a moment and softened. She sighed, shook her head, and turned her eyes to the ceiling. "I was thinking of going up to look at *Chronos* in the hangar." She looked over at the noisy atrium. "It's quiet up there, and somehow seeing the ship makes me feel better." She faced Will. "Care to come along?"

A lump in his throat silenced him.

She leaned in. "It's a beautiful ship, isn't it?"

He was grateful for the distraction. He nodded and forced the lump down. "Yes, she's a beautiful ship."

Kat curled up one side of her mouth. "There you go calling the ship 'she' again."

Will wasn't even sure which of his thoughts he was giving voice to. "Well, sure. Anything so beautiful must be a she."

She looked down. "Oh yeah, like all women are beautiful."

"All the women here are." He cursed loudly in his head, closed his eyes for a moment and shook his head.

Kat looked up with wide eyes just in time to see him shaking his head. She bit her lip and turned away for an instant that seemed to last an hour. "The memorial service will start soon, *sir,* and if you haven't heard, the director wants to see you."

Will's ears smoldered. *Not again.*

47

She hurried down the corridor toward their quarters.

Will looked at the elevators that led up to the hangar, then glanced at Kat walking away. Then he stared at the executive office behind the top of the atrium waterfall. He heaved heavy feet up a nearby stairway, stepped out onto the balcony, and looked down at the atrium floor. The cascading waterfall usually soothed him. Not this time.

He took a deep breath and walked along the balcony behind the waterfall. He was just about to step through a broad doorway when Jamie bumped into him. He raised his hands and stared at the floor.

"Oh, excuse me, Colonel Stark."

Man I'm being a jerk to everyone. Will nodded, and she continued past. A secretary inside stood and gestured into the office. "Good evening, Colonel Stark. The director is expecting you."

Will continued into the office. Dr. Sekulow stood and peered over the desk at Will but said nothing. Will took a seat and looked straight into Dr. Sekulow's eyes. Then the director settled back into his chair.

Will surprised himself with his own words. "Dr. Sekulow, I screwed up today. I shouldn't even be here. I'm not the man for this mission, and I certainly didn't ask to be recruited."

Dr. Sekulow looked down for a moment. "I thought you might say that." He looked up and tilted his head. "Colonel Stark... Will... I believe you are the man for this mission."

Will had expected a curt thank you and a short-notice plane ride home. "I'm sorry, but I can't see that I bring anything special to this project. I just want to return to the space program."

Sekulow removed his glasses and placed them on his desk. "You wouldn't be in the space program if it hadn't been for me, Colonel Stark."

Will blinked.

"I've had you in mind for this mission for years."

"Me? For years."

Sekulow was silent for a long time. Then he took a breath, stepped down to the floor, and shuffled to a nearby cabinet. He opened it, retrieved and opened a wooden box, and then pulled out a leather-bound book. It draped over the ends of his fingers until he carefully supported it with both hands. He laid it flat on the front of his desk where Will could see it. It was a Bible.

Will stared at the book and raised his eyes to the director. *Is this supposed to help?*

Sekulow returned to his seat and rubbed his chin with one hand. Will had never seen him at such a loss for words. For just a moment, he thought he saw grief sweep across the director's face.

"It was your father's, Colonel Stark."

Will's eyes went wide. The director might as well have slapped him in the face. "You knew my father?"

Sekulow stared in the distance behind Will. "He commanded the mission to retrieve *Snowman*." After another pause he choked the next words out. "It was his last mission."

Will shook his head. "You must be mistaken. My father died in Nicaragua, and I'm certain he never had a Bible in his life."

"I only knew your father for a few weeks, Colonel Stark, but in that time I saw him change."

Will opened the Bible to a few dog-eared pages and read the highlighted passages. Some obscure religious nonsense about being saved or whatnot. He felt a flush of heat and ground his teeth. *This doesn't bring Dad back any more than it changes his last words.*

He stared through the open Bible at all the memories, and it came to him. He leaned back and shook his head. *Of course. This is why they recruited me.* The mounting epiphanies boiled up in his chest. *And—why I was lucky enough to command two shuttle missions.* He exhaled hard. "All this time I thought I got into the space program by merit."

"You did, Colonel Stark. Don't underestimate your own role in your success. I only helped guide you toward your legacy."

Get a grip, Will. He stared at Sekulow and wrestled the anger down from his chest. "So you chose me to command your mission because you knew my father."

Dr. Sekulow looked intently into Will's eyes. "Your father was a hero, Will."

Will stood and ignored the Bible on the desk. "Not to me, he wasn't." He folded his hands behind his back and stared across the room. "Sir, I resign my command. I don't belong here, and now I've gotten someone killed."

"Don't fall into that trap, Will."

"Sir, with all due respect, you have no idea..."

Sekulow slammed the desk with an open hand and shouted. "I know exactly what you're going through." He paused and took a deep, shaky breath. "I suffered from false guilt for years, until I realized how ludicrous my expectations were." He stepped around his desk and gestured to the chair.

Will suddenly felt sorry for the director. He sat and stared at the Bible.

"You can't control everything, Will. I've tried, and trust me when I tell you this..."

Will looked at him.

"You didn't kill Dr. Stephens with your decisions any more than I killed your father." Sekulow turned his gaze to the wall to Will's left. Will followed the director's eyes and saw a framed picture for the first time. He leapt to his feet and hurried to the wall for a closer look. A college-aged Dr. Sekulow stood beaming with a SEAL team kneeling around him. Will leaned in and stared. His father knelt with his right hand on Dr. Sekulow's shoulder and the most placid smile Will had ever seen on his face. His left hand clasped the Bible Sekulow had just shown him.

It was as if he were looking at a stranger.

Sekulow picked up the Bible and moved beside Will. "I was a naïve, young scientist, full of myself, proud of the scientific coup I had pulled off. I invented an unbreakable means of secure communication and then detected an example of what I thought was my own technology coming from Siberia. My discovery thrust me into a world of secrets and power." He placed the Bible on the credenza below the picture.

Will grasped it in one hand, ran his other hand over it, then stared back at the photograph. "How did he die?"

The director stared into the distance and swallowed. His eyes grew wide and he paled, trembling. Will knelt and put a hand on his shoulder to regain his attention. Sekulow turned his eyes to Will and reached to his own shoulder to pat Will's hand, then stared at

Will's father touching his shoulder in the picture. "You're so much like your father." His jaw quivered as a tear rolled down his face. "I was the only one to survive. Commander Stark died saving my life."

"Who killed him?"

Sekulow drew a deep breath. "More like what." He blinked, shook his head, and wiped his eyes. "Your father was very sober that last day, like he knew what was coming. He gave this to me before we left the submarine, Will. I think he regretted something, but he didn't get a chance..." He swallowed and patted the Bible in Will's hands. "I've been searching for an opportunity to give this to you for years. The fact is, I haven't had the courage until now. I've tried so hard to forget that day." He lowered his voice almost to a whisper. "I've never been so scared."

After a moment of silence, Sekulow returned to his seat behind the desk. "With all due respect, Will... resignation not accepted."

Will held the Bible and turned back to the photograph. "They wouldn't tell us anything." He swallowed hard and his eyes watered. "They wouldn't even let us open his casket."

"Your father died a hero, Will, and I think this mission might be the key to your learning how... and why... he died." He let that sink in for a moment. "That is why I chose you for this mission, Will. This is your legacy and your right."

Dr. Sekulow folded his arms on his desk in front of him. "So what's it gonna be?"

Will wiped his eyes, glanced at the director, then at the Bible, and turned again to the photograph.

CHAPTER 8

The atrium waterfall rushed in the background. Several rows of empty chairs faced a lectern, left over from the memorial ceremony. Will stood and walked toward Chris, the Bible firmly grasped in one hand. Chris and Jamie kissed tenderly. Then Jamie threw her arms around him tightly before walking away.

Chris sat at one of the tables and buried his head in his hands.

Kat approached and motioned to the Bible in Will's hand. Her tone was icy. "Where's your football?"

Will looked at the Bible and understood her surprise. He loved turning that football in his hands during tedious meetings. "It's in my quarters, Major Dalton."

She softened and looked down. "Sorry, sir. My tone was inappropriate."

"It's all right."

She snapped her head back and blinked.

Will sat across from Chris, leaned forward in his chair, and looked intently at the grieving engineer. Chris straightened in his seat for a moment and then slumped with one elbow on the table and his hand on his forehead as if to shield his eyes from some non-existent sunlight.

Kat joined them and faced Chris.

Will broke the silence. "Chris, I know I've said this before, but it wasn't your fault."

Chris kept his eyes hidden. "You don't understand. I was supposed to engage the clamps. If I had, none of this would've happened."

Kat leaned toward Chris. "You don't know that. Even with the clamps engaged, there's no way to know..."

Chris shouted angrily. "You're right. There's no way to know it wasn't my fault."

"Chris, be reasonable, you have to..."

Will raised his hand in a respectful cue to stop. He let a moment of silence cool things off. Chris usually took care of morale, but now the man was in crisis. "Chris, Joe was a good man, and nobody blames you for his loss. He knew there was risk, but he thought it was worth it. He had his reasons for doing this."

Chris had calmed down. "I don't follow your point."

"My point is that you've known the risk all along, too. You must have your reasons for being here."

Chris's expression looked painfully empty.

"Lieutenant Commander Nur Saif-ad-Deen, why are you here?"

Chris looked away and swallowed. Then something registered in his expression, and he looked pointedly into Will's eyes. "I want the truth."

"About what?"

"About everything. About the universe. I've got questions."

Kat sounded dismissive. "We've all got questions."

"No. I've got questions. I've got doubts."

Will was concerned. "About what? The mission?"

Chris dismissed the thought with a sweep of his hand. "No. No. Nothing like that." He paused. Will and Kat waited patiently. "Okay, it's like this. You know my father came from Baghdad. He was Muslim."

Will wanted to make sure Chris knew this wasn't an issue for him. "Of course."

"Well in Islamic eyes, that makes me a Muslim, but my mother was a Lebanese Christian." My father died after I was born in the States, and I grew up caught between cultures. Arab and American. Islamic and Christian."

"So did you choose one?" Kat asked.

Chris grimaced. "It isn't that simple. My extended family and the community at my mosque all expect me to live as a Muslim, and for me to choose otherwise makes me worse than a *kafr.*"

Will and Kat looked at him with blank expressions.

"Kafr means... *not of the faith.* Infidel. But they would think of me as *mortadd,* or apostate."

Kat sounded indignant. "Why should you care what they think?"

"You don't understand. To leave Islam is the worst thing any Muslim can do. At best it leads to complete ostracism, which in Islamic countries means no hope of career or marriage. At worst it carries the penalty of death, usually at the hand of a close family member."

Kat blinked. Will couldn't hide his own shock. He never realized the burden his friend carried.

"That's why my father's name has always haunted me."

Will was curious. "Why, what does it mean?"

"It means *sword of the faith.*"

Kat gulped. "Have you talked to anyone about this?"

"Sure, I talked to my imam. I told him I want to decide based on evidence. I told him I wanted to compare the fruits of each religion." Chris mustered half a smile. "But I think I only said that to gall him."

"And what did he say?"

"He said evidence is irrelevant. Fruit is irrelevant. He said the only thing that matters is faith."

"In what?"

"Well, for him, faith that *God is One* and that *Muhammad is the messenger of God.*"

"But why can't you just be both?"

"Both Muslim and Christian?" Chris's expression brightened for just a moment. "Well for one, I'm not Gandhi."

Will was puzzled by the reference.

Chris looked disappointed his quip had fallen flat. "To unify India against Britain, he claimed to be Hindu, Muslim, and Christian." He shook his head. "Never mind. I can't be both because my fellow Muslims wouldn't tolerate that, and besides, I'm too honest for it. They can't both be true."

Chris stared over Will's shoulder for a moment. Will glanced behind to see what Chris was looking at, a tall cross behind the lectern.

Chris looked away. "Joe wasn't conflicted at all about religion. He talked to me a lot about faith. He told me he knew where he was going when he died. He was the strongest Christian I've ever met."

Kat leaned in. "Isn't that good?"

Chris looked distant. "I want to know for sure. I just want to know."

Will wished he had his football. "You're talking about religion, but you've dedicated your life to the Navy and to science."

"Yeah." Chris shrugged. "Maybe neither of them is true, but then, I haven't had the luxury of proving that before, either. After all, you can't reproduce billions of years in a laboratory." He wiped a tear and smiled at his next thought. "At least, you couldn't until now."

They laughed, and Kat seized the moment of levity to change the subject. "About that. Don't you think our mission is just a little, I don't know, *over the top?*"

Will looked around. They had the room to themselves, but that wasn't enough. "This room isn't secure, Major Dalton."

She lowered her voice. "I know, but really, *thirty-three thousand* years? What are they thinking?"

Chris scanned the room and spoke in a hushed tone. "You know exactly what they're thinking, Kat. Their best dating suggests the Ice Man died that long ago, and we're expected to learn the source of his technology."

"And why he was so healthy, I get it, but come on, *thirty-three thousand* years?"

Will ended the conversation. "Drop it both of you. Not here."

Kat huffed and looked away.

Chris looked thoughtful. "Sir, if I may, why are *you* here?"

Will swallowed. Despite his question to Chris, he didn't like whys. He preferred whats. "I'm here because it's where I'm supposed to be."

Kat straightened. "Is that enough for you?"

"Of course it is." Will thought for a moment and noticed the others were still looking at him. "I've been called to do a mission, and I can't fail."

"You can't?"

"I won't." Will turned directly to Kat. "I won't let you down." *Again, anyway.*

Will hoped that would end the line of inquiry, but Kat and Chris stared at him. He glanced at the Bible on the table. "I always wanted to be better than my father. We spent a lot of time arguing, and I suppose we still are."

He looked into Kat's eyes. They seemed soft now, concerned. Will didn't want to drive her away again. "Now, for the first time, I want to be like him."

Will took a deep breath and looked at Chris. "That's why I'm here." He smiled at the sudden realization. "That's why I want to be here." He leaned toward Chris. "I need to know you want to be here, Chris. If not, I'll cancel the mission."

Chris and Kat blinked and froze.

Will took a deep breath. "We don't have to go. If you're not ready, just say the word."

The rush of the waterfall filled their ears.

58

CHAPTER 9

Will raised his helmet visor to look out the window of the ground shuttle. His sleek blue, gray, and silver space suit was a technological achievement that more resembled a flight suit than the traditional, unwieldy affairs of the past. Outside, it was bright and sunny, the perfect day for a launch at Cape Canaveral. Will surveyed the circus of media production trailers, tents, and platforms as their ground shuttle crept along toward the launch site. He was surprised at the attention their launch was attracting. He glanced down at the thick, metal attaché case in his hand that housed *Snowman*.

Sitting nearby, Kat tapped Chris on the shoulder to point out the VIP seating where Kat's father and Chris's mother would be. Appropriate for the inconvenience of helmets and space travel, her pixie-cut hair was short and tidy.

Their out-of-proportion, elevated ground shuttle crept along on a tall suspension, rolling slowly as if stretched up on its toes, conveying the crew to the ship. By Will's count there were a dozen technicians on board with them. From one of the onboard terminal monitors, Will could just make out the sound of one of the news broadcasters: "...for the historic launch at Cape Canaveral of the *Chronos* spacecraft, a technological leap forward in time."

Will curled his lips up. *Now that's ironic.* They were truly hiding the truth in plain sight where no one would see it. He still shuddered at the destructive power *Snowman* could unleash in the wrong hands. A terrorist could change history, even erase entire civilizations from existence. That made their true mission the most closely guarded secret of the modern age.

"The brave crew of *Chronos One* will conduct the first-ever horizontal space launch and then spend a record three months in deep space, after which they will reenter the earth's atmosphere and glide to a landing at Edwards Air Force Base."

Will turned to face a technician who was looking at him. The technician quickly turned away, his hand steadying a wheeled crate next to him. Will had seen the look many times from naïve, starstruck fans at his hometown. He tried to offer a reassuring smile to the fellow but couldn't regain eye contact.

Moments later, Will saw their ship perched in the distance, surrounded by a mobile gantry and connected to a web of cables and hoses. He looked soberly at the ring of Humvees and light-armored vehicles that provided security. Apart from the three team members, only a few technicians and some privileged congressmen in the dark halls of Washington knew what they were truly guarding. Kat and Chris looked at Will, who returned a reassuring nod.

Their shuttle docked with a hermetic seal to *Chronos's* side hatch a short distance from the front of the fuselage, an act of precaution both to augment security and to maintain a clean, antiseptic atmosphere within the craft.

Will, Kat, and Chris carefully stepped through the hatch into the craft. Then just as Chris was turning back to secure the hatch and dismiss the ground shuttle, Will felt an unexpected breeze stroke his face. "Did you feel that?"

"I felt a gust of wind." Chris touched his face.

"Yep, me too." Kat took a step to the side to look through the still open hatch. "We shouldn't get a breeze from the shuttle. I mean, the pressures should be the same."

Will pursed his lips. "How 'bout it, Chris. Could we have a seal leak?"

"I don't see how. The seal was checked this morning, and we docked smoothly." There was a pause. "You want me to check it again; don't you?"

"Now would be easier than when we're in space." Will tried to keep a straight face.

Chris chuckled. "You pilots always want to play it safe."

Chris and a worker in the shuttle examined the seal. They found no signs of tampering or failure.

Will nodded his approval, and Chris secured the hatch and waved through the porthole to the ground shuttle crew. A hiss indicated the outside seal was broken, and light poured through the porthole as the ground shuttle backed off and drove away.

They took their seats in the command compartment that served as the bridge, and soon it came to life with flashing lights, active monitor displays, and the hums and beeps of all the systems designed to inform and empower its occupants.

Will looked around as he performed initial system checks and admired again the beautifully engineered bridge. A line of narrow windows ran from the entry hatch around the front to the opposite side. Above and below the windows, an impressive sphere of monitors provided a near-total view of what lay outside, including a pair of suspended monitors that displayed the view behind and an array of smaller monitors attached to the pilot and copilot stations that displayed system status, radar, and telemetry. Will's and Kat's stations were mounted on a clear, Plexiglas floor so they could see the display below. Will twisted in his seat and stared at the one extravagance he couldn't explain: an extra pair of seats at the back that Dr. Aelter insisted would provide flexibility for future missions.

A couple of hours of preflight checklists ensued, during which time Will sent Chris aft to install *Snowman* and inspect the apparatus of lasers that would control it. Chris soon returned to his engineering station behind the pilot and copilot seats to continue his preparations.

Will was so busy that the time passed instantly. After successful startup, the engines whined with massive, harnessed power. Elements of the mobile gantry disconnected one-by-one with pops, bangs, and hisses as the gantry slowly rolled behind. The last support vehicle in front of the ship disconnected its two hoses from the nosecone, and a puff of steam burst from the outlets as they sealed for flight. The support vehicle crept to the side and out of the way.

As they passed T-minus ten minutes, Will lowered a set of levers to engage their thrusters, and *Chronos* rolled for the first time under her own power and taxied slowly toward the runway.

Will breathed slowly and intently. His anticipation was visceral. Much of the world was watching, but he couldn't think about that now. Too much was on the line.

Will carefully moved the controls and turned the graceful craft to its position at the end of the runway. Then they waited. Will looked up and around as *Chronos* paused, leaned forward on her haunches, and spun her engines down to a low idle, eager to display her power.

He grinned from ear to ear. *What a rush.*

Will looked back. Chris took a break from his calculations to look above his terminal at Will, then turned his gaze farther up to look at the forward display. Will glanced at Kat in the copilot seat, poised and ready to assist. Will grasped the controls and steadied his heartbeat. A voice announced the countdown in increasingly short intervals, "T-minus one minute, thirty seconds..." Will's breath grew shorter and shorter, his heart drummed intensely. It wasn't fear. It was *thrill.* The countdown passed one minute.

A shrill voice in the cabin announced, "*Chronos One,* you are cleared for take-off. Good luck."

Will cued for a final status check.

Kat responded, "Flight Two ready."

Chris added, "Engineering ready."

Then Will reached to his right and deliberately pulled a set of levers back to engage the rear thrusters.

wwwwwwwwwww

The ship's narrow, rectangular thruster cones exploded with force. Streaks of red-hot flame extended behind the craft. Dust streaked away, and grass beside the runway waved furiously. Acceleration forced the occupants back in their seats as *Chronos* rolled down the runway and quickly gained speed. As cameras turned to follow its path, it nosed up and lifted off the ground the instant the countdown reached zero. Now supported by her backswept wings, *Chronos* retrieved her landing gear and soared into the sky at a sharp thirty-five degrees, heralded by a popping roar and thunderous applause from the crowded viewing stand. Airwaves flooded with commentary as tens of millions of viewers watched the new spacecraft leap into the air like an eager fighter jet. For just a moment the United States cheered, once again proud of their collective achievement.

Chronos continued to roll to the vertical, and the steaks of red-hot flame lengthened behind her. Now rocketing straight up, she raced for her natural home in space. Minutes passed by as her altitude increased more and more quickly. The exhilaration of a successful takeoff now behind, an entranced audience around the world looked on in hopeful silence from countless sports bars, TV lounges, and living rooms as the sleek craft grew smaller and smaller on their screens. The image grew more and more pixilated, and the high-tech cameras struggled to maintain focus across the growing distance.

wwwwwwwwww

Will, Kat, and Chris watched the earth's blue horizons slowly narrow and fall away. The sky above them steadily darkened from blue to purple to black. As they finally reached the calm of space, Will reduced their thrust to about half a G. It gave them at least a semblance of a floor, a floor that before takeoff had been their back wall. The roar of the engines dulled to a steady rumble, and they began the long process of preparing for their jump through time. Chris and Kat climbed from their seats and grasped a ladder that ran the interior length of the ship. They climbed down from the flight cabin into the series of compartments that ran along the top of the vessel. Will continued to monitor their flight in his seat high above them.

"*Chronos One,* this is Mission Control." The tinny voice echoed through static from speakers throughout the ship.

Will engaged his helmet mike. "Mission Control, this is *Chronos One.* We copy five-by five."

"*Chronos One,* confirm that all is secure."

Will blinked. This question was not part of the expected protocol. He turned back to see Kat and Chris poke their heads into the ladder tube, their puzzled expressions unmistakable. They gestured to Will with a thumbs-up. "Mission Control aye, everything is secure."

The brief silence that followed was deafening. They needed to be able to speak more freely, but comms weren't secure. "*Chronos One,* congratulations on your successful takeoff."

This was the prearranged cue to hand control off to the "alternate mission control."

"Roger, Mission Control." Will reached over and flipped a switch to their alternate, secure channel before speaking again. "Ivory Tower, this is *Chronos One,* do you copy?"

After a moment of silence and static, Jamie's voice rang through the speakers. "Roger, *Chronos One,* this is Ivory Tower. It's good to hear you." She paused for a moment before continuing. "We confirm a secure link. You can speak freely now."

"Ivory Tower, why did Mission Control depart from protocol?"

"*Chronos One,* we appear to have had a security breach on the ground. There was an unauthorized container on board the ground shuttle."

"What was in it?"

"Nothing. It was empty."

Will glanced again at his crew mates before responding. "The outer hatch was only open for a moment, and we didn't bring anything else on board. I don't see how anyone could have gotten past us." His gut wrenched at his next thought. "Mission Control, could something have been placed on the ship's hull?"

"Negative, *Chronos One*. We've reviewed footage from the gantry cameras, and all eleven of the technicians on board check out."

Weren't there twelve? No. I must have miscounted.

"*Chronos One,* Mission Control has recommended scrubbing the mission."

Will blinked, swallowed again, and turned to his comrades. They stared at him with wide eyes.

"Does *Snowman* check out all right?"

Chris echoed back through the speakers. "Aye aye. *Snowman* checks out perfectly. No problems here."

They waited. Will counted each breath. Jamie's response was sober. "*Chronos One,* the decision is yours. Do we proceed with the mission?"

This time, Will didn't turn to look back. He couldn't think of any way they could be compromised. His eyes moved back and forth as he reviewed every detail in his head. His crew's lives depended on him. "Ivory Tower, *Chronos One* will proceed with the mission."

Did I really just say that?

"Copy, *Chronos One.*"

CHAPTER 10

Will had gotten precious little sleep that night after he established a stable orbit and shut down the engines. He awoke to Ivory Tower's musical selection for them, the Fifth Dimension's "Up, Up and Away." Kat and Chris stirred from their own bunks, and excitement quickly eclipsed his fatigue. His first order of business was to reactivate their thrusters to break orbit and move them farther from the earth for their time jump. The maneuver had the added advantage of giving them the illusion of a "floor" before breakfast.

He pulled himself along the ladder hand-over-hand from his sleeping compartment to the bridge and then strapped himself into his seat at the controls. By plan, Chris made his way to the compartment that housed *Snowman* while Kat followed Will to the bridge before heading toward one of the labs. She checked some settings at the engineering station and floated to the ladder.

Will donned and activated a small headset, and his voice echoed through the ship. "Prepare for forward thrust." In short order, Will summoned *Chronos* to roar to life and carve a tangent away from her orbit around the earth. As the thrust regenerated a semblance of gravity, Kat paused and grasped the ladder while the force pulled her legs down and onto the ladder. Once stable, she continued climbing, *down* now.

Will heard someone go thump with a barely audible, "Mmph." He smiled. "Chris, you all right down there?"

"Sure, why?"

"Oh, no reason." *I did warn you.*

After a short while, Will climbed from his seat and down to the galley, where he found Chris and Kat waiting for him.

They hurried through breakfast, eager to get on with the mission. Will seized the opportunity to check on his crewmates. "Last chance to speak. Are you both ready?"

They nodded. Kat, still chewing a bite, added, "Absolutely."

"No concerns about the mission?"

Chris shook his head and smiled. "Bring it on."

Kat's expression changed. "Okay, I have one question that I've never been able to ask. Why didn't they send us, I don't know, to the Civil War or something? A shorter trip to test the concept? Shouldn't we have tried something other than one of Chris's 24-hour jumps?"

Chris wrinkled his nose and tilted his head back and forth. "I suspect they already have. I never got the impression they told us everything."

Will didn't like the sound of this. *We can't afford doubt.* "They shouldn't have to tell us everything. They told us enough."

Kat leaned in. "But we're the ones risking our hides."

Will thought for a moment. *There's no room for failure.* He took a deep breath. *Oh, come on. There's nothing wrong with a little reassurance.* "You're right, but do you think Dr. Sekulow..." He turned to Chris. "...and Jamie... would intentionally keep something from us that we needed to know?"

Their expressions softened, and they both nodded.

"All right. Let's do it."

They put away their meal implements and headed to the bridge. After they secured themselves in their seats and donned their helmets, Jamie's voice squawked from the speakers like a bad AM station. "*Chronos One,* this is Ivory Tower."

Will touched his mike control. "Ivory Tower, this is *Chronos One.* We read you five-by-five."

"Copy *Chronos One*—stand by... *Chronos One,* we have all indicators nominal. Do you confirm?"

Will glanced over and back to get a thumbs-up from Kat and Chris. "Confirm aye, Ivory Tower—all indicators nominal."

"Roger that, *Chronos One*—initiate mission countdown."

"Copy, Ivory Tower, countdown initiated, jump minus ten minutes."

Will turned back to Chris, who was already feverishly applying calculations. "Chris, the ship is yours."

He replied without looking up. "Yes, sir."

Will and Kat glanced at each other. Chris had told them that his twenty-four-hour jumps passed in an instant, but no one really knew what a 33,000-year jump would look or feel like.

With the computer's help, Chris guided the ship onto a carefully calculated course, sought the perfect speed, and conversed periodically with Dr. Sekulow's team to confirm his calculations. Focused and calm, he announced the countdown periodically as he continued to monitor his calculations and settings.

For Will, the countdown seemed interminable. He could tell it was the same for Kat. All they could do was wait.

At last, the moment arrived, and their anticipation grew. Chris finished his preparations, "Thrust is down to twenty-five percent... fifteen percent... five percent... thrusters deactivated."

Chronos's engines quieted as she continued to soar by inertia along her predetermined vector. The illusion of gravity faded away. Will and Kat grasped their armrests as Chris continued.

"Engaging maneuvering thrusters to reverse our position." The intermittent sound of pressure hissed from the thrusters and echoed from different directions. Slowly, the distant earth moved into view ahead of them. Chris adeptly moved his controls, focused on a monitor on his panel. "Position stable. Thrusters disengaged." The cabin grew silent.

Chris continued the countdown. "Jump in one minute and counting."

The speakers squawked with intermittent static. Will broke protocol to speak. "Ivory Tower, confirm comm link."

"Jump in forty-five seconds."

"*Chronos One*, this is Ivory Tower. We read you fivers."

The intermittent static continued.

"Jump in thirty seconds."

Will glanced at the large, red abort button in front of him. The static grew louder and more frequent. He thought he could almost make out fractions of syllables.

Chris seemed too engrossed to notice anything but his own calculations. "Activating device now." Chris pulled a lever to activate *Snowman* below deck. The spherical array of monitors grew bright as a field appeared and grew around *Chronos*. "Jump in ten seconds... nine... eight... seven..."

It was more spectacular than Will had anticipated. Streaks of white light dove from the ship in quick bursts. They formed an ellipsoid that encompassed the ship. Bright and clear in a separate monitor that displayed the view along the top of the ship, the hull glowed with brilliant energy.

"*Chronos One,* this is Ivory Tower. Say that again?"

Will responded. "Ivory Tower, this is *Chronos One,* we didn't—"

The static grew much louder and interrupted him. They strained to hear. "... *Chro... warn...*"

Will and Kat exchanged worried glances. Was someone trying to warn them of something?

A klaxon blared and a terse computer voice startled them. "*Collision warning.*"

Will tensed. It was too late to abort now. His eyes flicked from one monitor to another. *It must be a meteor.*

"...three... two... one..."

Just at that instant, a word echoed through the speakers. "... *emergency...*"

"Go."

A powerful force froze Will in his seat. The field around the ship distorted as it ripped through time and carried the ship with it. Bursts of blue light streaked toward them. In the large pair of monitors that displayed the view behind, similar bursts of red streaked away.

A powerful hum filled the air, a resonant chord replete with rich overtones. Will stared at the dazzling display outside the ship, his eyes wide, his jaw hanging slightly open. *I've never seen anything like it or heard anything like it.* The chord tickled his ears.

A large mass swept across their view with a percussive swoosh. It startled him from his trance.

Will tried to ask what it was, but in place of his voice, a deep, distorted rumble emanated from his mouth. He tried again and heard the same incomprehensible utterance, then paused, at a loss.

Will heard a few grunts behind him from Chris, whose first few attempts to speak were ineffective. Then Chris shouted one more time, projected as best as he could, and enunciated with crisp, exaggerated consonants. It worked.

"That... was... the... earth," he managed to get out, his voice deeply distorted but vaguely comprehensible. "See... here... it... comes..."

Swoosh!

"...again."

The earth flew by again in its backward orbit before he could finish his sentence. Then after an even shorter interval, it streaked by again. Will watched as the earth sped by over and over, picked up speed, and counted off the years as they traveled back.

Chris counted off their distance across time, spitting out the consonants as clearly as he could, "We've... traveled... fifty years... one... hundred... two... hundred..."

The earth pounded by percussively with increasing frequency. It beat along like a massive propeller, gained speed and hummed like a massive, celestial motor. The lights around the ship still created a stunning display.

"One... thousand... years..." Chris continued.

Will mused. *There's no powered flight on earth now... heck, my nation doesn't even exist yet.* He struggled to remember his history and tried to imagine just *when* they were at any moment.

"Two... thousand... years."

Kat was smiling.

"Three... thousand... years."

Will struggled against the invisible force and turned to Chris. The engineer grinned broadly while calculating. Chris raised his head to inform the others, took a deep breath, and readied himself to project his voice through the distortion.

"We're... just... approaching... six... thousand... years... At... this... rate... we'll..."

A powerful jolt stopped him mid-sentence. The impact forced them painfully into their seat restraints, and an unexpected and loud roar sent a chill down Will's spine. The previously harmonious chord crescendoed into a hideous and deafening shriek, and the ship's lights dimmed as if its energy were suddenly wasted away. The vessel seemed to grind gears in a vain attempt to continue its journey. The smell of smoke wafted up from the chamber below.

Unable to speak over the din, Will turned to Chris and gestured with a flat hand across his throat. *Cut it off.*

Chris nodded, threw the lever forward, and disengaged the laser. Their world went silent. They sat dumbstruck for a moment.

Kat finally managed to speak, "What the heck was that?"

Chris shook his head, "No way."

"What?" Will demanded. He had to gain control of the situation, whatever it was, and he needed information.

Chris was still shaking his head when the ship lurched again, this time backward. The resonant hum resumed, though this time it seemed strained and dissonant.

Chris blinked and shouted out, "It's... the... auto... return... sequence... It... was... triggered..."

Will could smell smoke. With great effort, he managed to interrupt. "*Stop it.*"

Chris stared at his station, his hands above his controls, apparently unable to determine what to do. "I'll... have... to... go... below." Just as he grasped his restraints to release them, the hum subsided, and the ship's journey through time came to a stop a second time. A few tools and implements, shaken loose with the turbulence, floated through the air around them.

Will broke the silence with controlled calm and turned back to his engineer. "Chris, what just happened?"

Chris blinked. "I'm not sure. I estimate we had traveled back 6000 years when..."

"When what?"

"When something stopped us. Something prevented us from continuing. I can't explain it. Whatever went wrong triggered the auto-return sequence, but I can't explain why we stopped again. We traveled forward exactly one thousand years, and then we just stopped." He stared at one of his monitors. "A good thing, too, because the *Snowman* control system is overheated. A moment more, and it would have been damaged beyond repair. We would have been trapped."

The thought made the hair on the back of Will's neck stand up.

Kat stared out the view screen. "Guys," she pointed outside. "What is that?"

"That's the earth," Chris said without looking up.

"No it's not." She shook her head and kept pointing.

They turned to the image in the array of monitors. Eyes wide, Will released his harness, leaned forward, placed his feet on the back of his chair, pushed himself through the air, and caught a handhold closer to the window for a look at the real thing. The others followed. A hazy green globe—too hazy—with spots and streaks of blue stretched before them. It was stunning, something between emerald and jade, beautiful and pure. If this was the earth, they were much closer to it than they had been when they started their journey through time. It filled their view. Chris couldn't hide his amazement. "Where's the cloud cover?" He scanned up and down. "And where are the polar icecaps?"

Kat scanned back and forth across the surface. "And the oceans." She paused for a moment, then pointed. "Look at the rivers."

Will and Chris turned their gaze to follow her gesture. A large lake appeared to be the source of a vast river, which split into four rivers that spanned the globe. Each of the rivers split several more times the farther they stretched from the headwaters. Several small seas—or large lakes—dotted the surface. Most of the surface was lush and green with tiny patches, suggesting agriculture. A significant distance east of the headwaters, on the other hand, the land looked untamed with scars that were scorched and barren.

Nothing about this world resembled theirs.

Kat turned to her comrades. "This can't be the earth."

Chris made his way back to his station, grabbed the back of his chair and awkwardly swung his legs over. He seized one arm of his seat and a handle on his workstation and steadied himself while he scanned his monitors. "No. This is the earth." He pointed to the right end of their display. "Look."

The bright, perfectly formed, pearl moon rose over the horizon. Kat watched in awe. "It looks brighter." She squinted. "And there aren't any craters." Kat and Chris leaned closer and stared.

Will was deep in thought. They were 28,000 years short of their goal. He quickly sorted priorities in his head. *Get the crew home safely, and salvage what you can of the mission.* He looked out the window again and noticed the world outside was growing larger. "Chris, make calculations for orbit before we get too close."

Chris clearly heard the urgency in that. He pushed back to his station, strapped himself into his seat and got to work.

Will turned to Kat. "Get down to the aft compartment and start checking for damage. I'll start here and work my way down."

Kat nodded. "Yes, sir." She made her way to the ladder and thrust herself down the tube.

Will considered for a moment longer. *Could we try again to continue our jump back in time?* The faint smell of smoke still wafted up from one of the compartments. *No way.* He turned again to Chris, who was bent over his terminal. "And Chris,... Launch the satellites. Let's get a better look."

CHAPTER 11

Chris held the charred circuit panel from *Snowman's* laser control system in his hand. Will looked at it soberly. "Can you replace it?"

Chris shook his head. "The replacement boards were seated adjacent to this one." He jerked his head forward and shook a fist. "Foolish design. I didn't catch that before. Even the least damaged board will only give us partial capability."

"Enough to get us home?"

"I don't know yet."

Kat's voice squawked over the cabin speakers. "Sir, you'll want to come down here to see this."

Will took a deep breath. *Please, no more bad news.* He spoke over his shoulder as he pushed himself down the ladder. "Do what you can and let me know."

He emerged into the aft lab. Kat gazed back and forth between a folder in her hand and a set of monitors. He secured himself next to her, glad for any chance to be this close. "So are the satellites working as advertised?"

"They're incredible. This technology has Dr. Sekulow written all over it. In fact, I'll bet this is how they detected *Snowman* in the first place." She gestured to one of the monitors. "All three satellites are nominal, and we're receiving telemetry, but the readings are all off." She stowed the notebook. "Satellite two got some great readings on the moon. There are no craters, and there's no surface dust whatsoever, which explains why it seems brighter."

Will nodded as if he understood. He wasn't sure he did.

"That led me to wonder why there are no craters, and then it occurred to me that our navigational radar hasn't detected anything."

"Strange."

"Very strange. In the hours since we arrived and established orbit, the system hasn't logged a single speck of space dust and not a single meteorite. So then, on a whim, I initiated a long-range imagery scan for planetary locations."

Will raised his eyebrows. *And?*

"It'll take a while, but the system already logged a serious anomaly. It scanned early for some of the larger elements of the asteroid belt, and they aren't there. None of them."

"Why would that be?"

"No idea. The readings below are just as strange. First, the spectrometers show O_2 levels on the planet to be several percent higher than normal. Second, the planet's magnetic field is tremendously strong."

"The planet's?"

She tilted her head and tightened her lips. "I still find it tough to believe that's Earth down there."

Chris's voice squawked from the speaker. "It has to be the earth, Kat."

Kat blinked and stared at the speaker. Will guessed she had forgotten it was on. She turned back to Will. "Look here. There are no fault lines. The climate is semitropical from pole to pole with no variations greater than ten degrees Celsius. There are no mountains taller than about three hundred meters."

"And the oceans?"

"That's the strangest part. The satellites' ground penetrating sensors indicate most of the water is below the surface. In fact, there's a global subterranean ocean layer between the surface crust and the upper mantle." She gestured to more readings. "It's under tremendous pressure, and look here: Spectrometer readings on all visible water show the salinity level is almost zero. The water is fresh." She gestured around an image of the earth on one of the monitors. "The rest of the water is suspended around the atmosphere as vapor. There's so much of it that the air pressure at the surface is more than doubled. That may explain why there are no icecaps." She returned her gaze to Will. "The canopy of vapor is acting like a greenhouse, and vapor currents help distribute the sun's energy and level the temperatures around the globe. It's also acting as a shield. Most of the cosmic radiation is reflecting off of the vapor canopy, which suggests only a fraction of the expected amount is getting through to the surface."

Chris interjected again through the speakers and grunted as he secured a panel. "Sounds like a great place to live."

Kat didn't smile. She focused intently on a set of readings she had apparently just noticed. She quickly turned, removed a binder, flipped to a certain page, and looked again at the indicators. She wrinkled her brow, then looked up with wide eyes, her face pale.

"What is it?"

Kat looked toward the ladder and back, then reached to the wall and deactivated the comm link. She moved back, spoke under her breath and pointed. "Look here. This indicator is our projected O_2 consumption level on board."

Will nodded.

Kat gestured to the next monitor. "And that's what we've actually consumed."

Will leaned in for a closer look.

Kat whispered, "It's almost exactly 33 percent higher than projected." She paused, looked him straight in the eye, and whispered. "You know what that means, right?"

Will's gut tensed. He nodded. "Head for the bridge." With that, he leapt up the chute along the ladder as Kat secured her binder and followed. Will stopped briefly in the next compartment, opened a storage panel, then removed a long, heavy flashlight. He considered its usefulness as a weapon. He longed for the Beretta 9-mil he had carried in his F-22, but even with the unknown risks for this mission, the consensus was that firearms weren't a good idea in a pressurized spacecraft far from earth. He scanned the entire compartment around him and watched Kat float past. He grasped the flashlight firmly and made his way back to the ladder.

He looked aft toward the lab and reviewed every facet of the ship in his mind. Then he looked toward the bridge and pushed himself to slowly, very slowly, float along the ladder. As he approached each compartment, he reviewed it in his head. As he neared the storage compartment just below the one where Chris was working on *Snowman,* Will abruptly reached to the ladder and stopped his motion. This was the only compartment with room to hide.

Thumps and taps echoed from Chris as he worked in the compartment beyond. Then the answer hit Will like a ton of bricks.

Sabotage. We've been sabotaged. He looked up. Kat stared down from the bridge. He flipped the flashlight around in his hand and grasped it like a club. Then he took a breath and steeled himself.

He slowly ascended into the compartment, then carefully moved his free hand from handhold to handhold. His heart thumped in his chest. *Steady Will. Steady.* He consciously measured his breaths—in and out—to calm his heartbeat. He scanned every centimeter of the cabin. Then he spotted it, a door slightly ajar and a frightened eye looking back.

Will secured his grip on the handhold and held the flashlight up in the most menacing gesture he could muster. The urgency of his shout was unmistakable. "Come out, now. Let me see your hands."

Slowly, the panel swung open to reveal a man with medium-length, jet-black hair. His ethnicity was strangely ambiguous. His slightly olive skin suggested he could have been Mediterranean, but his square jaw and chiseled features looked more Scandinavian. The man slowly emerged, one hand in the air in obvious surrender, the other hand wrapped firmly around a handhold. He wore a simple tunic, loose pants, and leather boots.

Will shouted at the stowaway. "Who are you, and how did you get aboard?"

Chris poked his head down from above, his eyes wide with curiosity.

"I said, who are you?"

The man opened his mouth, his eyes frozen on the flashlight, and took a deep breath. His voice was a deep baritone. "There's no need for that."

Will stared at the man intensely. "What did you do to the ship?"

"I didn't do anything to your ship."

"Then why did we stop traveling back?"

"You stopped because you had to."

Will wasn't satisfied. "You mean because you sabotaged us."

The man blinked. "Sabotaged?"

"You heard me."

The man looked up at Chris for a moment, then fixed his gaze on Will. "The only thing I did was to stop your auto-return sequence before you melted the sequencing coil. I also chose a good year to stop us. You can thank me later."

Chris's head still protruded down from above. "Before we melted the what?"

The stranger looked up at Chris. "The sequencing coil that surrounds the core of the sub-nuclear phase inducer. I think you've been calling it *Snowman*."

Will wasn't ready to stand down. "Where are we?"

The man furrowed his brow. "Why, you're orbiting Earth, of course."

"You're telling me that's Earth down there."

The man shook his head. "You really don't know, do you?"

Will wouldn't tolerate a diversion. "Why are you here?"

The man stared squarely into Will's eyes. "I'm here to help." He gestured around. "Look, I have nowhere to run, and if I had wanted to hurt you, don't you think I would have done it while you were asleep?"

Will thought for a moment and lowered the flashlight.

Just then, a loud bang echoed from one of the aft compartments, followed by a loud hiss.

Chris was quick to identify the problem. "O$_2$ tank rupture. We need to seal it off before..."

An explosion rocked the ship. Will covered his ears and grimaced in pain. The overpressure thrust Chris up the tube, but before he reached the next compartment, the aft cabin started to depressurize and sucked him back down. He flew past Will and the stowaway. Will crashed into the ladder and grabbed it to keep from getting sucked down, too. The impact knocked the flashlight from Will's hand. It streaked down the tube with the suction. Will looked down.

Chris threw one arm into the ladder to keep from getting sucked out. His arm caught and his legs flailed around him, still caught in the powerful suction. *Crunch.* He cried in pain. Blood from a gash on his arm streamed past him, sped into the next compartment and carved a rapid arc to where the air was escaping.

The stowaway lunged toward Will and allowed the pressure to pull him down the chute headfirst. He grasped the ladder, swung his legs around, straddled the opening into the next compartment and grasped the bulkhead hatch just past Chris. He grimaced, fought the pressure, and moved himself clear of the opening. With a grunt he gave the hatch a pull, and the pressure drew it closed with a violent clang. The sound of rushing air subsided, and a klaxon, inaudible in the din before, replaced it.

Will struggled to breathe. They had lost precious air. He reached into a nearby compartment and removed a small, portable oxygen mask. He quickly donned it and activated the breathing device, then tossed two more to the stowaway, who donned his own and placed the other on Chris, who floated unconscious, his injured arm contorted around the ladder.

Will removed the mask to shout his command. "Bring him to the bridge."

The stowaway nodded as Will leapt up the ladder chute to the bridge, where he found Kat activating the O$_2$ supply in her helmet and strapping herself into her seat.

He shot to his own seat, removed the mask, and put on his own helmet. "Kat, we need the emergency air supply."

"I'm on it." She worked at a set of controls as Will activated his helmet mask. A hissing indicated the slow increase in the ship's pressure.

A few minutes later, the stranger entered the bridge with his arm around Chris, who was now conscious but groggy. Will twisted in his seat.

Chris grimaced again as the stranger carefully placed him in his seat and moved his arms through the harness restraints.

Chris squinted from the pain. The man looked at Chris and spoke through his mask. His voice was calm and reassuring. "Try to relax."

Chris stared at the stranger. The man pressed on the area around Chris's shoulders. Chris made no effort to hide the pain.

"It seems dislocated."

"It feels dislocated."

The stowaway smiled. "At least it didn't break your sense of humor." He placed one hand on Chris's chest and firmly grabbed the dislocated arm with the other. Chris closed his eyes and looked away, and the man gave his arm a firm jerk.

Will heard a stomach-turning pop.

Chris grunted and drew a long, labored breath. A moment later he moved the arm. It was clear it still hurt, but it was functioning as it should.

"Better?" The stranger gently palpated the shoulder.

"Yeah. Better. Hurts. But better." Chris paused. "I guess I should say thanks."

As the air pressure approached normal, the klaxon silenced. Will motioned to the pair of empty seats at the back of the compartment, suddenly grateful for them. The man made his way to one of the seats and secured himself in place. His portable air supply ran out, but he no longer needed it. He carefully secured it, so it wouldn't float away.

"What's your name, stowaway, and who are you?"

"My name is Kemuel. I'm a Guardian."

"A Guardian?"

"I go where the phase inducer goes. I'm responsible for making sure it doesn't fall into the wrong hands—among other things."

Chris cradled his injured arm with the other and scanned his workstation. "Sir, our emergency air supply will only last us about twelve hours. We have full use of *Snowman's* thrust capability, but not time travel. I might be able to jury-rig a way to jump back forward, but whether in the here-and-now or back in the future, we need to set down soon for repairs."

Will considered their situation. "Can the hull survive reentry?"

Chris scanned his readouts for a moment, his face still tense from the pain. "It looks like the damage was to the dorsal shielding on top of the ship, which we could repair. The ventral shielding below absorbs most of the heat and shock of reentry. If that survived undamaged, we should be able to reenter safely. The only way to know for sure is a spacewalk." Chris's face lit up with an idea. "We could also use *Snowman's*... I mean, the phase inducer's... thrust to minimize the shock of reentry. We considered that possibility before but ruled it out as unnecessary and too risky."

"What's the risk?"

"Well, wear and tear for one, but mostly, our systems weren't designed to maintain stable hover flight under reentry conditions." He looked at Will and Kat. "You'd have to wing it, but I think you could do it. Besides, it's the best way to land discreetly."

Will was decisive. "We'll do it. I'll conduct a spacewalk to survey and repair damage enough to get us to the surface. Then we'll de-orbit and reenter, using *Snowman*, so we can complete repairs on the ground."

"Do you want me to go below and find a way to return us to the future?

"Not yet. Priority one is to repair the ship. Besides..." Will turned to look out the window. "I'd like a closer look down there." He turned to Kemuel. "You don't look surprised."

Kemuel shrugged innocently.

Will faced Chris again. "Can you find a good landing site?"

Chris spent a moment calculating at his workstation. "Satellite imagery suggests the flattest surface is about nine thousand kilometers east of the headwaters."

"No. It is better to land west of the headwaters." There was note of concern in Kemuel's voice. "I assume you've noticed the land to the east is barren. Trust me on this. There's a reason for that. Let me show you a good landing site."

Sure, what better navigator than a stowaway. "Let's see it. Chris has..."

Kemuel released his harness to move next to Chris before Will could finish the sentence. He pointed to a display on Chris's workstation. "There, see that city?"

"Yes."

"Take us here, west of that populated area, and make sure we land at night."

Chris worked in silence for a few moments. "We'll need to de-orbit in just over three hours to land at his proposed site after sunset." A moment later, he added, "We have sufficient air supply for that schedule, but any longer would be risky."

Will nodded. "Get started." He looked at Kemuel and thought for a moment. "You help Chris. He'll need an extra pair of hands."

"Yes, sir..."

Will wasn't done. "Kemuel, I don't know what a Guardian is or does, but I know this: You tamper with this ship or my crew, and you'll reenter the atmosphere all by yourself and without benefit of this ship. You understand what I'm saying?"

"I do."

Kemuel helped Chris from his chair and led the way from the bridge.

Kat was clearly uncomfortable trusting Kemuel so quickly. "But sir..."

"I know, Kat, but we have no choice. Besides, without him we might not have survived the decompression." He released his harness and removed his helmet. "Come with me. I need you to work with me from inside the ship."

CHAPTER 12

Will tugged at the tether that secured him to the ship. The emerald-green earth above stretched far in each direction as the ship sailed backward in low Earth orbit. The air system in his spacesuit hissed intermittently. He pushed against the hull with his feet and pulled a large, cube-shaped apparatus, roughly two meters across, away from the hull. It was a state-of-the art metallurgical system worth almost as much as the ship. A bead of sweat found its way to one of his eyes, and he squinted in discomfort. *Yup. That's the worst part about spacewalks.*

Kat's voice squawked from the headset in his helmet. "How does it look?"

He blinked repeatedly to clear his vision and surveyed a patch of glowing metal on the hull as it cooled. "It looks good. We should be able to restore pressure to the aft compartments shortly. How are we on time?"

"Ninety minutes to spare."

Finally. Good news. "Great. I'm coming back in."

"Roger."

Will maneuvered the repair apparatus back to the airlock and secured it to a hook nearby. He reached into a circular hatch that was temporarily open for the spacewalk, grasped a rotary latch with both hands, and then pulled it out to turn it. He looked through the outer door porthole. Kat looked out through the porthole on the inner door. He turned the latch with a grunt.

The main thrusters glowed for an instant, and the ship lurched hard. Will held onto the handle tightly.

It happened again, this time more violently and for several seconds. The ship decelerated hard, and Will's inertia pulled him toward the rear of the ship. Will grunted, eyes wide. He held on to the airlock latch with one hand and struggled to bring his other arm forward. The repair system broke loose and dropped back until it reached the end of its tether, which pulled taut and jerked it to a stop just before the thruster deactivated.

Will drew a hard breath. "Chris, what's happening?"

Chris sounded agitated. "A thruster control circuit is firing sporadically. We must have a short somewhere. Are you okay?"

The ship lurched again. "No. Find it and stop it."

"Already on it."

Will turned to the repair apparatus just in time to see it floating toward him, centimeters away. It hit him head-on, knocked his grip loose from the airlock latch and snapped his tether hook loose from the ship. Will saw the end of his tether cord float free, disconnected from the hull. His gut wrenched. The thrusters fired again, but this time, they stayed on. The ship moved past him with growing speed. Will was just inches too far away from the ship to grab it, but the repair apparatus floated next to him. He jerked his hands out and grabbed its handles just in time. Its tether again pulled taut, and the cube jerked hard, pulled with tremendous force along with the ship. Will's legs whipped around him and snapped straight, and he hung below the cube. He let out a long, desperate grunt and held his grasp with all his might. The thrust had to be about one-and-a-half Gs. It was like hanging above a cliff with a lead weight tied to his feet. This continued for what felt like an eternity. Will breathed through grunts and strained to maintain his grip.

After a couple of minutes, the thrust abated but continued with less force. With all the strength he could muster, Will reached one hand up to the next handhold on the system and slowly, hand-over-hand, climbed up the cube toward its tether line. Its connection to the cube was visibly strained.

The thruster deactivated again. The cube floated forward and slightly away from the ship with Will still attached. As quickly as he could, he walked his hands to the tether line and grabbed it. He pushed off the cube and slid along the cord toward the tether's connection next to the airlock. He held his grasp to the tether with one hand and reached for the airlock latch with the other.

He grabbed the hatch. The thruster ignited again, and the force pulled him hard toward the back of the ship. He struggled to hold the latch with one tired hand and strained to reach up with his free arm before he lost his grip. The cube's tether again pulled taut. The apparatus snapped loose and floated away. Its empty tether hung from the ship. Will lost his grip. His hand slipped off the latch, and the ship pulled away from him. He grabbed the empty tether line that once held the cube and gripped it hard. It slid through his hands.

Before he reached the end of the cord, the thruster deactivated again, but only for a moment. Will quickly wrapped the tether around his arm twice. The thruster reignited and pulled the cord taut again with a hard jerk. He managed to hold fast as it pulled him with the ship. This time the force stayed lower, about one G.

Will looked up. He hung about five meters below the airlock. With a loud yell, he pulled his free arm above him and wrapped it around the cord. Then he carefully unwrapped his lower arm from the cord and, with another yell, pulled himself up again. His muscles strained, and he forgot all about the sweat in his eyes as he continued his labored climb. With a final, loud yell, he grasped the airlock latch with one hand, pulled his other arm up, and grasped the latch with his other hand.

He breathed hard and struggled to hold onto the latch with exhausted hands when mercifully, the thruster deactivated. Will wasted no time. He pulled his legs up for leverage and turned the latch with all his might. He heaved the door open and reached into the dark airlock just as the thruster fired again. His mind raced. He searched quickly for something to grab. There was nothing.

Will's arms slipped from the airlock. Will was powerless against the force. *No, no, no, no.* Then two gloved hands grabbed one of his wrists and held him fast. Will looked up. Kat's face strained in the helmet of the other spacesuit. She braced herself with her legs and held on. Will heard her sustained yell through their comm link. With the current force, she was holding onto three hundred pounds. Their grip slipped a few millimeters, and Will searched for something else to grab with his free hand. He found nothing. He looked back up at the desperation on her face. Their grip slipped again.

Chris's voice rang through the speakers. "Found it!"

The thruster deactivated, and Kat pushed her legs straight to heave Will into the airlock. She closed the outer door, spun the wheel on the inside, and slammed her hand against the control to pressurize the compartment. As soon as the indicator turned green, they removed their helmets, both breathing hard.

Will gasped deep breaths, and his body trembled from exhaustion and shock. Kat held him against the airlock wall and looked into his eyes. His gaze met hers. He wanted to kiss her even more than he wanted to wipe the burning sweat from his eyes. He managed a whisper between gasps for air. "Thank you."

She opened her mouth to say something. Her eyes moved back and forth for a moment before she closed her mouth, turned away, and opened the inner hatch. Kemuel pulled Kat through and reached in again for Will.

Will was still shaking and unable to move. *Man, I've never had to rely on others so much.*

Kemuel pulled Will through the hatch to his chest, then held his arm around Will from behind to secure him in the zero-gravity. He allowed Will to rest there for a moment, his arms floating beside him.

Will was the first to speak between heavy breaths. "I think I'm through with spacewalks."

The ship hit something and shook from turbulence. Will's mind raced with the question. *Wait, turbulence?*

Chris shouted as he raced past them up the ladder chute to the bridge, hitting the wall several times as the ship rocked with impacts. "We're not out of the woods yet. The thruster misfire decelerated us, and we're falling out of orbit."

Will looked up at Kemuel. "Help Kat out of her suit now; then help me." Kemuel hurried to Kat as Will shouted up the tube. "Chris, turn us around and fire the main thruster to reestablish orbit."

"I'll turn our nose forward, but I can't fire the main thruster. I had to disable it to stop the malfunction."

The turbulence grew in intensity. The compartment echoed with the rumbling, and the hiss of maneuvering thrusters sounded from different directions.

Chris found another moment to shout down the chute. "I'm positioning our ventral shields down for reentry, but I'm not a pilot. I need you up here."

Kat was nearly free from her spacesuit. Will looked at her intensely. "Use *Snowman* to decelerate us and take us in slowly using hover flight."

As soon as she could, Kat pushed herself up the tube. More turbulence slammed her against the ladder as she left Will's view. She gathered herself quickly and pushed off again.

When Kemuel finished helping him with his suit, Will pushed his tired body up the ladder chute. The resistance from the Earth's atmosphere created a partial—and unwelcome—sensation of gravity. Will grimaced and moved his arms and legs up the ladder by sheer willpower. As he emerged onto the bridge, the windscreen glowed with blinding flashes of red.

Kat operated the controls from her station as the turbulence continued. "We're traveling belly-first. Preparing to engage *Snowman* for vertical thrust at two Gs."

Will pulled his harness straps on and tried to ignore his muscles' complaints. Kemuel secured himself in the back and braced for the deceleration.

Kat grasped a control next to her station. "Engaging *Snowman*... now."

A panel near Chris blew open in a burst of sparks. Chris whipped his good hand to a switch and cut off power to that system. He pulled himself free from his harness, jumped to the floor, placed a hand on his injured shoulder, and cried out for an instant. He composed himself and ripped another panel open. "We just lost *Snowman's* hover control system. Until I can restore it, you'll need to reenter traditionally."

Will lifted his exhausted arms and grasped his controls. "Understood. I'll pilot us down until you do."

Chris shouted toward Kemuel. "We had hoped to land discreetly using *Snowman's* hover capability, but now we're going in hypersonic. Our arrival won't exactly be a secret."

Kemuel's eyes widened for a moment. He clutched his armrests with white knuckles. "Where are we now?"

"Thirty degrees west of the headwaters, heading east."

"Is our trail visible?"

"Yes, for a little while longer, but that's not the worst of it. As we get lower, we'll drag a sonic boom across a pretty big swath of territory."

Kemuel's voice shook. "We have to slow down, then."

Kat interrupted. "Our current speed is 28,000 kilometers per hour, and we only have maneuvering thrusters."

After a while, the turbulence subsided, and Will lowered the nose of the craft. The flashes of red in the windscreen diminished, and *Chronos's* wings lifted them on the surrounding air and completed the sense of gravity. "We're in the atmosphere now and gliding conventionally." He glanced at the darkness in the monitors below. The barely visible headwaters disappeared from view behind them. He heard Kemuel mutter something from behind him. *Is he praying?*

Will turned back to Chris. "I need to hand control to Kat for hover-flight after we go subsonic. What's your status?"

Chris worked feverishly in an open panel. "I don't have it yet. You might need to land on a runway."

Kemuel's eyes nearly popped out of their sockets. "A *runway?* The people down there don't have much use for runways."

Will snapped his eyes to Kemuel. "Get up here and help us find a good landing spot, then. I'll have to glide us all the way in, and we'll only have one shot."

Kemuel slipped from his harness and crept forward to kneel beside Will, one arm on the back of his seat. He scanned the display beside Will. A short distance ahead, the last shadow of night slowly gave way to the approaching sunrise. Kemuel pointed north of them on the display. "Can you arc us back around to land in this area?"

Will nodded and banked the ship to the left just as they crossed into daylight. Even in the shadow of twilight, it was clear that most of the target area was a flat, barren wasteland.

Chris shouted from the back. "There. I've shunted the laser control system over to backup power. You'll have *Snowman's* hover flight capability for two minutes."

Kemuel brightened, focused on the monitors around Will, and pointed. "There."

Will nodded and reduced their pitch to adjust course. Unlike the flat wasteland nearby, their new target landing site was hilly with dense patches of trees and vegetation. Will continued their long banking turn and settled into a course back toward the darkness to the west. "We're subsonic now. Three thousand meters... twenty five hundred meters..."

Kat grasped her controls and readied herself.

"Fifteen hundred meters."

Kemuel slipped over beside Kat and pointed to the display in front of her. "Right there, do you see?"

She nodded.

"One thousand meters. Velocity three hundred knots." Will nosed the craft up to decelerate more quickly. "Five hundred meters. Velocity two hundred knots... prepare for handoff... now."

Kat carefully manipulated the throttle with her left hand, the *cyclic* with her right, and the *anti-torque pedals* with her feet. "Acknowledged. I have control." Apart from the hum of the laser system below them, *Snowman's* thrust was remarkably silent.

Chris interjected. "*Snowman* is active. You have two minutes of power."

Kat kept the nose up, decelerated them quickly and descended toward their target site. Her eyes moved back and forth across the virtual external view in the monitors around her.

Will activated a control next to him. "Deploying landing gear."

Chris stared at his readouts. "One minute, thirty seconds."

Kemuel pointed at one of the monitors. "There."

Kat adjusted course. "Got it."

"One minute."

Kat slowed them to hover over a small clearing in the middle of a densely forested area, then carefully descended between some tall, thick deciduous trees.

"Thirty seconds."

As they neared the ground, Kemuel pointed at the displays to one side. "Can you get us under there?"

Kat manipulated the controls to turn the ship and backed it carefully into an opening underneath a dense tree canopy.

"Ten seconds."

Kat carefully stopped their horizontal movement and lowered the ship. Just before they touched down, the hastily connected wires next to Chris's station flashed brightly and burned out. The ship fell the last fraction of a meter and landed with a loud thud.

Kat clutched her controls firmly for a moment.

Chris reassured her. "That wasn't you. The hover control system just burned out." A moment later: "Some of my wiring is fried. I still have readouts. I read outside pressure at two-point-one atmospheres. We'll need to equalize before we can get out."

Will removed his harness with a slight grimace and a lot of effort. "Do it." He looked at Kat and Chris. "Great job, both of you."

"Shutting flight systems down." Chris worked at his panel. The spherical array of monitors went dark. Only vital and research-related systems remained active.

Will peered through the front windscreen. The sky had been growing brighter with the sunrise, but a fog rose from the ground and slowly dimmed the sunlight.

Kemuel looked relieved. "Good." He leaned over and squinted at the sky through the angled window. "The moon must be overhead. The mist will help hide us during the first few hours of daylight."

Kat sounded puzzled. "The moon?"

"The moon's gravitational pull draws a daily mist from the ground. Much like the daily tide you're accustomed to."

"How can things be so different?"

Kemuel let out a heavy sigh and shook his head. "You future dwellers and your shoddy epistemology."

"Shoddy what?"

Kemuel's expression softened. "I'll make time to explain everything later." He addressed Will. "Sir, I concede you're in command, but it'll take several hours to equalize pressure before you can leave the ship, and we're pretty well hidden for now. You all need some rest."

Will had to admit he was exhausted. It had been over twenty-four hours since they slept, and they had spent much of that time fighting for their lives.

Chris massaged his temples with his good hand. "The aft compartments are re-pressurized, so we can get to the sleeping compartment."

Kemuel looked straight at Will to reassure him. "I'll stay here and keep watch. I'll wake you if anything happens."

Will looked warily at Kemuel but couldn't find any deception in the man's face. Still, he wasn't completely ready to trust a stowaway with their lives. "We'll take shifts."

Kemuel nodded. "Fair enough."

Kat interjected. "I volunteer for the first shift. Chris is injured, and you must be worn out from the spacewalk fiasco."

Will nodded and headed for the sleeping compartment.

CHAPTER 13

"**Sir, you need** to wake up and come see this." Kemuel's voice was calm but urgent.

Will sat up and rubbed his eyes. He took a deep breath and felt a refreshing rush. "How long?"

"Six hours. The mist has gone. We're equalized to the outside pressure. It's about noon."

Kat sat up in her own bunk.

Will looked at Chris's empty bunk. For the first time, he noticed a picture of Jamie on the wall behind. He turned back to Kemuel. "Where's..."

"He took over for Major Dalton a couple of hours ago to assess damage. Follow me please."

Will followed him forward to the bridge, where Kemuel ducked down and approached the front windscreen almost at a crawl. Will followed his example, ducked down, approached the window, and poked his head up beside Kemuel's to look outside. Kat followed in like fashion.

Kemuel raised a hand to point outside. "There, see? Behind that tree."

Will fixed his gaze in the direction Kemuel indicated. At first he didn't see anything, but then a head poked out from behind a tree and quickly drew back. It was a short, grotesque creature with ears stretched back, almost to a point.

"They're called se'irim." Kemuel looked up as if searching for a better word. "Imps. If one is here, you can bet there are others around. We can't stay here long."

The creature poked its head out again, took a long look, and abruptly turned away. It scampered awkwardly into the trees.

Chris joined them and stared out the window. "What on earth?"

Will turned to Chris. "What's our status?"

Chris sat on the floor, leaned against the wall, and placed a hand on his injured shoulder. "Okay, first the good news. Your repairs to the hull worked fine, which is great, since we lost the metallurgical system during the thruster malfunction." He rubbed his eyes. "We had enough spare parts to restore the main power system, which filters through the battery bank to power the lasers. The batteries are drained, but they're recharging. Part of the hover control system got fried as we landed, but I think I've narrowed it down to a single circuit board that I can access from outside. If I can repair that, we'll have silent hover-flight capability."

"And the bad news?"

Chris massaged his temples. "Space travel is another story. The main thruster control system is heavily damaged. It could take days, maybe weeks. Life support needs some major work before we can return to space. We have the parts, but it'll take time." He lowered his hand from his head to look at Will. "And I don't know how to restore our time jump capability. I'll need to engineer a new control system for that, and right now, I don't know how."

Will reached out and gave Chris's good shoulder a firm squeeze. "You're doing great. Focus on restoring flight capabilities. We'll worry about space travel and time travel later."

Chris looked up and mustered half a smile. "I've done nearly everything I can from inside the ship for now. I could work from the crawl tube, but it'd be easier to effect repairs from outside. Permission to disembark?"

Will looked at Kemuel. "Anything stopping us?"

Kemuel shrugged blankly. "Whatever it takes to get us out of here. We should leave at nightfall."

Chris interjected before Will could ask. "That might be possible. I'll let you know."

Will stood. "Permission granted, then. We'll all go out, but stay within view of the ship."

Kemuel nodded. "All right, but first..." He walked back to the compartment where he had hidden from them. Will followed. Kemuel opened a panel. "You should put these on." He pulled out a set of simple outfits and leather boots much like his own.

Will didn't bother to hide his shock. "You brought clothes?"

"It was important."

wwwwwwwwwww

Will was the first to climb down the ladder to the ground. He tugged at the loose tunic Kemuel had given him while the others followed. Chris moved directly to the stern of the ship to access the thruster control system. Kemuel paced the perimeter and scanned the surrounding trees. Kat walked a short distance into the trees and knelt down to look at the vegetation.

Will followed Kat and kept a close eye on her from behind. He threw an occasional glance back toward the ship.

Kat was engrossed. "I've never seen this species before." She crept along the ground, moving from plant to plant. "And this one has only been seen in the fossil record."

Will blinked. "Do you mean you really remember that from your studies in... "

"Botanical science. Sure."

"Yeah. And I suppose you know what kinds of trees we landed the ship between."

"A sugar maple and a bur oak, with a giant red cedar nearby." She looked up, stood, and pointed to a tree a short distance away. Dense clusters of red fruit draped from its thick branches. "And look there. Have you ever seen fruit like that?"

Chris shouted something. Will turned to see if anything needed his attention. Kemuel walked calmly toward Chris with a hand extended. By the time Will turned back, Kat had walked ahead to the strange tree. She reached up and plucked one of the red fruit.

Something brushed through dense leaves and broke limbs nearby. Will caught movement in the tall, dense brush to his right, close to Kat. She heard it, too, and turned toward it. She looked up and froze, the fruit still in her hand.

A ten-foot-tall lizard stepped out and stood on its sturdy, hind legs several yards in front of Kat. Every muscle in Will's body tensed. He first thought it could be a tyrannosaurus, but not as big as what he had seen at the Smithsonian, and its narrow head didn't look quite right. Still, its massive frame and long tail were a fearsome sight. Kat stared at the beast but didn't move. She seemed to be debating whether or not a sprint away might trigger a reflex to chase.

Will was impressed. *Good instincts.* He wanted to give Kat a chance to get away. He broadened his stance and bent his legs, ready to run toward the beast to distract it. Before he took his first step, though, the beast lunged straight for Kat.

Will shouted. "Kat, run."

Kat wheeled around and bolted past the tree and across a clearing. Will was about to shout and wave his arms to get the dinosaur's attention when it stopped and craned its head up to pluck some of the fruit in its toothy jaw. Will blinked. He walked cautiously around the munching lizard and, once past, jogged in the direction he had seen Kat run.

When he caught up to her, she was standing behind a thick tree, eyes fixed on the dinosaur. She carved her hands through her hair, held it back for a moment, then released it and pointed to the lizard, eyes wide in disbelief. "Is that..."

"A dinosaur? It sure looks like it. We must have traveled further back than we thought." Will stood in front of the tree and looked back to watch the creature feast on more fruit.

Kat scratched her jaw, then extended one finger in front of her mouth. "I just ran a hundred-yard-dash with my tail on fire, and I'm not the least bit winded."

Kemuel's voice surprised Will. "It's the air." He gestured back toward the ship, which was now too far away to be seen. "You should see the lieutenant commander's wound, and his injured shoulder.

They're healing quickly, thanks to the higher oxygen pressure. You'll start noticing a lot of benefits."

Will considered that and stared again at the dinosaur.

Kemuel was dismissive. "Oh, he's just hungry." He squinted a little. "A young iguanodon if I'm not mistaken."

Kat took a deep, trembling breath. "I thought it was a T-Rex."

Kemuel shook his head quickly. "No, no. There are no tyrannosaurs or anything like them. Not yet, anyway." His expression grew distant. "It will be a dark day when they come." He took a deep breath and focused on Kat. "I'm surprised there are any dinosaurs here, since the land nearby is so barren and ravaged."

Will found it tough to wrap his mind around the presence of a dinosaur. He turned to Kemuel. "Ravaged by other dinosaurs?"

"Goodness no." Kemuel's voice grew gravely serious. "Ravaged by the sons of the Watchers."

"The sons of the Watchers?"

Will heard movement. A black-gloved hand reached down, grasped Kat by the arm, and pulled her around hard.

Oh no you don't. Will jumped out to confront the hand's owner and found himself staring at his leather-clad belly. Slowly, Will lifted his gaze to the stranger's head. He was well over three meters tall, dressed in dark leather with a sweeping cape that nearly touched the ground. He had broad shoulders and a handsome face. A large broadsword hung in a gold sheath at his waist.

Will clenched a fist. *Here's trouble.* He recognized a bully when he saw one.

Another voice shouted. Will leaned his head and noticed others behind the giant. Two were dressed and armed similarly but were normal height, about two meters tall. *And more trouble.* They were lean and strong and walked with arrogant confidence. Behind them, half a dozen other men and women watched, clad in simple clothing like Kemuel's.

The giant held onto Kat's arm and knelt on one knee. He put his other hand under Kat's jaw, lifted her head and looked her over. He took a deep, quivering breath and pulled her head closer to his. Then he narrowed his eyes and breathed in again to smell her. Kat stared daggers into the giant's eyes, grabbed the wrist of the hand under her chin, pushed it away hard, and stepped back.

The giant bared his teeth and lifted his arm to backhand Kat. Will jumped between them and crouched with his arms up, ready to block the swing. He stared into the kneeling giant's eyes, which were now just below Will's.

The giant's mouth fell open, his arm frozen in position. Will continued his stare-down. A grin crept slowly over the giant's face. He bellowed a deep laugh, lowered his arm, and looked back at his comrades. Then he turned back, still laughing, and stood. He took his first steps around Will toward Kat.

Will stepped into his path again and cut him off. The giant stopped and exhaled hard. He thrust the butt of his hand into Will's chest and pushed him back several meters along the ground.

Will slid to a stop on his back, the wind knocked out of him. He pulled himself up quickly, took a deep, labored breath, and again crouched in front of the giant, his arms up and ready to block or punch. The giant pulled back one side of his cape and reached across his waist to grasp his sword with a gloved hand. Only the sound of stretching leather from his glove could be heard. Everyone else stared in silence.

Will didn't budge.

Kemuel stepped around the tree and said something Will couldn't understand.

The annoyed giant glared at him and responded with seething anger. "*Anno Adrok ben Semyaza.*"

Kemuel paled, took a breath, and spoke again.

Tense silence followed. Then one of the giant's armed comrades spoke with an impatient tone and motioned away.

The giant wheeled around and shouted with flared nostrils. His comrade spoke again, gestured toward the six men and women with them and pointed away. Even in the strange language, the message was clear. *Come on, let's go.*

The giant turned back, glared through narrowed eyes at Will, and stared at Kat. He clenched his free hand for a moment; then he let go of his sword and led his group away.

Will watched them leave until he realized Kat was looking at him. She approached and reached to one side of his head. "You're bleeding." She touched him behind his ear and gently turned his head so she could see. "It's a pretty bad scrape."

Will touched the wound and surprised himself by placing his hand on hers. *This is still inappropriate, Will.*

She didn't pull away, instead she let her gaze linger on him. "Thank you."

Will nodded. They slowly dropped their hands to their sides and turned to watch the giant's entourage walking away.

Kemuel let out a tense sigh. "You have no idea how much danger you were just in."

The indignation in Kat's voice was pointed. "I've got some idea." She glared at the group as they disappeared from view. "Who was that?"

"They're called the *nephilim,* the Sons of the Watchers. The giants call themselves *overlords.*"

"You mean there are more people his size?"

"Oh yes. Some are much, much larger. The two others with him, the ones who are about normal height, are called the *sheddim.*" He thought for a moment. "They call themselves something that roughly translates to *nobles.*" His eyes looked hard as flint. "The nephilim see themselves as sons of the gods, destined to subdue the earth." He gestured with an open hand toward Kat. "They and their fathers are manipulating animal bloodlines to breed the wicked, man-eating creatures you were thinking of earlier. They first began crossing their own bloodlines and failed, leading to their lowest class, like the creature you saw spying on your ship, the *se'irim,* or *imps.* They're short, androgynous, and grotesque, but don't underestimate them. They're also wicked and fiercely strong."

Will led them back to the ship. "All of those people were nephilim?"

"Technically, the title *nephilim* is reserved for the *overlords,* but all too often we use the word to refer collectively to all three castes." His expression softened. "The six others following them were humans."

"Are they prisoners?"

He shook his head. "In a way. They're fools. They've submitted to a terrible lie. They choose to worship the nephilim because of false promises of pleasure and wealth." His voice grew edgy. "The nephilim are enemies of humanity. They're psychopathic, wasteful murderers, consuming everything. We're deep into their territory." Kemuel looked around. "I thought we were in Havilah, since so much of the ground has been scorched through strip mining." He turned back to Will and Kat. "Gold and other materials useful for weapons. This isn't Havilah, though. It's Nod."

"And that's worse?"

"Much worse. Nod is where the Watchers first began their conquest of Earth."

"The Watchers?"

Kemuel stopped walking and looked gravely at Will. "Servants of God who rebelled."

Will blinked.

"They're angels, Colonel Stark, and I cannot overstate their power. You don't want to encounter one. The nephilim are nothing compared to the Watchers."

Kat looked more surprised than Will. In fact, she sounded impertinent. "Angels. You mean to tell me those punks are children of angels?"

"Yes. Two hundred angels, in fact. They descended onto Mount Hermon, just east of the headwaters, more than three centuries ago and together swore an oath. Then they moved east..." He gestured around with his eyes. "...here... to Mount Taneen Sharr, took wives from among the human descendants of Cain, and sired a new race of demigods." He looked down. "The first generation grew to become..." His eyes grew wide. "...*massive* giants and could easily have wiped humanity out." He shook his head and blew through pursed lips. "Fortunately for us, they destroyed each other in a war... a war like nothing you can imagine, but not before they gave birth to their second generation, including the *overlords* and *sheddim*."

Kat lowered her head and stared up at Kemuel. "Angels."

Will let Kat express his own disbelief for the moment.

Kemuel sounded determined. "You saw him. Do you have a better explanation?" He shook his head and sighed. "Look, I know this is a lot for you to process all at once, but even if you don't believe me, at least heed my warnings."

Will led them toward the ship and considered everything Kemuel had said. After the ship came into view, he stopped and turned to Kemuel. "What did the *overlord* say to you that frightened you so much? You looked like you had seen a ghost."

Kemuel smirked. "It's funny you should say that." He took a deep breath, and his expression sobered. "The *overlord's* name is Adrok, son of Semyaza. His father... *grandfather*, technically, is the leader of the Watchers. That's how I realized we're in Nod. They're probably heading to Semyaza's palace right now."

Will looked in the direction of the giant's entourage. "And that's why we need to leave?"

"Yes. Their power hasn't reached the West yet, thanks to Enoch's revival. We will have friends there."

Every answer raised more questions, but Will knew what had to be done. He turned to Kat. "All right, no more work except for repairing the ship." He turned back to Kemuel. "We leave at nightfall."

CHAPTER 14

Will, Kat, and Kemuel arrived back at the ship to find Chris hard at work in an open panel near one of the rectangular thruster cones.

Will stopped next to him. "How's the arm?"

Chris moved his arm up and down and winced. "It still hurts, but it's much better. I guess I heal faster than most. I've repaired the hover control system, by the way, but it'll be offline until I finish this." He removed a shiny, platinum cylinder from the panel, followed by several other parts, examined each, and carefully arranged them on the ground. The faint smell of burned insulation wafted out from the open panel. Chris shone a light into the compartment and scrutinized the interior.

His voice rang with success. "There you are." He reached in, pulled out a charred circuit panel, and held it up to show the others. "This is what caused the thruster to malfunction, and ultimately it led to a chain reaction that blew out the hover control. It must have shorted during the time jump. It's an easy fix. We have replacements in the engineering storage compartment."

Kat took the panel from Chris and looked it over. "I'll get one for you." She headed for the ladder.

"Thanks, Kat." Chris turned to Kemuel. "It takes two people to move some of the storage bins."

Kemuel nodded and followed Kat. "I'm here to help."

111

Chris picked up the parts and arranged them just inside the open panel to speed up reassembly.

Will took another look around before he spoke. "Do you need my help here?"

Chris shook his head while inserting a part. "No thanks. As soon as Kat returns with the panel, I'll reassemble and close up. We can take off any time after that."

"Good, but we'll wait for the cover of darkness." Again, Will scanned the area. "We ran into a little trouble while we were gone."

"Trouble?"

Will laid out the events with the giant and his cohorts. He did so without emotion, like a man giving a report about his trip to the hardware store. He sounded detached, but his gut told him otherwise. "Be alert, Chris. I've got a feeling there's more danger here than we know."

"Got it. I promise to scream like a little girl at the first sight of a giant man with a sword."

The bravado brought a smile to Will. "Yeah, you do that. That alone might drive the guy off."

Will left Chris to his work and climbed the ladder into the ship. Once inside he heard Kat and Kemuel grunt as they lifted a crate in the storage compartment. The crate thudded on the floor. Will was headed back to help when he heard Chris shout angrily outside. Will jumped to the ladder, quickly slid down, and looked toward the stern of the ship just in time to see Chris sprint into the woods. Will looked up for an instant to consider Kat and Kemuel. *No time.* He raced into the woods after Chris.

After he rounded several trees and climbed a short ridge, he saw Chris running farther ahead, and it all became clear. A dozen yards in front of the engineer an imp scampered into the brush. It jumped back and forth from foot to foot with its arms in the air, one hand brandishing the platinum cylinder. The imp's amused cackle echoed through the trees. Chris nearly caught up but was slowed by the brush. Will heard him growl angrily as he jumped in after the imp and parted sharp branches as well as he could with one good arm.

Will bolted forward and sprinted some distance to the left around the brush so he could maintain speed. He planned to out-flank the imp and get their part back. He was surprised by his own endurance. He had already covered quite a bit of ground at a full sprint and wasn't breathing hard at all. He bounded down a gully and back up the other side to where he expected to see the others. Just as he reached the top, he spotted a dozen other imps crouched behind some trees. *Ambush.* He didn't have time to warn Chris before they burst out, surrounded the hapless engineer, and pointed several spears menacingly at his belly and throat.

Chris stopped, his hands in the air.

Will crouched behind the top of the ridge. He heard the first imp shout at Chris, waving the cylinder in the air. Its voice was squeaky and guttural, and it spoke in what sounded like the same strange language Will heard from the *overlord* earlier. He couldn't make out a word. Chris wisely stayed silent, and the imp moved closer and shouted louder. When Chris didn't respond, the creature shouted to the others and led them off into the woods. The other imps prodded Chris along with their spears.

Will moved from tree to tree to follow at a safe distance.

They had covered several kilometers when Will reached the end of the forest. He stopped behind a large tree that bordered an endless, barren plain. A hundred meters ahead the hoard of imps prodded Chris along toward the only visible structure a couple of kilometers beyond, a broad, square wall about five stories high. Several narrow plumes of smoke rose from within it, and Will guessed the wall protected a village or city. Thousands of people walked and knelt around the wall in what appeared to be some ritual. The hair on the back of Will's neck stood. Something about this place felt terribly wrong.

He scanned the horizon. Beyond the city, a deep quarry gouged the valley and stretched for many kilometers. The unsightly canyon separated the fortress from a single mountain that rose on the horizon. An occasional deep rumble echoed across the canyon from the mountain. *The mountain Kemuel mentioned? Mount Sharr... or something?* Will looked at the sky. It was a deep azure blue, darker than he was accustomed to, even though there wasn't a cloud in the sky. He could look almost directly at the sun without squinting from the glare. By its position, he guessed it was mid-afternoon.

He heard voices to his left and moved, his head down, around the tree to look. Several dozen people stepped from the forest some distance away and headed straight for the city. They wore simple clothing, and some carried baskets of fruits and grains. As Will watched, dozens more emerged from the woods. Some paused and smiled at first sight of the place. Others knelt and kissed the ground before they continued. All kept their awestruck gaze fixed on the walled city as if it would vanish if they looked away. After a few hundred passed by, Will took a breath and stepped out to walk alongside them. No one seemed to notice.

Will watched Chris and the imps disappear into the distant crowd around the city. When he finally got close enough, Will moved into the crowd while the others around him began their ritual circumambulations.

Will had little choice but to walk with the crowd as they circled the city clockwise. Each time he found an opening, he made his way closer to the center. Ahead, on a balcony above the tall, broad-arched entry that served as the city gate, a dozen people in dark, hooded robes raised crude horns and blew a dissonant call to the crowd.

At once, the crowd stopped in place, wailed at the top of their lungs, and waved their arms crazily or beat their chests. Will crouched, covered his ears, and looked around at the wild-eyed, screaming mob. This continued for nearly a minute until another dissonant blast from the horns ended it. The throng resumed their ritual walk, and Will hurried through them toward the center as they approached the massive, arched entryway some distance ahead.

He emerged from the crowd just in time to see Chris and the imps disappear through the archway.

Will looked the city up and down as he walked with the pilgrims. The walls were strong and imposing, but there was no gate in the archway. Several leather-clad *sheddim* stood in front of the entrance and watched the crowd pass by, but no one guarded the entryway, and there were no sentries on the city wall. *Whoever built this place doesn't see others as a threat. Probably more for secrecy than security.*

As Will approached the archway, the *sheddim* occasionally pointed to select pilgrims and directed them in. Those who were chosen responded with shouts and tears of joy. Other pilgrims congratulated them. Some wept with jealousy and anger and implored the *sheddim* as they walked by.

When Will reached them, one made eye contact with him. He looked Will up and down, took him by the shoulder, and pointed into the entrance. Will nodded and walked in with a handful of others. The archway was large, at least twenty-five meters across. It formed a long tunnel that emptied into a vast courtyard lined with rows of tents and small buildings, as well as countless piles of provisions, apparently offerings from the pilgrims. A broad, clear path led directly ahead from the tunnel to a massive citadel that bordered the city walls on each side.

The others with Will looked around joyfully as if they had finally found paradise. One of them looked behind with wide-eyed awe. Will turned to look, and above the tunneled entryway, an ornate palace rose against the front city wall. He looked back and quickly found the imps who forced Chris toward the citadel directly ahead. In front of its open gateway, another group of *sheddim* held the assembly of select pilgrims outside.

Will slipped between several piles of rocks and looked back and forth. No one seemed to notice. The other pilgrims hastened toward the citadel, apparently impatient to realize the pleasures they had been promised.

Will glanced around from the rock piles. There were dozens of light structures and tents in the courtyard between the palace and the citadel. Prominent among them were several sizable armories of spears, bows, swords, and shields.

Closer to the citadel, an open, mud-brick structure housed what looked like a smelting furnace. Several people heaved rocks inside, supervised by more armed *sheddim.*

Will picked up a small rock in front of him and moved his hand up and down. It was very heavy, like lead.

A large cape swept across an opening between the rock piles. An *overlord* walked by but did not spot Will, who crouched down silently and watched the giant from behind. Another *overlord* joined the first and engaged in quiet conversation. They both watched the assembly in front of the citadel.

Will looked to his left and spotted an opening in the city wall a short distance away. One of the laborers from the smelting furnace approached with a wheeled cart to gather more rocks, and Will took the opportunity to hurry between several tents and into the opening in the wall. Inside, he turned and peered up a dark set of shallow steps that led to the top of the city wall. Will bounded up and carefully emerged from the top. He was alone.

A walled passage about a meter-and-a-half wide led along the top of the city's rampart. The passageway walls were just short enough for Will to lean over and look in either direction. He peeked at the citadel's entrance: no sign of Chris. *They must have already taken him inside.* Will crouched and ran along the passage to where the citadel bordered the city wall.

When he reached the citadel, he found another passage that branched to his right and ran along the front wall of the structure.

He paused to look cautiously around the corner and then hurried past it, farther down the outer passage.

A short distance in, he peeked over the wall and spotted Chris and the imps. They were in a broad antechamber that stretched below, open to the sky above. Directly below, a long series of opulently furnished chambers ran along the outer edge of the huge room, secluded by walls but still open to the sky above. Across the antechamber in the distance, a group of *overlords* and *sheddim* stood around a long, stone table and feasted on bloody carcasses. Closer to Will, another one of the *sheddim* took position beside a log that weighed at least a ton, hefted it on his shoulder, and carried it toward a chamber beyond that appeared to be one of the sources of smoke. A growing number of *nephilim* gathered just inside the entryway to the citadel, and most who were feasting at the table abandoned it, wiped blood from their mouths, and joined the others. When most of them had gathered, they walked out with their chests out and heads held high. A dissonant fanfare and deep thumps of large drums heralded their exit, and Will heard the crowd outside the citadel cheer.

Will moved back along the outer wall to peek outside the citadel. The *nephilim* chose men and women from among the crowd and took them in, often with their arms around the pilgrims' shoulders. The pilgrims still rejoiced and celebrated, some tearfully. Will shook his head. *You'd think they won the lottery or something.* Soon, the *nephilim* escorted the last of the pilgrims into the citadel.

Will hurried back to where he could see the antechamber. The *overlords* and *sheddim* led their chosen into the lavishly furnished rooms. A chill ran down Will's spine. *Pretty sure I don't wanna*

118

see this. He looked up. The hoard of imps scampered away from a small group of *sheddim* with Chris still trapped between them. They poured through an entryway into the next chamber.

Will crouched and ran farther. He reached the boundary between the antechamber and whatever lay beyond. A stairway on his right led to the ground. The passage ahead opened into a large, upper chamber. Watchful, Will stepped in and crossed the ornate, marble floor to a railing that overlooked an enormous amphitheater below. It was many times larger than the first chamber, large enough for tens of thousands of people, with a gentle slope down to the front and an unrestricted view of Mount Sharr in the distance. Several balconies ran along the back at the same level as the side chamber where Will stood. Torches lined the amphitheater walls, and tall, narrow, red tapestries hung between them from the top of the outer wall to the floor. A stone platform spanned the front. At its center, a large fire burned in an ornate pit. Attendants dressed in hooded robes were throwing pieces of something onto the fire. It hit Will: he was looking at an altar.

Behind the altar, pilgrims circled behind the city, and beyond them, the view stretched across the canyon beyond toward the distant mountain.

Will looked down at the back of the auditorium where the imps had stopped below one of the overlooking balconies. They bickered loudly and pointed at Chris while several dozen others scrambled awkwardly toward them.

He breathed out hard and searched for any opportunity to rescue his friend. From this vantage point, he could just see over the auditorium's back wall into the antechamber. With many of the *nephilim* occupied in the smaller chambers, this would be a good time to make a break for it. He turned back toward the front of the auditorium, leaned over the railing and scanned the long tapestries that stretched to the floor.

Something set off Will's instincts, and he wheeled around to find one of the *sheddim* standing only a couple of meters away, his sword pointed at Will's neck. They stared at each other in silence. The *sheddih* turned to look at Chris and the growing mob of imps below, then stared malevolently at Will. He shouted in the same strange language Will had heard before. Will put on his best poker face and stared back silently. Slowly, the warrior sheathed his sword and gestured impatiently toward the stairs Will had just passed. Will descended the stairs to the auditorium floor, and the *sheddih* pushed him several times while they walked toward Chris.

Chris was visibly relieved to see Will, who gave his friend a serious but reassuring nod. A fierce argument ensued between the warrior and the gaggle of imps.

This went on for several minutes until someone shouted from the passage into the antechamber. They turned to see Kemuel walking toward them, flanked by two *sheddim*. As he arrived, he gave both men a serious glance. His unspoken message was clear. *Don't say a word.*

The *sheddih* who had caught Will said something to the others as they approached, and another long conversation followed. Kemuel said little but maintained a confident demeanor. Soon, he appeared to come to some agreement with the warriors while the lead imp protested loudly. Kemuel walked to Will and Chris, placed his arms around their shoulders, and ushered them a short distance into the auditorium away from the others.

He whispered urgently. "Has either of you said anything? And I mean *anything.*"

They shook their heads.

"Good. Please follow my cues and keep quiet." He looked at Will for approval.

Will nodded.

Chris grabbed Kemuel's shoulder and leaned in to whisper in his ear. "The imp stole something from the ship."

"What is it?"

Chris gestured in front of himself. "It's a platinum cylinder about twenty centimeters long. I'm sure it looks valuable to them, but we can't take off without it."

Kemuel thought for a moment. "Has either of you seen any mined ore here, say gold or silver?"

Will remembered what he had seen in the courtyard. "Yes, I saw them refining ore from rocks in a smelting furnace."

"Did you see what kind of ore?"

"Not exactly. It was heavy, like lead."

"Not gold or platinum?"

"No."

Kemuel considered this, and a grin crept over his face. "Please stay close... and act confident."

His expression serious again, Kemuel turned and walked back to the others. Will followed closely and stood at an official looking *parade rest* next to Kemuel. Chris followed suit at his other side. Kemuel said something to the apparent leader of the *sheddim* and gestured toward the lead imp. Now that they were close, Will recognized it as the one they had seen spying on their ship.

The *sheddih* commander listened, then bared his bloody teeth with a snarl. He turned to the imp and shouted a furious rebuke. The imp cowered and protested, its arm raised to shield itself.

The commander gestured to one of his comrades, who pushed the other imps aside and grabbed their cowering leader. He reached into the trembling imp's garment, retrieved the platinum cylinder, and held it up to his commander. The leader thought for a moment and gestured with his head toward Kemuel.

On cue, the *sheddih* warrior handed the tube to Kemuel, who accepted it with a nod and a slight bow. Kemuel flashed a look at Will and Chris and headed quickly through the passage into the antechamber. As he and Chris followed, Will glanced over his shoulder. One of the *sheddim* swung a sword and decapitated the screaming imp while the others scattered.

Another dissonant blast from the horns outside the city walls initiated a long scream from the throng. Behind the closed doors of the small chambers to their side, bloodcurdling screams of pain and terror from the pilgrims inside echoed out and across the antechamber. Will saw Chris shudder and turn to him. His face was ashen, and his breaths grew tense. Will gestured forward with his eyes. *Just keep going.*

Then it hit Will. He remembered the bloody carcasses on the table in the distance and realized what the attendants were casting into the fire at the front of the auditorium. More screams of protest, pain, and terror echoed off the stone walls. Will's every instinct screamed that he should run, but he knew that would destroy Kemuel's ruse. Chris looked like he was about to throw up.

Kemuel never paused. He walked straight across the vast ante-chamber toward the citadel exit. After they went through, they continued across the courtyard to the tunnel under the palace. The screams from the dying pilgrims at last subsided, and another blast from the horns outside ended the shrieks from the mob around the city. Several *overlords* and *sheddim* stared suspiciously as Will and the others walked by. After what felt like an eternity, they exited the arched passageway and walked into the crowd. The sun was dipping over the horizon.

After they pushed their way through the crowd, they started across the barren plain, Chris broke their silence, his wounded arm cradled in the other. "How did you..."

Kemuel continued with his gaze fixed on the forest beyond. "Once they saw your platinum, they assumed we were servants of a rival *nephilim* clan. I let them assume. Clearly, they don't mine platinum here."

Will spoke for only the second time since he had followed Chris into the woods. "Do you think they'll follow us?"

"I'm certain they will. The dead imp told them about your ship. They don't know what it is, but they know it looks valuable. Besides, the imps will blame us for their leader's death."

A hush swept over the crowd behind them. Will and the others turned to see the worshippers prostrate themselves on the ground. A man in ostentatious, royal attire appeared on a high balcony on the city wall with a beautiful woman at his side. An *overlord* stood behind them. Even in the distance, Will immediately recognized the *overlord* as Adrok.

Kemuel's voice seethed with indignation. "That's Adrok's grandfather and his latest queen."

Chris asked Kemuel, "Should we kneel, too?"

"Absolutely not. I bow only to the Most High, not to this... *devil.*" He wheeled around and continued with all haste.

When they reached the trees, they turned to look again. The sky was dimming. Halfway between them and the walled city, hundreds of angry imps scampered toward them, followed by several dozen *overlords and sheddim.*

"No time to lose." Kemuel ran into the woods.

Chris followed quickly. Will stared for a moment. The army of *nephilim* was heavily armed. He turned and followed the others back to the ship.

Chris still cradled his wounded arm and ran the slowest. Will stayed at his side and allowed Kemuel to run ahead.

They arrived at the ship to find Kat looking out from the top of the ladder and Kemuel below her. Chris shouted, "The replacement board... I need the replacement board." Kat disappeared for a moment and emerged with the part. She handed it down to Kemuel, who met Chris at the open panel near the aft thruster. Chris took the board, reached into the open panel, and carefully inserted it where they had removed the charred panel earlier. He installed the platinum tube and hastily reassembled the other parts.

Angry battle cries grew louder as the *nephilim* approached. Will sent Kemuel inside the ship and stood guard near Chris until he secured the panel and ran for the ladder.

Will followed up the ladder just as the *nephilim* emerged from the trees. He retracted the ladder and secured the hatch just as the first arrow struck the hull. Chris and Kemuel were strapping themselves in as he jumped to his own seat and secured his harness. Kat was already at her controls. The hull resounded with hollow clangs as the *nephilim* outside struck it with clubs and spears.

Chris threw several switches and shouted from behind. "You've got power. *Go, go, go.*"

Kat pulled up on the throttle with her left hand and pushed the *cyclic* forward with her other. The ship obediently rose from the ground and leaned forward. As they lifted through the trees, they could see the angry *nephilim* below on the monitors. The hull clinked with more arrow strikes until they rose to a safe height. The sun was just disappearing over the horizon to their left.

Kat continued to lift them above the trees. "Heading?"

Will watched the furious *nephilim* shrink below. "West."

"Aye, sir."

Kat adjusted the *anti-torque pedals* to yaw the ship around and then pushed the *cyclic* forward and pulled up hard on the throttle. The ship leaned forward and accelerated west.

Will took the controls at his station and looked over his shoulder at Chris. "Transition to aerodynamic flight."

Chris adjusted the settings in front of him. "Transitioning now. Rotating *Snowman* forward... thirty degrees... sixty degrees... rotation complete."

Will throttled up and pulled on the yoke to climb to a safe altitude. "Kemuel, where are these friends you talked about?"

Kemuel leaned forward. "Three hundred kilometers south-west of the headwaters, on the west bank of the river that runs that direction."

Chris studied a monitor at his station. "That's nearly fifteen thousand kilometers." He tapped in figures while he spoke. "If we can maintain five hundred knots, then the earth will be rotating about twice as fast underneath us. We should have sixteen hours until the sun rises behind us."

Will recognized the problem. "We won't make it all the way. We'll need another place to set down for the day."

CHAPTER 15

Will walked the underground corridors of the secret base. It was late, the lights were dim, and the halls were empty. He thought of the mission. *Was it all a dream?* He couldn't help but feel relieved. They weren't lost. The mission hadn't happened yet. Then he felt a strange sense of urgency. He needed to get back to his quarters fast.

Just then, an imp peeked around a corner ahead and disappeared from view. Will shouted and ran for it. He rounded the corner and found nothing but a long, empty hallway.

Kat, Chris. They need me. I can't let them down. Will sprinted to the dormitory entrance and flashed his badge. A red light flashed, and a buzzer squawked disapproval. He flashed his badge again and again, until finally, he got the green light and beep he wanted. He pushed through the door. Inside, a dozen imps and *sheddim* stared at him.

He raised his arms to fight, only to hear their taunting laughter in response. Then he saw Adrok stare at him and smile as he walked into Kat's room.

Will bolted forward and into Kat's room. She tossed and turned in her bed, and Adrok stood over her. The *overlord* unsheathed his sword and held it over Kat. Will yelled and lunged forward to attack, but he was too late. Adrok plunged the sword down.

Will sat up in his bed and gasped. After he caught his breath, he looked quietly at the ship's sleeping compartment. The reality of their circumstance came back to him. Kat and Chris slept soundly in their own bunks nearby. Will found himself staring at Kat. Whether the dream was grounded in reality or not, it gave him a deep sense of compassion for her.

He got up, wiped his forehead, headed forward to the bridge, and peered through the drops of water on the outside windows. It was early afternoon, and here, more than eleven thousand kilometers west of their first landing site, the mist had risen outside.

The external hatch clicked and opened, and Kemuel climbed in with a basket of fruits, vegetables, and bread. The fragrance of warm bread filled the bridge. He kept his voice to a near whisper. "Good morning, sir. Are the others awake yet?"

Will shook his head.

"I'm not surprised." He set the basket down. "I thought you all might like something that hasn't been freeze-dried, reconstituted, and microwaved." He found his seat near the back of the bridge and sat. "I got the food from the nearby village. We're fortunate that the people there are friends."

"How can you be certain?"

Kemuel thought for a moment. "Because they've chosen to reject everything the *nephilim* stand for. They've called on the Name."

Will was about to ask about that when Kat and Chris emerged onto the bridge. Chris was the first to speak. "Do I smell bread?"

Kemuel smiled and gestured to the basket. "Help yourself." He turned to Will. "Better yet, there's a hill next to us where we can enjoy our food with a view. We'll be within sight of the ship, and it'll be a great place to talk about what's happening."

Will considered that. It would be safer to stay in the ship, but they needed to learn everything they could about the world around them to salvage their mission. "Are there *nephilim* here?"

Kemuel shrugged. "I didn't see any, and their home is a considerable distance east of here."

"All right then, but everybody take earpieces. I should have required that the last time we left the ship. If we get separated again, I want comms." They each inserted a small, nearly invisible earwig, and Chris handed an extra to Kemuel.

Kemuel was right. They climbed above the mist, and the view was remarkable. The sky above, even in broad daylight, was a rich, deep blue with no glare whatsoever. It cast a crisp, golden glow on everything. Just as they reached the top of the hill, the mist settled, and the view below cleared. A village with several dozen tents and finely crafted huts lay next to another hill in the distance. The fields immediately around it were lined with rows of grain and vegetables, and the trees were rich with all manner of fruit. The rest of the land was pristine, with green grass and lush vegetation.

The grass at the top of the hill was dry, so Kemuel invited the others to sit while he distributed food from the basket. Chris sat first and took a large bite of fruit.

Kat remained standing and looked over the village. Then she tilted her head up, closed her eyes, and took in a deep breath. Will watched her and smiled. The fragrance of jasmine and lilacs wafted in the breeze from the valley below, and with the high air pressure, every breath was invigorating. She stretched out her arms, wheeled around, and then let herself fall into the grass. She lay on her back in the grass for a moment, then sat up and leaned against a tree. Kemuel lowered the basket of food next to her. She took a piece of bread and a handful of grapes. After taking a bite, she drew one knee up and gazed into the distance.

Will was entranced. Kat's blue eyes and short, auburn hair caught the warm glow of the sun, and her skin looked soft and radiant. On top of that, she seemed playful and relaxed. He was grateful Kat didn't have to see Semyaza's palace.

It wasn't until she looked at him that he realized he was staring. He looked away and found his own seat on the grass and, with one hand, accepted some bread from Kemuel. He glanced at Kat one more time to drink in the image. Then he noticed Chris watching him. He wore a broad grin.

Will regathered his thoughts and faced Kemuel. The strange man had offered some explanations, and Will was eager to hear them. "How did you get on our ship?"

Kemuel shifted uncomfortably. "Not without help. I couldn't have done that alone." He sat in the grass in front of Will. "I can't tell you how exactly, not yet. Please trust me on this."

Will looked Kemuel straight in the eyes and decided their new friend had earned his trust. "All right."

A deep, trumpeting grunt echoed across the fields. A large herd of brachiosaurs emerged onto a distant field and foraged in the surrounding trees.

Kat interrupted her repose and sat up. "Why are there dinosaurs here? Just how far back did we go?"

Kemuel gazed at the herd of brachiosaurs. "This is the year 1000."

"BC? No way."

"No. The year 1000 of creation. Around five thousand years before your time. Your chronometers are working fine." Kemuel thought for a moment. "You've noticed how different things are in this time, right? Well, between the increased atmospheric pressure, the higher percentage of oxygen in the atmosphere, and the vapor canopy filtering out most cosmic radiation, everything lives longer."

He watched a pair of pterodactyls rise on the wind above. "You realize that pterodactyls wouldn't be able to take off in the atmosphere you're accustomed to, right? Have you never wondered why the insects in the fossil record are so large? They stop growing when they can no longer absorb oxygen, which makes them smaller in your time." He gestured toward the brachiosaurs in the distance. "And massive creatures like that don't have large-enough lungs to survive in your time. Lizards never truly stop growing, and here, there's little to stop it, so they can get pretty large, especially after a few centuries."

Kat's surprise was apparent. "Centuries?"

"Sure. How old do you think I am?"

"Maybe thirty-five?"

Kemuel smiled. "Well you got the first two digits right. I'm three hundred fifty years old."

Will furrowed his brow. "But you came from our time."

"Yes, technically, but I was born of this world." He thought for a moment. "Here, the average man or woman lives about nine hundred years."

Chris dropped his jaw. Kat didn't sound ready to believe that. "Nine hundred years."

"Yes. But when we enter your world, we won't be able to live much more than five centuries, and each successive generation born to us will live a shorter life until ultimately, lifespans land below one century."

Kemuel paused to let that sink in. Kat tore off another piece of bread, ready with her next question. "Why didn't the dinosaur attack me?"

Kemuel smirked. "Why should he have? There's no need to eat meat here. In your day and age, it can be tremendously difficult to subsist without meat, but here..." He looked around him. "It's much easier to get all the nutrition you need without it."

"So no one eats meat here?"

"Well, people don't, and few animals ever do. The *nephilim* do, and some of the foul beasts they'll soon breed will, but God hasn't ordained it yet, so it's considered an abomination."

"God?"

Kemuel's expression turned very serious. "You all seem surprised by everything, but isn't this exactly what you find in the Bible?"

Kat shrugged. "I've never read it."

Kemuel shook his head with a look of deep compassion. "The curse you all live under is so quiet, so deceptive." He turned his attention to the east. "At least here, you can see the war right in front of you."

Will had been listening intently. "Tell us about the war."

Kemuel's expression grew distant. "I suppose the war really started almost a thousand years ago when Father Adam and his wife Eve were cast from the garden, and it continued when their son Cain was sent wandering east to Nod as punishment for murder. His brother Abel was the first martyr." His sober expression brightened for a moment. "The tide first began to turn when Adam's grandson Enosh called on the Name, and many others followed his example." He paused. "But I don't suppose that's the part of the war you're concerned about."

Will let his silence communicate agreement.

Kemuel's gaze disappeared into the distance again. "The Watchers—two hundred of them—landed on Mount Hermon during the days of Jared." He appeared to calculate in his head. "About five hundred twenty years ago."

Will blinked. This all felt more like legend than real life.

"They took an oath binding themselves to each other and moved east to rule Cain's descendants from Mount Taneen Sharr." He shifted his glance between his three listeners. "Mount Sharr is the mountain you could see from the great hall in the citadel of Semyaza. Then in an act of brazen rebellion against the Lord of All, they took human wives, made them their queens, and began to father children: half angel, half human."

"The *nephilim?*"

"Yes. The *nephilim* claim to be demigods. I told you earlier the first generation were unspeakably large giants. They echo in your own history as the Titans. They reigned for five centuries and very nearly unleashed a complete genocide on humanity." He shuddered.

"But war broke out among them, and instead they destroyed each other, only a couple of decades before this time. That's why I stopped your auto-return sequence here. This is the most peaceful time since the Watchers arrived—much more peaceful than what's to come." He stared into the distance.

Will couldn't suppress his curiosity. He cleared his throat to regain his attention.

Kemuel blinked and focused on Will. "Today's *nephilim* are their descendants. You've seen all three of their orders: the *overlords,* the *sheddim,* and the *se'irim.* The *se'irim* are despised even by the other *nephilim,* so they live as scavengers and robbers. As you can well imagine, the *overlords* dominate."

Kemuel's expression grew indignant. "The Watchers claim to have ushered in a millennial kingdom of the gods, one in which they will rule all humanity through their *nephilim* spawn. It's all a counterfeit of what God will truly do at the end of the age. Enoch made that clear."

Chris cocked his head. "Enoch?"

"Enoch was born forty-four years before the Watchers came. He was the seventh generation of the patriarchs, the first-born of each generation, and he was a great prophet."

"Shouldn't he still be alive, then?" Kat said.

"God took him up thirteen years ago when he was only three hundred sixty-five. It was a powerful testimony."

"To whom?"

"To everybody. To the *nephilim.* To the Watchers. God confirmed Enoch's testimony by taking him up. Enoch had long since warned the Watchers that God had exiled them to the earth, and he warned the *nephilim* that God would deny them rest."

Kemuel furrowed his brow and tilted his head. "When people die, they either go to reward or to punishment, where they await judgment. But when *nephilim* die, they are cursed to wander the earth as unclean spirits, never again to be satisfied through the flesh, always parched, bitter, and empty. Have you never wondered where ghosts come from?"

Will's mind flooded with the memory of his nighttime encounter at the secret base. He glanced at Kat. Her expression was distant and troubled, and she placed a hand on the back of her neck.

Kemuel continued. "Enoch's ministry exploded during the last fifty-seven years of his life." He leaned forward and rested his arms on his knees. "Seventy years ago, in the year 930, Adam died. That was a big deal. You see, when Adam and Eve were cast from the garden, God warned that they would die, but until Adam's death, the only people who died were either murdered or fell to terrible accidents. Humanity had naïvely believed itself to be immortal. Adam's was the first *natural* death, and it rocked the world. The realization that death is inevitable spread fear like an epidemic. Millions mourned his death. At the funeral, Enoch warned them to call on the Name. Revival spread like wildfire."

Will tried to imagine millions of people attending a funeral.

"The Watchers countered by promising to end death by the end of their rule, but anyone with discernment knows they intend to destroy all of humanity by then. With no one left to die, they will have destroyed death." Kemuel's gaze dropped to his side. "They'll nearly succeed, too."

Laughter echoed across the valley below as a group of children played in a field a short distance from the village. Will and the others paused to enjoy their food, the beauty around them, and the unbridled joy of the children below.

After a few minutes, Will caught movement in the distance to their right. He leapt to his feet and moved to a better vantage point. Once he was certain, he announced it to the others. "Imps, and they're heading for the village."

CHAPTER 16

Kat, Chris, and Kemuel dropped their food and jumped to their feet. The band of imps scampered across the valley below.

Kemuel stood next to Will to look. "They're marauders. Dozens of them. We have to warn the village."

Will turned to Kat and Chris. "Guard the ship. Take off if you have to, but keep her safe. I want open comms. Keep your mikes hot."

All four of them touched their earwigs to activate the microphones as they parted ways.

Will and Kemuel ran down the hill and headed to the field where the children were playing. Will tried to formulate a plan. "Will the villagers have weapons?"

"Not likely. The imps are poorly formed, and most are slow, so they aren't good fighters, but don't underestimate their strength. They'll try to spear or club you, and a single blow would probably kill you. Keep moving. Don't just block their attacks; redirect the force."

Their run became a sprint until they reached the clearing and saw the children. Kemuel shouted and pointed in the direction of the approaching imps. "Se'irim! Se'irim!"

The oldest of the children, a teenage girl, quickly gathered the others, made sure everyone was accounted for, and ran them back toward the village. Will and Kemuel followed. By Will's count, there were eight other children less than ten years old and two toddlers. Will and Kemuel carried the youngest, so they could make better time.

They ran through a forested area and emerged from the trees where they could see the village across the clearing. The teenager stopped, cupped her hands around her mouth, and sounded a loud, warning shriek. Within seconds, someone rang a warning bell in the center of town, and the villagers ran in every direction to get their families to safety.

They were a short distance into the clearing when more than fifty imps emerged from the trees some distance to their right. They shrieked and waved clubs and spears. Kemuel shouted to the children, and they stopped.

He turned and asked the teenage girl something, and a brief, urgent conversation ensued. The girl pointed to the village and back into the woods.

Kemuel turned to Will. "The villagers have a safe house underground, but we won't make it. She says they have a treehouse in the next clearing."

Will watched the band of imps. One of them spotted the children, shrieked at the others, and pointed toward their newly intended victims.

Will shouted to the girl. "Go! Go!"

She didn't need to understand. She quickly ushered the children back into the woods. Will and Kemuel ran behind, the toddlers clutched in their arms. The girl shouted to Kemuel and he translated for Will. "She said we must follow her carefully."

The imps shrieked behind them. The children filed into a tidy line and followed the teenage girl. Will and Kemuel did the same.

She led them over several obstacles and avoided the clearest path, where Will spotted a well-camouflaged pit. Soon after, the sound of breaking branches and the dying screams of a handful of imps echoed from behind.

As Will and the others ran through the trees, a dozen of the faster imps started to close the distance. The girl shouted an instruction and led them single file through a hidden path in some brush. Will and Kemuel had to crouch awkwardly to get through, careful to keep the branches around from hitting the small children in their arms.

As they ran from the other side of the brush, Will turned to see the first imps scamper around the brush. One of them tripped over a cord and released several large logs that rolled over their position. Their blood-curdling shrieks made the hair on Will's neck stand.

Will was impressed. *These villagers are resourceful.* At last, they emerged from the forest. A tall, thick tree stood in the middle of the clearing ahead. A sturdy platform straddled its branches about ten meters off the ground. A single wooden ladder led from the ground to the platform.

They ran across the field and reached the tree just as the first few of the angry imps scampered from the forest behind them. The girl ushered each of the children up the ladder.

Will watched as the rest of the imps burst from the forest. Three of them were approaching fast.

He looked at Kemuel. "We won't have enough time. Get the children to safety and pull the ladder up." He handed the toddler to the girl, then ran toward the approaching imps.

Will reached the first imp, who wielded a wooden club over his head. The imp swung down with enough force to break bones.

Will dodged the blow and rolled on the ground. The imp's club struck the earth with a thud. It growled fiercely, charged, and swung the club a second time just as two of his comrades arrived with spears. Will dodged again, but this time he managed to grab the end of the club. He pulled it to his chest, spun, wrenched it from the bewildered imp's grasp and pulled the creature off its feet. One of the other imps thrust a spear at Will. He jumped to one side. The spearpoint missed him by an inch. He flipped the club around and seized it by the handle. He swung with all his might and crushed the second imp's skull. Then he dropped the club, grabbed the imp's spear, wheeled around to the third imp, and impaled it before it could spear him.

Before he could draw the spear back, the first imp tackled him at his waist. He hit the ground hard. One of the approaching imps stopped to throw its spear like a javelin. Will tried to roll out of the way, but the first imp held him in place. The creature jumped up and grabbed Will's neck just in time for the flying spear to pierce its back and protrude from its chest.

Will pushed the dead imp off and scrambled to his feet. He glanced toward the tree. Kemuel was pulling the ladder off the ground and into the treehouse. Will turned to the hoard of imps. They were only seconds away, and there had to be thirty more of them.

Kemuel shouted from the treehouse and Will turned to see him drop a rope ladder. He sprinted toward the tree. The remaining imps were slower than their dead counterparts, so Will gained some distance from them by the time he reached the rope ladder. He grabbed it as high as he could and swung one foot through the bottom rung. He heaved himself up with his arms several times and carried the bottom of the ladder off the ground with his foot. It was just out of reach when the imps arrived below.

One of the attacking imps swung a club hard, but Will was too high. Will pulled himself up again. Then another imp thrust a long spear, cut a deep slice in Will's calf, and sent him swinging. White streaks cut across Will's field of vision. Every muscle tensed from the pain and stole his breath away. He grimaced and clung to the rope ladder, careful not to let the bottom fall to the ground. *No matter what happens, keep the children safe.*

Will's leg throbbed, and his body surged with each heartbeat. He gritted his teeth, continued to haul himself up, secured his free foot into a rung, and reached down to pull the ladder's slack off his injured leg. He pulled it higher to keep it out of reach of the imps below and held himself in place. A stream of blood from his calf fell onto the imps below. He felt dizzy, and his vision began to tunnel.

He looked up. The children watched from above as Kemuel readied himself to pull Will up to safety. Then some of the children yelled and pointed down. Below, a handful of the imps ignited arrows and mounted them in their bows.

Will's mind raced. The imps were going to burn them out. He searched for options. The imps drew their bows and aimed.

Then the ground began to shake, and dozens of deep, trumpeting cries rolled across the valley. The archers turned to look across the clearing, and their malevolence melted into fear. A large herd of brachiosaurs stampeded directly toward them. The imps abandoned their attack and fled. A few struggled briefly to climb the massive trunk before they gave up and scampered across the field.

Will watched the thundering stampede. *What on earth could scare them so much?* Then he smiled as *Chronos* crested the trees and hovered behind them. Kat deftly maneuvered the ship in swinging dives across the brachiosaurs, and the terrified beasts thundered around the tree and crushed the fleeing imps.

Once he was certain the dinosaurs were gone and the imps dead, Will carefully lowered himself toward the ground while Kemuel lowered the main ladder and hurried down. Will's head spun, and the world slowly closed in around him. He was still a couple of meters off the ground when Kemuel rushed to his side. As Kemuel helped him to the ground, Will could just hear Kemuel's voice as the light tunneled to black.

Will awoke later to find himself on a cot in the village, surrounded by grateful parents. He forced deep, tense breaths as the village doctor stitched his wound. The parents around him lavished their children with kisses and wept with joy and relief.

Kat, Chris, and Kemuel stood nearby while the teenage girl continued to relate their adventure to the adults. Will still couldn't understand any of it, but he had a good idea what she was saying. Listening helped distract him from the pain.

The doctor cut off the excess thread, cleaned his leg of residual blood, and applied a thick ointment to the wound. The skin numbed, and Will immediately felt relief. He nodded gratefully to the doctor.

The doctor said something to Kemuel, who reported it to Will. "You'll be surprised how quickly you heal. Their medicine is quite good, and by now, your body is saturated with oxygen from the higher pressure."

Will was still groggy but managed to push himself to a sitting position on the cot. "Are the villagers safe now?"

Kemuel frowned. "For the moment, but more marauders are sure to follow. I'm surprised to see them so far from Nod already."

Will was concerned for the people around him. "What will they do?"

"The same thing as everyone else who refuses to submit to the *nephilim*. If they can't fight, they'll migrate farther west. Their elder tells me they've already been planning it. The surrounding villages fear the *nephilim* more than they fear God, which makes them unreliable."

Interesting way to put it. "I hope they leave soon, then." He looked straight at Kemuel. "We need to get the ship someplace safer."

Kemuel nodded.

As the doctor stepped away, the little boy Will had carried earlier ran from his parents and threw his arms around Will's neck. He uttered one word. "*Ashakkerka.*"

Will put his hand on the back of the boy's head and held him to his chest. "You're welcome, little man."

CHAPTER 17

Will held the ship in a steep bank. It carved a broad circle around the city's outskirts. If it hadn't been for the occasional need to employ his wounded leg to manipulate the rudder pedals, flying wouldn't have caused him much pain at all, but he had little choice. Kat needed to be at her own station, ready to take over for hover-flight.

The monitors employed spectral enhancements and glowed green or red to display the nighttime city below. Will was surprised at its size. Kemuel had told them several hundred thousand people lived here.

Kemuel gestured to a monitor display ahead. "It's the most obvious structure on the mountain in the center, there."

Will nodded and leveled their course across the broad river toward the three-hundred-meter-tall mountain in the center of the city. "Let's make this a quiet landing."

He handed off controls to Kat and deployed the landing gear as Chris rotated *Snowman* back for hover-flight. Kat took them in for a smooth approach. An ornate structure had been carved into the mountainside with a broad ramp that spiraled from the base to the top. At the summit, a stone tower rose above a broad, open amphitheater.

Kemuel knelt between Will and Kat and pointed to the monitor display. "There, do you see the large enclosed chamber that opens onto the floor of the amphitheater?"

Kat focused on the image while she carefully manipulated the controls. "The tower entrance at the end zone opposite us?"

Kemuel laughed. "No, the large opening on the left at the fifty-yard line."

Kat nodded and continued their descent.

Chris adjusted the view on one of the screens. "We're being watched." Will and Kemuel looked where Chris pointed. "There, from the chamber at the top of the tower." In the magnified view on the screen Chris indicated, two men watched *Chronos* descend.

Kemuel reassured them. "If they're in that tower, they're friends."

Kat took the ship down until they were just above the center of the amphitheater floor, yawed around ninety degrees to face the rear of the ship toward the adjacent chamber, and carefully backed them into the opening before she set them down for a smooth landing.

Will turned to Chris. "Get to work on the ship. I want her spaceworthy ASAP."

Chris responded with a thumbs-up. "Yes, sir."

Will turned to Kemuel. "Will your friends see us as a threat?"

Kemuel shrugged. "Possibly."

"Then you should introduce us."

wwwwwwwwww

The sky above slowly grew brighter as dawn approached. Will walked slowly to the center of the manicured, grass amphitheater floor. He forced his own breaths whenever the pain stopped it, careful not to stress the stitches in his leg. Kat and Kemuel followed and waited with him. They watched as one of the sentries from the tower descended the last steps to join them on the field.

Will studied the man as he approached. He was dressed in a tunic that reached to just above his knees. It was secured at the waist by a belt from which, on his left, hung a sheathed longsword. He had olive skin, jet-black hair, and a trimmed beard. He looked strong, and his gait was confident but not arrogant. He also appeared to be about Will and Kat's age, but Will had given up guessing ages in this place.

When the man reached them, he stopped a few paces away, reached across his body, and grasped the handle of his sword.

Kemuel spoke first, and after only a few words, the man let go of his sword, closed the last distance, and grabbed Kemuel in a tight-fisted bear hug. They exchanged a few more words until Kemuel gestured toward Will and Kat. Will stepped forward and extended his hand. The man looked at Will's hand and then at Kemuel, who spoke a few more words.

The man grinned, accepted Will's handshake, drew him in for a hug, and said something in a welcoming, bass voice. Will couldn't help but smile. *I like this guy.* He couldn't understand the words, but he suspected it was something like *"any friend of Kemuel's..."*

Kemuel shifted back to English. "This man is Khaliil. He's a tower guardian, and he has already sent word to the Council."

Khaliil stepped in front of Kat and bowed his head with his fist on his chest. She smiled sheepishly and bowed her head in return. She looked awkwardly at Will.

Khaliil followed her gaze to Will, looked him in the eyes, turned back to Kat, and looked again at Will. Then he grinned even more broadly as he took one step back.

Will hoped no one could see his face flush. *Why is it so obvious to everyone?*

Mercifully, a group of men and women emerged from the tunnel entrance in the "end zone" opposite the tower. Determined to show respect by helping to close the distance, Will led Kat and Kemuel toward the approaching party despite the pain.

Kemuel sighed as they walked. "This will be tough to explain."

There were twelve men and twelve women in all. Their attire was simple but looked somehow important. By their expressions, Will surmised they bore heavy responsibility. They stopped a short distance away. One member of their entourage continued forward. He stepped in front of the others and escorted one of the women— his wife, by all appearances—with him.

Kemuel approached and greeted them with a bow. After a moment of introductions, Kemuel spoke to Will and the others. "This is the Council of Twelve. Their wives compose the Council of Women." He searched for the right words. "You might think of them as a cross between church apostles and a ruling assembly."

Will mimicked Kemuel's bow from earlier. Kat followed his example. The council members nodded in response.

Will scanned the group as Kemuel began to speak again. His eyes landed on one councilman, and he couldn't hide his shock. "Dr. Aelter, is that you?" Kat followed Will's gaze, and similar recognition flashed on her face.

147

The councilman looked back and forth, clearly puzzled. Kemuel turned to Will and dropped his jaw, aghast. "You know this man?" Will measured his words carefully, uncomfortable saying anything about the secret base. "He basically built the ship, but he didn't know specifically about the device. At least, I didn't think he knew at the time."

Kemuel shook his head. "I had no idea the council were conducting such operations. It sounds like they were helping you from a different angle than I was working."

Kemuel seemed to struggle to regain his verbal footing and resumed his discussion with the council. Over the course of several minutes, members of the council nodded and interjected questions while Kemuel explained their situation. At one point, it seemed clear he was relating their experience in the village. As Kemuel gestured toward Will's leg, Khaliil's expression turned grave at the sight of the wound. He gave Will's shoulder a firm shake. Several of the women—and a few of the men—wiped tears at the apparent reference to the rescued children.

Much to Will's surprise, he started picking words out of the conversation and recognize their meaning.

As Kemuel finished, the council members' expressions grew serious. A moment of painful silence ensued. Then their leader announced something and waited for Kemuel to translate.

"They've invited you to their meeting hall." Kemuel gave Will a serious look. "*Both* of you."

Kat looked at Will. "What about Chris?" She lifted her hand to her earwig.

Will took her arm to stop her and nodded subtly to Kemuel. "Tell the council we'll *both* be happy to accompany you."

Kemuel looked conflicted but nodded in agreement.

After a few more words, the council members left. Kemuel stood by silently.

Will waited until Kemuel came back to him. He spoke under his breath. "What was that about?"

Kemuel responded quietly. "There'll be a conflict of interest here." He gestured around them. "This place..." He struggled for words.

Kat interjected. "Is this some kind of temple?"

"No. Not a temple. A temple is where God's presence resides for covenant reasons. No, this is primarily a meeting place for worship, and secondarily a fortress."

Will knew that was significant. "To protect what?"

Kemuel pointed up to the tower. "That. The Council and their followers are responsible for protecting the first device. Since we came from the future, they deduced the bad news that you have a second one. We didn't even know Enoch made a second device until you came up with it in the future." He placed one hand on the side of his forehead. "Of course, now that you've met them here in the past, they will have known about the second device ever since this time." He shook his head. "Time travel makes my head hurt."

Will cocked his head and waited for more information. "Tell me about the first device."

Kemuel lowered his hand from his forehead. "In the future, we still have the device safe and secure in our own hands, but then word reached us that you had found a second one." He shook his head.

"Lord only knows why on earth Enoch made a second one, but he must have had his reasons."

"What will they want to do with it?"

"Our primary imperative has always been to keep it out of the hands of the Watchers and the *nephilim*." He scratched the back of his head. "I neglected to mention Lieutenant Commander Saif-ad-Deen. I didn't mean to. I just found myself leaving it out."

"It was good thinking. Besides, if everything turns out all right, you can offer that later." For Khaliil's sake, Will pretended to speak to Kat as he touched his earwig. "Chris?"

Will, Kat, and Kemuel all heard his response through their earpieces. "Yes?"

"Stay with the ship and don't let anyone see you for the time being."

"Roger, sir."

Will and Kemuel looked at each other and then turned to Khaliil. Khaliil glanced suspiciously at the ship and then turned to lead them into the tunnel exit. Will thought it spoke volumes that a warrior like Khaliil chose to expose his back to them. It made him like the man all the more. As Khaliil led them through the tunnel and out onto the broad ramp that spiraled down the mountain, Will resumed his interrogation to distract himself from the pain. "So they built this place to protect the device?"

"Yes. Enoch told his followers to build it."

They followed the ramp down along the mountainside and gazed occasionally at the view across the river that bordered the city's east side.

"And Enoch constructed the device? Why?"

Kemuel looked baffled. "I always assumed it was because God told him to. Maybe Enoch thought it was the best way to fight the *nephilim*. After the catastrophe, it turns out to be a priceless power source, but in this time, we have little need for such power."

"Sure, you barely need a roof here. No rain, no snow, no winter cold. It's almost paradise."

Kemuel nodded.

"Why is Dr. Aelter here?"

Kemuel shrugged. "His name is Joachim. I have no idea why you met him in the future." He turned his head to face Will. "A group of us will travel to the future to protect the device. The Council and their wives will form the core of that group, forty people in all. We call ourselves the Guardians."

Kemuel stared at the ground, lost in thought.

Will put his hand on Kemuel's shoulder to regain his attention. Kemuel looked up. "I was born to one of their families. We've been fighting the *nephilim* for centuries."

"You mean there are *nephilim* in the future?"

"Yes, but not as many." Kemuel sounded incredulous again. "Your own Bible says so in Genesis 6:4, 'The *nephilim* were on the earth in those days—*and also afterward.*'" He emphasized the last three words. "King David dispatched a *nephilih* in battle when he killed Goliath." Something flashed across Kemuel's face. "Don't get me wrong, none of them will survive the catastrophe, but we think part of the *nephilim* bloodline survived in the wife of Ham, allowing other giants to be born to the Canaanite descendants of Anak."

"Ham?"

"The second of Noah's sons: Shem, Ham, and Japheth. To our knowledge, after Enoch's ministry, no angels dared to sire first-generation *nephilim* again."

"Why not?"

Kemuel raised his eyebrows. "Fear. The two hundred are under a grievous curse, and after their judgment, no others dared to defile humans directly as they did. I know others will continue to manipulate humans more subtly, but my knowledge on that is scant. We haven't been completely privy to the angelic side of the War."

Angelic? Will pondered that for a moment.

Kemuel dropped that line and continued. "Ever since Enoch's ascension, it appears to have become either impossible or too frightening even for the two hundred to directly father children again. The penalty for them will be severe."

"Penalty?"

"Imprisonment in the Abyss, a terrible place of torture deep under the earth. Even the disembodied spirits of the *nephilim* will be terrified of it throughout history. That won't happen for some time yet, though."

Khaliil stopped them. They stood in front of what appeared to be the council chamber, carved into the mountain one level below the amphitheater.

Will worked hard to wrap his mind around everything he had just heard. "So how do you fight an angel?"

Kemuel took Will's shoulders in his hands. "You don't, Colonel Stark, you don't. You leave that to God, and you do that by calling on His Name."

Khaliil watched silently, his brows furrowed in concern.

Before they could continue, someone stepped from the council chamber and ushered them in.

Will, Kat, and Kemuel followed Khaliil into the chamber. The twenty-four members were seated in large chairs set in a semicircle.

The leader stood, gestured for them to stand in front of the council and issued an official-sounding proclamation. Kemuel protested emphatically. Several different council members made statements, and Kemuel argued with each of them. Finally, Joachim stood and shouted angrily at Kemuel. He fell silent.

Will knew something was wrong. "What is it?"

Kemuel faced Will and Kat. "They will not permit you to leave with the device."

"But we can't get home without it."

"They know. I've told them you must return to your own time, but they see keeping the device from the *nephilim* as the greater imperative."

The council members abruptly rose. From behind Will and the others, two men entered the hall. Will couldn't be sure how long they had been listening at the entrance. The older of the two looked to be in his fifties or sixties, his hair and beard a snowy white, and the youngest had the appearance of a man in his thirties. They acted like men of great authority, and humility. As they passed by, Kemuel bowed deeply, but the younger took him by the shoulders and lifted him up straight. Then they stepped in front of the council, and the elder spoke.

Will leaned his head over to Kemuel. "Who are they?"

Kat leaned in to listen, as well.

Kemuel responded in a whisper and watched the man speak. "They are two of only seven surviving men in this world the Council must listen to: Enosh and Lamech, the oldest and youngest of the Patriarchs."

"Patriarchs?"

Kemuel appeared to calculate in his head. "Enosh is seven hundred sixty-five years old, the first man to call on the Name. Lamech is only one hundred twenty-six years old, younger than any of the council members, but he's also Enoch's grandson. Their line is formed by the firstborn of each generation, with the sole exception of the second generation. Adam's son Cain murdered his brother and lost his inheritance to the third-born, Seth. Most of the humans you saw in Nod are Cain's descendants." Kemuel gestured toward the two men. "Enosh is the third generation of the firstborn. Lamech is the ninth generation."

"You're losing me," Will said.

"Think of it this way, if Adam had been king, Seth would now sit on the throne, Enosh would be the heir apparent, and Lamech would be the youngest in line for the throne. Theirs is the holy bloodline. Lamech is only twelve generations from Abraham. The bloodline will continue until the birth of the Messiah."

Will felt a rush of epiphany. *Of course.* The story around him suddenly began to make sense.

While Will and the others listened, Enosh finished his address to the council and left with Lamech without waiting for a response.

They turned to face the Council, who slowly took their seats. Their leader spoke to Kemuel and waited patiently for him to relate it to Will and Kat.

"Lamech has graciously offered to host you and your crew for as long as you stay. He has offered you protection."

"Does that mean they'll let us keep the device?"

"No."

Will weighed his options. "What if we don't agree to give it up?"

"Then they'll destroy your ship and take it by force."

"Do they have the means?"

"Yes, I'm afraid they do."

Will looked at the council members, who stared down at him dispassionately. After a moment's consideration, he flashed a sober glance at Kat and touched his earwig. "Chris."

"Yes, sir."

"I want you to remove *Snowman* from its housing and bring it outside of the ship."

"You want me to do what?"

"You heard me."

CHAPTER 18

The waning half-moon dipped toward the horizon. Will sat alone under its light, some distance from a large fire in the center of Lamech's vast courtyard. He listened to conversations in the distance. After three months in Lamech's household, Kemuel's translations were now only occasionally necessary, and apart from a pronounced scar, Will's leg was as good as new. Kemuel was right that healing came faster here.

Will's mind flooded with thoughts he had never entertained before. He always had his life and career mapped out, always determined to succeed, always ready to achieve the next milestone: play football, be a quarterback, win the championship, get into the Air Force Academy, and become a distinguished graduate. He would succeed at pilot training, be the best F-22 pilot in the squadron, get into the space program, fly a shuttle mission, and *command* a shuttle mission. The driving force of his father's voice echoed in his head. *There's no room for failure.*

But now what? Everything here had changed all that. This place was beautiful—and awful. Will longed for what these people had, and yet this was not his world. It wasn't home. Will pushed that thought away. Nothing made sense any more, and for the first time, he found himself asking the one question he had always ignored.

Why? What was it all for? Then another question hit him head-on as if another voice had spoken it.

Not why, but who?

Someone laughed in the distance and burst his bubble of thought. One by one, Kat, Chris, and Kemuel joined him for one of their regular meetings to catch up on their progress. Kat ran her hand over her ear to control some of her growing hair, which touched the back of her neck. Will's and Chris's "high-and-tights" had filled in as well. Their hair formed a few waves they hadn't seen since joining their respective services.

Kemuel seemed shaken, but before Will could ask about it, Khaliil approached from behind and placed his hand on Will's shoulder. Even when he spoke quietly, his bass voice resounded off the surrounding walls. "Come and join us, my friend. We'll be feasting and dancing soon."

Will gave Khaliil's hand, still on his shoulder, a couple of pats and managed a comprehensible reply in the new language. "Soon, my friend. We won't miss it."

Khaliil nodded and walked back toward the fire.

Will turned back and shifted to English. He studied Kemuel for a moment, then decided to start with Chris. "What's our repair status?"

Chris leaned in and spoke quietly, an unnecessary gesture since no one else spoke English. "Better than expected. Life support and the main thrusters are fully operational. She's fully space-worthy."

An ensemble stuck up a vibrant tune near the fire, and the gathered attendees wailed with delight and began to clap.

Kemuel leaned in. "I've helped with a few... augmentations of my own."

Chris brightened and pointed at Kemuel. "I gave Kemuel root access to the laser control system, and I tell you what, this man is a programming machine."

Kemuel mustered a faint smile and let Chris continue.

"He has shown me how to make use of more phase inducer settings. We now have hover-flight capability without any need for the conventional maneuvering thrusters." He looked at Kat. "He tied the capability to your virtual helo-controls, but I can also perform limited maneuvers from my station using software controls."

Will was impressed. "That could prove helpful."

Kemuel furrowed his brow, opened his mouth to speak, then stretched his lips into thin lines and paused for a moment. "Colonel Stark, I also engineered a way to cause the phase inducer to overload and melt down. Given the proximity of your device housing to your fuel storage, it would almost certainly detonate your ship."

The music ended with a swell of laughter and applause.

Will's shoulders felt suddenly heavy. "A self-destruct capability."

"In effect. If we're confronted by one or more of the Watchers, there might be no choice."

Will thought Kemuel was holding something back. Someone spoke a few words at the fire, and the ensemble struck up another fast-paced tune. The crowd broke out in jubilant song.

Once the music resumed, Will spoke to everyone. "All right, we all want to go home, but we can't let *Snowman* fall into the hands of the Watchers. With that kind of power, they would destroy this world and ours. If it comes to it, we blow up the ship. Agreed?"

First Kemuel, then Kat, and then Chris nodded in agreement. Will watched Kemuel stare at the ground to one side. He had never seen the man so troubled.

After a sober moment of silence, Kemuel took the floor again. "Of course, this is all for naught without *Snowman*."

Will nodded. "The important thing is that we've done everything we can."

Kat leaned in. "Have we?"

Will wanted to respect Kemuel's privacy, but the stakes were too high. "Kemuel, what else is bothering you?"

Kemuel turned his eyes to the sky for a moment and swallowed hard. "Rumors have been coming in of increased *nephilim* raids to the east, and they're closing in. They're running out of resources in their homeland, so they're reaching out to consume more."

"Like what we saw at the village?"

Each time Kemuel made eye contact with Will, his gaze dropped again to the ground. "Yes, but that's not the worst of it. Joachim is fearful of the *nephilim*." He heaved a sigh and looked up for a moment. His eyes watered. "He fears them more than he trusts the Lord, and he has convinced the Council to make a terrible decision."

Kemuel paused, but Kat wasn't ready to wait. "What?"

"They've decided the existence of the second device—and the ship—is too great a risk. They're going to destroy them both."

Kat dropped her jaw. Chris's eyes widened and tensed.

Will sat silently for a moment and weighed his options. He watched Kemuel's expression. "Do you see any choice for us?"

Kemuel stood, folded his arms and dropped his head. "No, I don't. While we're here, we must obey the Council. I'm sorry. I'm so very sorry." He walked away.

Will drew Kat and Chris closer and spoke urgently. "Meet me at the ship before dawn. I won't let them destroy her."

They nodded quickly and sat in silence.

Will looked at the fire. "Let's go enjoy the party. This will probably be our last night here." The thought pained him, and that surprised him. He looked around. *I'm gonna miss this place.*

Will led them to the crowd gathered around the fire. Khaliil gestured to them, so Will joined him, followed immediately by Kat and Chris. They joined in the clapping, listened to the words of the song, and picked out what they could understand. With each repetition of the chorus, it became clearer, "Call on the Name of the Lord. Praise the Name of the Lord." After some time, even Kemuel rejoined his friends.

The song ended, everyone sat, and a woman began a beautiful, mournful solo in a rich contralto. It told the story of the Fall, the expulsion from paradise, Cain's decision to murder Abel, and Enosh's decision to call on the Name. Will noticed Kat and Chris were as engrossed in the story as he was. The soloist began a chorus, and an ensemble of other women joined in rich harmony. They sang an exhortation to call on the Name. Then the soloist continued with the arrival of the Watchers, deception, betrayal, destruction and murder.

Will remembered the poor fools he had seen at Semyaza's palace. He could still see the crazed looks on their faces. He had first thought it was delirium, but now he knew it was the desperate yearning of souls without hope. He could well imagine that at least a few of those pilgrims knew death awaited them, because after all, bad attention is better than none, and they were finally getting noticed *by their gods*. Maybe they thought death was a fair price to pay for a few moments of rapturous pleasure with the objects of their worship. Will's heart ached for them.

The chorus repeated the exhortation to call on the Name, and the soloist continued with a third verse. It was a prediction of sacrifice, redemption, rescue, and restoration. Will realized he knew something the people around him could not—how that sacrifice was going to happen—and he felt ashamed that he had always seen it in such trivial terms. He wiped a tear from one eye with the butt of his hand. He wasn't even certain why he wept. Maybe it was for those poor souls in Nod. Maybe it was for the villagers fighting for survival. Maybe it was because for the first time in his life, he didn't see God as distant and indifferent. God was reaching into time and space *to rescue him*.

Will saw the whole truth for the first time, and against that backdrop, his life finally made sense. The enemy was attacking him even when he was a boy. The enemy was attacking his father long before the fatal mission in Siberia, and yet, they were never alone. The Savior had fought for them all along. The vault in Will's heart opened, and the twelve-year-old boy inside at last found healing. Will's tears became a flood.

The music ended, replaced only by the crackle of the fire. Will placed his arm across his eyes and let the sleeve soak his tears. His heart quieted, and a powerful call tugged at him, different from anything he expected. *Come to Me, Will. I understand you. I understand it all.*

Will's heart swelled and groped for words. *But it hurts so much, Lord.*

I know, Will, and it grieves me to see you hurt. Now come to me, and let's deal with it together. Let's fight the enemy together.

Will's heart surged, and his eyes widened with hope. This was nothing like the dry liturgy or hollow traditions he was accustomed to. It was a call to join *the war.* It was a call to give up control of his life and follow his true Commander, his true King. He might have resisted, too, might have fought to maintain control of his own destiny, had he not seen such unmitigated evil when they arrived. Will didn't even know it was going to happen, but he found himself whispering, "Yahweh... Yahweh." The rest of the crowd broke out in quiet praises as if Will had opened a floodgate.

He turned to Kat. She looked at him as if she saw something wonderful for the first time. Beyond her, Chris wept bitterly, his head buried in his hands, his shoulders moving up and down with each sob. Kat followed Will's gaze, turned to Chris, and put a hand on his shoulder. Chris looked up and smiled through his tears. Will watched Kat wipe a tear of her own.

I suppose Chris has found his answers.

Kemuel had his hands opened to the sky and his eyes fixed upward. He muttered a tearful prayer of his own.

From Will's other side, Khaliil put his arm around Will's shoulders and gave him a firm squeeze and a look of heartfelt compassion.

Then an old man with a snow-white beard and a walking stick ambled to a spot in front of Will. A hush fell over the crowd. The fire snapped. Some of the wood settled and sent a burst of sparks into the air. The man looked Will straight in the eyes, and Will understood every word he said.

"Young man, you are from another time."

Will saw Kemuel in the corner of his eye lean forward, a look of deep concern on his face.

The old man continued. "And you are responsible for calling on the Name of all Names. It has been revealed to you."

It swept over Will like a wave, and it was on his lips before he knew it. "Jesus... Save me, Jesus."

Kat repeated the call, "Save me, Jesus," and a tearful group of her new friends hugged her.

Chris shouted in Arabic. "*Yessoua... khallassany Yessoua.*"

The old man smiled with satisfaction and looked heavenward. A moment of exuberant celebration followed until Lamech joined the old man and gestured for silence.

Lamech placed his hands first on Chris's head and spoke with tremendous authority. From that moment on, Will understood every word spoken. "Nur ibn Saif-ad-Deen, you have taken the name Chris, which Kemuel tells me is short for Christopher, meaning 'Bearer of Christ.' You have searched for knowledge and found the truth. You will bear the Name of all Names to a people in slavery to false law and to hopelessness. You are gifted with knowledge and teaching, and you are called to great sacrifice, but greater still will be your reward if you persevere."

Lamech moved to Kat and placed his hands on her head. "Katherine of the family Dalton, you recognize and discern evil, both in the physical realm and the spiritual." Lamech wept through his words. "You will endure great pain, but you will also be a courageous rescuer."

Then Lamech moved and placed his hands on Will's head, his eyes closed. "William of the family Stark. Your family's name means 'strong,' even as my name Lamech means 'strength.' Though your birth is seventy of your lifetimes removed from mine, you are my son in the Lord, and although the legacy was broken with your ancestors, I pass on to you a part of mine. Pass that legacy on. As a bearer of an orb of my grandfather Enoch, you will be gifted with great power, and your own legacy will bless you."

Lamech seemed weighed down with knowledge. He pulled Will up and into a fatherly embrace. He whispered in Will's ear. "Your fight will begin again soon. Fight well, my son."

Will returned the embrace, content to stay there for a while. He didn't realize until then how much he had yearned for such a father, or for such a father's blessing, and now that he had both, he felt stronger than ever.

Lamech drew back, held Will's head in his hands for a moment, smiled, and stepped around the fire. Will saw the old man who had advised him earlier and walked to him. He repeated the word the boy had spoken to him in the village: "Ashakkerka."

The old man smiled, put a hand on Will's shoulder, and whispered, "You're welcome, little man," before he ambled away.

Kemuel's eyes nearly popped out of his sockets. Then Will realized he had just heard English. He hurried to follow the old man, but well-intentioned friends from Lamech's household surrounded him and lavished him with congratulations. Will had little choice but to watch the wise old sage walk from the courtyard.

Khaliil laughed boisterously. "Blessed by a patriarch, my friend. You are truly blessed indeed." Then he shouted praises to God.

Joy swept over the whole crowd, and they broke into loud, joyful praise. Friends who were now brothers and sisters continued to surround them. The ensemble led them in a rousing chorus, and they ate, drank, and danced around the fire for hours. Will spent much of the time watching Kat, and he didn't even mind when she noticed. The smiles she threw his way stirred his heart.

Will looked up at the mountain that overshadowed Lamech's household and thought about the ship. For the first time, Will's determination was accompanied with the sure knowledge of his purpose. He knew *why* they needed to get home. They had to share what they had seen with the world. He also knew *who* he was doing it all for, and his heart thrilled that the Creator of the Universe was now his Friend, his Father, his Captain, and his King.

He watched Kat. The new change in their lives, their commitment to their Savior, completely stripped away her guarded exterior. Now she was serene, graceful, and beautiful beyond measure. Will watched her joyful dance, and his desire surprised him. He thought such a change in his life would render such things trivial, but instead, she became part of his calling.

The voice in Will's heart confirmed it, the voice he had always ignored—until today.

I made you for each other, Will.

Kat tossed a pleasant smile toward Will, excused herself from the crowd and stepped slowly away from the fire. She glanced over her shoulder for a moment as she walked away. Will was about to follow when Khaliil dispensed with any charade and gave him a firm push from behind. Will looked back at Khaliil with a grin and walked to Kat. She stood with her arms folded and gazed up at the moon.

He wasn't certain where to start. He stood next to her, gazed at the moon with her for a moment, and turned to look at her face bathed in soft moonlight.

Her head still, she turned her eyes to him for a moment, looked up at the moon again, and let him watch. "You aren't the same man I met in that hangar at Cape Canaveral."

Will looked at the ground and paused, lost in a wave of shame. "I was driven, misguided, and full of myself. I'm sorry if..."

Kat turned and gently touched his mouth with her fingers to silence him. "None of that matters. You're none of those things now."

Will gazed into her eyes, content to stay there a long time. A blue-tinted image of the half-moon shone in those eyes. Will couldn't tell if the glow came from the moon or something else within. Her fingers still gently touched his mouth. He reached up, took her hand into his own, and caressed it with his thumb. He lowered his head and gave her hand a soft kiss. "Please forgive me for being so difficult."

Her smile bathed him in warmth.

Will placed his other hand on her shoulder, caressed it, and held her arm gently. Then his other hand found its way to her other shoulder. He didn't even realize he was bending down until his lips were millimeters from hers.

She closed her eyes and waited.

Will paused, then closed his eyes, touched her lips with his, and stayed there for a long, sweet moment.

CHAPTER 19

Will emerged cautiously onto the amphitheater floor. The sky would soon brighten as dawn approached. He stared at the top of the tower. The chamber glowed with torchlight, which confirmed that no one was looking down at him. He quickly made his way around the perimeter of the field toward the bullpen that housed his ship.

His father's words echoed in his head, "There's no room for failure," but this time, another voice spoke to his heart.

Don't you believe that, Will. You're no failure.

Despite the seriousness of his situation, an unfamiliar lightness lifted Will's chest. He couldn't help but smile. *Thank you, Father God. I don't need to fear failure any more, do I? Last night changed that. Nothing the enemy can throw at me will change your gifts or your calling, and it certainly can't stand in your way.* Will took a deep breath and looked up. *If this is your will, Lord, then I trust you to bring it about even if I die trying.*

Will stopped and swallowed hard. *But Father, please protect Kat and Chris.*

He wondered if Kat and Chris were already aboard the ship. He rounded the corner into the bullpen and ran square into Kemuel.

Will stared at him intensely. "You can't stop me, Kemuel."

Kemuel whispered. "Of course I can't, and I wouldn't. I know what the Council cannot." He pulled Will into the shadow. "But now would be a very good time for silence. There will be a tower shift-change at dawn."

Will followed Kemuel's example by whispering. "Kat and Chris..."

"Lieutenant Commander Saif-ad-Deen has been aboard since midnight. I haven't seen Major Dalton."

They spotted movement at the entrance to the field and watched Kat run from the tunnel, turn, bound up the stairs, and duck behind the top of the entrance. Soon after, two men emerged and crossed to the opposite end of the field. Will squinted to confirm that one was Khaliil. A twinge of regret struck him. *I'll miss you, friend.*

Khaliil turned his head toward the bullpen for a moment but continued straight for the tower.

Once the men disappeared into the tower, Kat hurried to the ship and disappeared into the shadows, careful to keep her eyes on the field. Will startled her from behind and gently covered her mouth. She tensed for a moment; then she relaxed and nodded. Will removed his hand.

After a moment, the relieved tower guards emerged onto the field in the dim twilight and crossed to the opposite side. Chris quietly joined Will and the others and distributed communication earpieces while they watched the guards enter the tunnel. When they disappeared from view, Will spoke quietly.

"Chris, ready the ship for flight. Can you move her out onto the field yourself with Kemuel's enhancements?"

Chris looked at Kemuel for a moment before he responded. "Sure, but I'll need Kemuel to help, since they're new to me."

"Do it. Kat, come with me to the tower."

Chris and Kemuel headed for the ship's ladder.

Kat sounded enthusiastic but cautious. "How do you plan to get the device?"

"I'm hoping Khaliil will be sympathetic to our cause. We have to get home."

Kemuel turned to Will. "He's your best chance, but he won't disobey his orders."

Will stopped. "Wait, Lamech called me a bearer of an *orb* of his grandfather. Why would he call it an orb?"

"The cylinder you see contains an orb."

Chris stepped toward Kemuel. "The orb inside is the sub-nuclear phase inducer?"

"Yes. It's the true source of power. The cylinder simply helps to channel it."

Will nodded and led Kat toward the tower. They entered the tower's broad base. A long rope hung to the floor in the center with a metal weight secured to the end. A stone staircase with no railing spiraled up the tower's interior and narrowed as it rose thirty meters above the amphitheater floor.

As they neared the top, they paused on one of the landings. A thick, metal ring secured the top of the rope to a large pulley suspended from the ceiling. An apparatus of gears was connected to the pulley, and a large basket of food and fuel with a sturdy hook on the handle sat on the top landing just outside the chamber.

Chris's voice squawked in their earpieces. "Ready to taxi on your order. Shall we proceed?"

Will tapped his earpiece twice to signal, *No.*

"Acknowledged. Awaiting further orders."

Will led Kat up the last stairs and peeked into the chamber. It was round, roughly five meters wide, with a ring of thick columns around the center and broad windows open to the morning air. One of the cylindrical devices glowed slightly on a mount in the center of the chamber, and the second lay on a marble table next to it. A single stone at the end of both orbs glowed brightly. Some kind of commotion echoed up from the city below. Khaliil and the other guard looked outside to see the cause.

Will saw his opportunity and moved quickly across the entrance, then leaned against the wall on the other side. He gestured quietly to Kat and pointed to the two nearest columns on each side. Kat nodded.

Will searched for options. He had no plan. He took a deep breath. *Father God, please help me.*

He dove into the chamber and behind one of the columns. Kat readied herself. Just as she leapt through the entrance toward another column, a woman screamed in the distance behind the tower. Khaliil and the other guard turned to look and spotted Kat.

The second guard shouted, ran across the chamber, and grabbed Kat by the arm. Will remained hidden from the second guard and moved around the column into Khaliil's view. He looked at Khaliil, who kept his eyes on Kat and the second guard. Will crouched, ready to leap out and free Kat.

Khaliil shouted, "Stop," and held his arms up as if to calm the situation.

The second guard looked at him, bewildered. "We have to take her to the garrison to await judgment."

Khaliil paused, conflicted. "Yes, we have no choice. No one violates the tower without severe punishment."

The commotion outside grew with the morning light, and more screams and shouts echoed across the city. A plume of smoke rose in the distance.

The second guard pulled Kat toward the stairs while Khaliil looked outside again. He wheeled back to the second guard. "Wait. Take her to the council chamber."

"But our orders..."

"...are from the Council, and I'm certain they will want to speak to her. Besides, something's happening below. We shouldn't leave the mountain."

The second guard shrugged and pulled Kat away. Khaliil gave her a look of reassurance as the guard escorted her out. More screams and shouts echoed across the city, and two more plumes of smoke appeared, closer than the first.

When the others were out of earshot, Khaliil turned to Will. "I've bought you some time, Brother. I won't stop you from taking your ship, but I can't let you take the orb."

Will looked at the device on the table, and Khaliil placed one hand on his sword. Will knew what had to be done. He had to leap at Khaliil before he could unsheathe his sword. Will saw the determination in his friend's eye and knew at once that one of them was about to die.

Then something stopped him. He froze and took a tense breath while his heart pounded. A question flashed across his mind. *Is this God's will?* Never so conflicted in his life, Will choked down a lump in his throat, then relaxed and stared at his friend.

The shouting outside grew closer still, and more plumes of smoke stretched skyward. Horns sounded in alarm. Khaliil then turned to look outside. Will joined him and scanned the city below. Will spotted it first. "Nephilim."

A large army of *overlords* and *sheddim* plowed through the city straight for the mountain.

Khaliil looked puzzled. "They aren't taking anything, and they don't seem to be attacking anyone. They're just ransacking whatever they pass."

Will knew at once. "Adrok." He turned to Khaliil. "Do they know about the orb?"

Khaliil shook his head. "No. It is a well-kept secret."

Will ran across the chamber to look over the amphitheater. The second guard escorted Kat into the tunnel at the opposite end of the field. "Then he wants the ship."

He tapped his earpiece. "Chris, Kemuel, do you copy?"

Chris answered, "Roger."

"An army of *nephilim* is about to storm the mountain. Move the ship onto the field."

"We can't leave without you and Kat."

"You'll leave when I tell you to. Now move the ship into the open."

"Yes, sir."

Khaliil was puzzled. "What would they want with your ship?"

Will ran back across the chamber and stared at the approaching *nephilim*. "To project their power. We traveled well over eleven thousand kilometers in one night and encountered a band of *se'irim* in a village east of here. If any imps survived and reported what happened, then he knows how fast the ship can travel." He looked down.

A handful of *sheddim* started to climb up the mountain toward the tower. Will whispered, "Man, they're fast."

"But the Watchers can already fly."

"How many *nephilim* can they carry at once?"

Kemuel's expression registered his understanding. "No more than two. I see now. They want your technology."

"And we can't let them have it." He pointed to the orbs. "Any more than we can let them have the orbs."

Khaliil nodded. He moved to a cabinet on the opposite wall and pulled out two leather pouches with straps. He carefully removed the first orb from its mount, placed it in one of the pouches and secured it over his shoulder. Then he placed the second orb in the other pouch and placed it on Will. "There. The orb is your responsibility now, Brother. Guard it with your life."

Will nodded.

Khaliil opened another cabinet and revealed a small armory. He took a sheathed sword and handed it to Will, who secured it around his waist. Then he pulled out two bows and quivers of arrows. "Can you use one of these?"

Will slung a quiver over his shoulder and grabbed one of the bows. He moved to look outside, pulled an arrow from over his shoulder, drew, and released. A *sheddih* grunted in pain and screamed.

Khaliil stood next to Will and watched as the *sheddih* hit the ground below with a gruesome crunch. "I'll take that as a yes."

More *nephilim* scaled the wall toward them. Will and Khaliil fired again and again until they ran out of arrows and the ground below the tower was littered with corpses. Then they discarded their bows and drew swords. Will looked over the amphitheater. *Chronos* rolled slowly onto the field. Apart from the ship, the field was empty. The *nephilim* appeared to focus on the point of greatest resistance: the tower.

Khaliil shouted and swung his sword as an *overlord's* head emerged from below. Will joined his friend and held his sword up. The giant's hands clung to the wall for a moment while his head rolled down the tower wall. As the body fell it knocked two screaming *sheddim* down on the way.

Will swung hard at a *sheddih* just below, wounded him and broke his hold on the wall. Then another climbed to the opening further around the chamber. By the time Will ran there, the *sheddih* had grabbed the top of the opening and swung his legs in. Will ran him through, raised one leg, and pushed him off the sword and back out the opening.

Will looked down. A dozen more *sheddim* were closing fast. He turned to Khaliil. "We can't hold them off for long."

Khaliil dispatched two more *sheddim* and pointed to the chamber entrance. "The pulley."

"Show me."

Will followed him through the entrance and looked down the tower's interior. Khaliil sheathed his sword and hefted the pouched orb around in front of him. Will swung his own pouch around and kept his sword pointed into the chamber.

Khaliil pointed to the pulley. "You have to jump and grab the ring."

"Do it. I'll be right behind you."

Khaliil nodded, took a deep breath, leapt over the deep drop down the center of the tower, and grabbed the ring. The wheel and adjacent gears turned as he fell. Their punctuated squeak grew faster as two globes orbited each other amidst the gears. Then the globes swung out with the centrifugal force and slowed his fall.

Will watched the rising counterweight reach the top of the tower and looked down as Khaliil touch the ground. Khaliil looked up and released the ring. The counterweight fell back to the floor and drew the ring up.

Will heard a growl and spun. Three *sheddim* charged him from behind. He jumped to one side, pulled his first attacker past him, and sent him flailing to the floor below. Then he lifted his sword, ran the second through, and kicked him off the sword just as the ring reached the top of the tower.

Khaliil's voice echoed up the staircase. "Jump!"

Will turned toward the pulley and crouched, ready to grab the ring with his free hand. The third *sheddih* grabbed him from behind, snarled in fury, and pulled him to the ground.

Will tried to break free, but the *sheddih's* strength was overwhelming. The attacker tightened his hold around Will's chest. Will struggled to breathe.

An *overlord* stepped over them. He ignored Will's pouch and instead took Will's sword. Then he shouted in a booming bass voice, "Pick him up."

The *sheddih* pulled Will hard to his feet. Will gasped for air in the *sheddih's* vice grip. Shuffling sounds and clinking armor told Will more *nephilim* had climbed into the chamber. He stared down the point of his own sword into the *overlord's* eyes.

The giant looked down the staircase, turned back to Will, and grinned with sick pleasure. Then he swung the sword around with his long arms, neatly cut the rope, and watched it and the ring fall to the floor. He pointed down the tower and shouted at the *sheddih*. "Throw him down."

The *sheddih* pulled Will off his feet and started forward, close to the *overlord*. Will saw his opportunity. He lifted his legs and kicked the surprised giant hard enough to make him lose his balance. The *overlord* tried to right himself with a step back. It was a step into nothing. The giant fell through the opening in the floor. His deep, terrified scream hurt Will's ears. Shocked, the *sheddih* loosened his grip. Will broke free before the creature could tighten its hold again, spun, and punched him in the face. Furious, the *sheddih* grabbed Will by the collar, lifted him and pushed him toward the edge of the opening. Powerless to stop it, Will grabbed his foe by his own collar, drew him close, sneered in his face, and pulled the terrified *sheddih* over with him.

Desperate, the *sheddih* thrust to one side in a vain attempt to reach the stairs. His scream echoed down the tower, and Will found himself falling alone. Adrenaline surged through his body. Every muscle tensed with the rush of weightlessness, and the world went slow motion. Will closed his eyes and clutched the pouched orb with all his might. *This is it. Protect the orb from impact. Please, God, let Khaliil pass it on to my crew.*

He braced for crushing impact but instead felt searing heat. He opened his eyes. The device glowed brightly enough to be seen through the pouch. With a hard lurch, he stopped inches above the ground just as the *sheddih's* body crushed into a disfigured lump of flesh with a gruesome crunch.

Will jumped to his feet and shook hard from the adrenalin. Khaliil stared at him with wide eyes. Will thought he might have to push his heart back into his own chest. He took a breath, stepped over the dead *sheddih,* retrieved his sword from the lifeless *overlord,* sheathed it, and looked at Khaliil while he stepped out onto the field. Once he was outside, three *sheddim* surprised him from one side with swords raised. Will's device glowed hot again, and he instinctively raised his free hand toward the attackers. An invisible force exploded from the orb through his hand and slammed them to the ground unconscious.

Will looked down at the device for a moment before he ran across the field. He could just hear Khaliil mutter behind him. "Does mine do that?"

Will tapped his earpiece and shouted. "Open the hatch, I have *Snowman.*" He arrived to find the hatch open and Kemuel reaching down. Will removed the cylinder from the pouch and handed it up. "Have Chris install it. I'll get Kat."

Kemuel nodded and closed the hatch. Will and Khaliil bolted into the tunnel.

They ran around the path to the council chamber below. Kat, the second guard, and a group of soldiers fought fiercely to hold a line on the path in front of the chamber. Three soldiers fired arrows from atop the wall next to the path, while most of the rest fought at close range with swords. Dozens of *nephilim* lay dead or unconscious nearby and on the road below after failed attempts to pass to the amphitheater above.

Will reached them just as Kat swung a bat-sized club at a *sheddih's* head like she was picking off a fast ball shooting over home plate. The *sheddih's* skull cracked, and he fell limp to the ground. Will felt a rush of satisfaction. Kat lifted the club again, ready to swing at the next pitch just as Will approached her from behind. She lowered the club and turned to face him.

The second guard approached, sword in hand. Will lowered his sword. "I need to get her to our ship."

The guard looked at the attacking *nephilim* and nodded. Will and Kat sprinted up the path and into the amphitheater.

They emerged onto the field. Hundreds of *nephilim* climbed around the tower base and closed in on the ship. Will touched his earpiece and shouted. "Chris, take her up. Take her up."

"Aye, sir."

The ship lifted off and hovered thirty feet off the ground. Will looked around and directed Kat up the stairs nearby. "There, we can jump on board from the top."

Kat sprinted the first few steps and stopped. Will stopped behind her. Hundreds of *overlords* and *sheddim* climbed over the wall above, all around the amphitheater. Will and Kat bolted back down and into the tunnel only to see Khaliil and the soldiers sprint toward them from the other end. The guard who had arrested Kat shouted, "They've broken through. They've broken through."

Will drew his sword, turned, and held Kat behind him. The other soldiers joined them with hundreds more *nephilim* hot on their tails. Together they moved a short distance into the field and formed a circle. Kat and the bowmen stood in the center, and the swordsmen pointed their weapons out.

Everything grew quiet. Will looked around him and up at the hovering ship. It was a standoff.

Then Adrok stepped out onto the field and glared at Will with satisfaction. "Your ship is mine, human, and so is the woman." He looked up and shouted at the top of his lungs. "Everything is ready, Father."

The soldiers tensed. They kept their swords pointed out but looked up wide-eyed. Khaliil growled.

Then the most glorious creature Will had ever beheld flew over the amphitheater and circled the ship. He was fearsome and radiant, arrayed in glowing armor. Will and the others shielded their eyes. The angel swooped down and landed gracefully next to Adrok, who led his fellow *nephilim* in an obsequious bow.

Will and the others remained standing.

Adrok looked up at them and snarled. "Bow to your god, Semyaza."

Khaliil retorted with bared teeth. "We'll die first."

Adrok drew his sword. "I can arrange that." Several dozen *sheddim* stood with him, lifted their swords, and closed in to attack.

Semyaza raised his hand and spoke with quiet arrogance. "Stop."

The *nephilim* halted in place and held their swords up.

Semyaza turned to Adrok. "Be careful not to kill the ship's crew, my son. We will need their expertise."

Will tapped his earpiece and spoke while Semyaza and the others stared at him. "Chris, the situation we talked about has arrived."

There was a moment of painful silence before Chris responded. "I was afraid of that."

"You have to do what we agreed to. Detonate the ship now."

Semyaza taunted him. "You pathetic fool. You cannot kill me."

"Maybe not, but you won't get my ship."

"*Your* ship? It's mine now, and the only thing you can do is to kill yourself and all your friends."

Khaliil shouted angrily. "Yes, along with all of these abominations you call sons. I look forward to watching their souls cry for mercy while Yahweh's angels take us to our rest."

Adrok roared, but Semyaza restrained him. "Patience, my son."

Chris's nervous voice squawked in Will's ear. "Sir, we're ready."

Will's mouth went dry. He and Kat looked at each other, and he opened his mouth to speak. Before Will could utter a sound, Semyaza shouted, pointed a glowing sword at the ship, stretched his wings, and leapt into the sky.

Will watched as the angel streaked toward *Chronos*. "Chris do it! Now! Now!"

With a loud bang, a bright energy field surrounded the ship. Semyaza stopped, startled, a short distance away. Bolts of lightning struck from the field around the ship to its hull, grew in speed and intensity, and then reversed. They struck the ground with bursts of smoke. A rush of wind blew from the ship and knocked dozens of *nephilim* off their feet. Will fell to his knees with Kat and the other men, ready to die praying. The army of *nephilim* scattered in terror and fled into the tunnel. Some even dove over the side of the amphitheater.

The field grew brighter, and the bursts of energy scorched the ground with deafening cracks and booms. Will put his arms around Kat and held her tight. They closed their eyes and braced for the explosion. Then with a violent blast of wind in the opposite direction, the ship imploded with a deafening crack.

The sound echoed over and over. Will looked up through misty eyes. His ship was gone without a trace. *Chris, Kemuel, I'm sorry.*

Stunned *nephilim* returned to the field while Will strained to hear the last few audible echoes of the implosion. A moment of silence followed. Then Semyaza shook the entire mountain with a furious roar.

The angel landed with a violent crash and marshaled a group of *nephilim* to his side. Then he pointed to Will and the others and shouted, "Kill them." The *nephilim* drew swords and closed in on the circle.

Will braced for death a second time with Kat and the other men. Then a commanding voice resounded from the tunnel. "Stop this wickedness at once."

They turned. Lamech and the white-bearded old man walked toward them. Semyaza spat at them bitterly. "Get out of my presence, Patriarch."

Lamech stopped a short distance away and folded his arms. The old man walked slowly up to Semyaza and stared him in the eye. His old voice rang with weariness and wisdom. "You have no authority here, Semyaza, and you know it." He gestured to the circle of soldiers. "These brave men..." He looked toward Kat for an instant, "...and this fearless woman, have not submitted to you. They have called on the Name of the Lord."

Semyaza growled through his words. "That doesn't mean I can't watch them die painful deaths before your God takes them."

The old man gestured around the top of the amphitheater. "It does today."

Semyaza looked soberly around the perimeter of the amphitheater. Will looked around but saw only the sky.

The old man poked Semyaza with his walking stick. "See to it that your wicked spawn harms no one as you leave."

Semyaza bent down and stared into the old man's eyes. "Very well, *old man.*" He turned to the *nephilim,* shouted, "Get out," and stared for another moment around the perimeter of the amphitheater above. "If you harm anyone, you'll answer to me." Then he stretched his wings up, pulled them down with a whoosh, streaked away, and left his bewildered army behind.

Unceremoniously, the humiliated *nephilim* abandoned their dead and walked out. Adrok stared at Kat with wide, tense eyes before he followed his brothers. Lamech looked at Khaliil and gestured with his head toward the tower. Khaliil nodded and led the other soldiers across the field, the pouched device still slung around his shoulder. Then Lamech escorted the old man away.

After everyone else had left, Will turned to Kat. She stood alone and stared where the ship last was, her arms folded tightly across her chest. He stood next to her and put his arm around her shoulder. She gazed into the sky for several moments and then lowered her eyes to the ground. Her shoulders heaved with a gentle sob. A single tear streamed down her face. Will reached around, carefully took her by the shoulders, and stepped in front of her. He looked into her eyes, touched her chin with one hand, and gently lifted her gaze to meet his. She smiled through her tears.

Will had never seen her cry—not like this—and it surprised him. He longed to make her feel better. "It'll be all right, Kat. I know it seems you've lost everything..."

She shook her head. "That's not why I'm crying." She swallowed. "I mean, I'm crying for Chris and Kemuel." She wiped a tear. "What they did was more courageous than words can say, but that's not all. I'm crying because... I've wished for a long time that our careers, our mission, and everything else would just go away and leave us alone." She smiled sheepishly, sniffed and shrugged. "Now they have."

Will's heart flooded with yearning. The night before, he had become a new man. Now he wanted to be *her* man. He remembered his father, and as terrified as he was of losing someone again, he didn't care.

Will remembered his thought when he first met Kat and smiled. *If only we had met at another time, another place.* He no longer had any reasons left to hold back. "I love you, Kat. I've loved you since the first time we met."

She looked at him with an intensity that stirred his heart and a serenity he longed for. "And I've loved you back."

He kissed her for the second time. She slipped her hands up his chest and around his neck. He slipped one hand behind her back and held the back of her head with the other. Their tender, gentle kiss grew warm and passionate.

CHAPTER 20

Their lips parted with a gentle smack. Will stroked Kat's hair from her head down her back and drew some of it over her shoulder. Kat drew back from Will's embrace, smiled, pushed her hair off her shoulder, leaned on the sturdy balcony railing, and gazed with him at the sunset and the foggy mist that settled slowly to the ground.

A youthful voice sounded behind them. "Mom, Dad, I'm ready."

They turned and looked at the fine-looking young man showing off his new tunic and trousers fashioned to express his transition to manhood.

Kat stepped to him and smiled. "You look great, Joel."

Will gave his shoulder a firm squeeze. "I'm proud of you, Son. You've grown into a fine man." He slapped Joel's shoulder affectionately.

Joel grinned and beamed, then his smile melted. "I only wish my brother and sisters..." He turned his head and swallowed.

An unstoppable lump rose in Will's throat. He drew his wife and son to him in a firm embrace and let one tear pass unchecked. "We all miss them, Son."

After a moment of silence, Khaliil cleared his throat. His gentle, bass voice drew their attention to his sad smile at the door. "All right, enough of your strange language already." He fixed a serious gaze at Joel. "Sixteen years, and what a man you've become." His eye

184

twinkled. "You aren't planning to keep Lamech waiting, are you? He's only got seven hundred years left, and we mustn't waste them."

They grinned and wiped tears. Will ushered them through the door to the top of the staircase ahead of him. Khaliil's eyes met Will's, and the warrior's smile melted into a knowing look of compassion. Will stopped.

Kat saw the look on Will's face and spoke over her shoulder as she followed Joel down the stairs. "We'll see you two in a few minutes."

Once they were out of earshot, Khaliil looked at Will. "What's on your mind, my friend?"

Will shook his head. "How do you do it, Khaliil?" He looked up as another wave welled up in his chest. He closed his eyes, swallowed hard, and stared into the distance. "How do you go on?" He paused long enough for the wave to subside. "I've lost three children, but you've lost everyone."

Khaliil took a step toward Will and put a firm hand on his shoulder. "I trust God, Will. My wife and children are safe in His hands."

The next wave engulfed Will. He clenched his fists as if he wanted to hit something. "But they were so scared..." His lips tensed and his eyes welled up. "And I couldn't do anything to protect them." His face contorted and his shoulders shook.

Khaliil grabbed Will's shoulders and looked intently into his eyes. "They aren't scared now, Will."

Will swallowed and took a deep breath. "I can't lose Kat and Joel, Khaliil. I just can't lose them, too."

"I know, Will. I know it's hard. You've just got to trust God's heart. He isn't just your King. He's your Father, and a loving one at that. More loving than your earthly father could ever have been."

Will wiped his eyes with the butt of his hand. "I do trust God. It's just that I grew up, I don't know, *guarded*. After my father died, I didn't want to lose anyone else I was close to. Now, it's like I'm..."

"Vulnerable."

Will nodded. "Yes. Exactly."

Khaliil straightened. "And don't you ever stop being vulnerable, my friend. Just imagine how vulnerable God makes Himself with us. It takes courage, Will, but take heart. You *are* a man of courage. I don't say such things lightly, either." After a moment, he gestured down the stairs with his head. "Now, your son is waiting for your blessing."

Will wiped his face with a sleeve. "Man, I'm so proud of him."

"And well you should be. That son of yours is a hero in the making."

"Amen to that." Will gave Khaliil a playful punch in the gut on the way by. Khaliil doubled over with a mocking, "Oomph."

Will emerged into the courtyard and paused to take in the scene. His pain melted away with the warm crackle of the bonfire, the rich fragrance of burning wood and baked bread, and the joyful sounds of music and laughter. A feast of warm breads, rich pastries, fruits, and savory vegetable dishes covered a long row of decorated tables. Will found Kat and Khaliil in the crowd and joined them near the fire. Joel took a seat of honor. Then Lamech stood to address them.

"Council members, honored guests, dear friends, we gather tonight to celebrate Joel Stark's passage into manhood." A cloud passed over the Patriarch's face. "And while we grieve for those who are no longer with us..."

Will put his arm around Kat.

"...We also rejoice with them in the knowledge that they are in the presence of our mighty and gracious Lord and Redeemer." He looked at Will. "Will Stark, it has been my pleasure and honor to welcome you into my family, and it was nearly seventeen years ago that I blessed you as a new member of the host of the redeemed, and I bestowed part of my own legacy onto you. The time has come for you to pass that legacy on and bless your own son."

Will stood, shared an embrace with Lamech, and turned to face Joel. "Son, there are no words, either in this language or my native tongue, to express how deeply proud I am of you..." He stopped, swallowed, and let a tear fall from his eye without wiping it. "...or how very much I love you."

Joel looked up with eager, hopeful eyes. Will stepped behind him, placed his hands on his son's head, and closed his eyes.

"Joel Elias Stark, it is the greatest honor of my life to bless you as one who has called on the Name of all Names, the Redeemer to Come, Jesus Christ..."

A rush of wind made the fire roar.

"...making you not only my beloved son, but also my brother, a fellow heir of our great inheritance to come."

Will felt a surge in his spirit, and his voice swelled with authority and indignation. "That inheritance will include *this* Earth, and in the mighty name of our Redeemer we proclaim that to the enemy. No matter what destruction the enemy may wreak on our lives, we will prevail. We will prevail for our victory is sure, and all of us will one day return with our Lord to reclaim what is rightfully His."

Will's soul quieted, and a calm fell on everyone gathered there.

"Son, I call you a man of wisdom, strength, stature, integrity, and courage. You have a refreshing spirit and a heart after the Lord's, and I have known since your birth that the purpose of my fatherhood has always been to prepare you—to shepherd your heart—to guide you, so that you would follow your Father God all the days of your life. Our family's legacy has been restored, and I pass that on to you today. I give you to our Lord and Savior, Jesus Christ, and, Joel, I *unleash* you on the world against the enemy. However God calls you to fight, whether it is through the sword, the pen, the pulpit, or any other manner of service, I call on you to *fight well*."

The attendees applauded. Will stepped in front of Joel, drew him up into a tight embrace, and then looked at Kat. She smiled through her tears.

Lamech stood and raised his hands for silence. "Well said, my friend. A father's blessing is one of the greatest weapons a man can have. With your permission, Will, I would like to bestow my own blessing on your son."

Will's chest surged with joy and pride. He smiled, nodded, and took one step back, but Lamech pulled him by the arm to stand next to him. Then as Joel knelt respectfully, Lamech placed his hands on the young man's head.

"Joel Elias Stark. Your names mean 'Yahweh is the Lord' and 'The Lord is my God,' and you *will* follow Him all the days of your life. You have already shown courage through great loss. You have not grown bitter, nor have you despaired of hope. You will continue to persevere and will be a man of great character. Always cling to the sure hope that does not disappoint..." Lamech's expression tightened with pain. "...especially when there seems to be no hope at all. You were born out of time, Joel, and time will remain central to the battle you are called to. Your father has been a bearer of an orb of my grandfather, Enoch. Both he and your mother paid a great price to keep that orb out of enemy hands. As your father's son, you, too, will be blessed with great power, but your father's gift will not be yours."

A single pair of leather-gloved hands clapped slowly. Joel rose and stood next to his father and Lamech. Adrok walked slowly through the gathering, and several people gasped. He stood a couple of feet taller than before, and his long cape flowed behind. He stopped in front of Will, Lamech, and Joel and stared down at them. "Bold words, both of you. Bold words." He smiled at Will with bitter malevolence in his eyes. "I especially liked the part about your *sure victory.*" A vein pulsed in his neck and his face reddened. He spat on the ground.

Lamech took a step forward and planted his feet. "Why are you here, Adrok? You have no part in this ceremony."

"I am come with a message from my father." He gestured across the broad courtyard to the sky over a low part of Lamech's house. "You will all remember the village of Sha'ar el Qedem, thirty kilometers east of here. Perhaps you know that yesterday we notified the village elders of our claim on their territory. We are generous leaders, so we gave them a choice. Submit to us or suffer the consequences. Now what do you think their decision was?"

A bright arch of light flashed on the horizon and swept across the sky. Will remembered the heavy ore he saw mined in Nod, and the hair on the back of his neck stood. *No way. That's impossible.* For a moment, the east glowed bright as if the sun were rising.

Adrok stared with raised eyebrows while the people murmured amongst each other.

Lamech's indignation was transparent. "What is the meaning of this?"

Adrok held up a hand. "Patience, Patriarch. Patience."

Will's mind shouted to him. *Shock wave. There'll be a shock wave. Thirty kilometers is a safe distance, right?* Then a deafening crack swept over the house, followed by a terrifying roar. The stars to the east grew dark as a shadow rose above the horizon.

Will flushed with anger, clenched his fist, and glared at Adrok.

The *overlord* lifted his hands to regain the party's attention and spoke matter-of-factly. "Sha'ar el Qedem is no more." He turned to Lamech, and his voice seethed with bitterness. "We now lay claim to your own City of Enoch."

Lamech stepped toward Adrok. "You still have no authority here, Son of the Watchers. We have called on Yahweh, and we will not submit to you."

Adrok mocked sympathy. "You may not submit to us, but others in your precious city already have. Their voices have reached my father as they have cried for freedom. We are simply here to end your repression."

"By destroying the city?"

"Better to die than live under God's repression."

"You wicked servant of Lucifer."

Adrok bared his teeth and shouted. "My father owes nothing to that snake. That coward sits in the heavens while my father leads the fight here on Earth."

"Leads the fight against whom? Against Yahweh? Or against all the sons of Adam who bear His image?"

Adrok stared at Lamech. "My father has spoken. Because of his grace and beneficence, he grants you thirty days to prepare for our arrival. If you refuse, you will suffer the same fate you saw tonight."

Adrok wheeled around and walked through the gate that led out of the courtyard. His long cape drifted through after him.

wwwwwwwwwww

The Council Chamber had never been so crowded or so loud. Word of Semyaza's threat spread to every corner of the city and drew the leading men and women there to seek help. Given their history with Adrok, Will wasn't willing to let Kat and Joel out of his sight. The three stood against a wall and watched the proceedings. One by one, citizens took the podium to shout their opinions.

"This is the angel Azazel's doing. He has served Semyaza by creating all manner of weapons."

"The Watchers have been invading lands bordering us for a decade now. It's only a matter of time until this city falls."

"We have to fight. We cannot allow the *nephilim* to take any more territory. If we fall, then only the West will remain."

"We cannot fight Semyaza. If we do, they will destroy us as they did Sha'ar el Qedem."

"No, no, we have to accept the reality of *nephilim* rule. At least they can guarantee order."

"Order? They only want to destroy us."

"Our only choice is to flee west."

"Flee how far? If we keep running, we'll soon run out of places to go. They'll take everything."

Soon the discussion descended into an incomprehensible shouting match.

Only Lamech was finally able to establish order. He raised his hands until he got the silence he needed. "Men and women of the city, you shout and argue in fear. May I remind you that we serve the Almighty Yahweh? Let us pause to seek His face and His guidance in this troubling matter."

The focus was just what the crowd needed. They knelt without a word.

Lamech remained on his feet so the crowd could hear. "Yahweh Elohim, Maker of Heaven and Earth, we seek Your perfect will. We know we cannot submit to our enemy—Your enemy—because that would mean rejecting and denying Your Name. We will die for Your Name first. Father, if it is Your will for us to fight, we will lay our lives down. If it is Your will for us to be destroyed to testify to the descendants of Cain and the rest of humankind so that they, too, may call on Your Name, then we submit to that will. Please show us what You would have us do. Amen."

Slowly, the people rose to their feet.

Lamech looked soberly around the chamber. Every eye was on him. "It is clear what the *nephilim* want. Our blood. The blood of every last son of Adam. They spill blood for food in direct defiance of Yahweh's decree to Adam. They spill blood to conquer. They spill blood to satisfy their own, perverse lusts. They rape, kill, and consume men, women, and animal alike."

Lamech swept his indignant gaze around the room. "Any of you who may be considering life under *nephilim* rule would do well to remember that. Yahweh offers you life, even life after death. The *nephilim* offer only death and destruction. Do not be fooled. God's will for us is clear, no matter what befalls us. We cannot submit. We cannot fight for long, but we will fight to defend ourselves. If we fall, or if we are captured and taken east, we must witness faithfully to the Name of Yahweh and to His promised Redeemer, the Son of Man, even to our dying breath."

Lamech took a deep breath. "Any family not willing to submit to *nephilim* rule must leave the city quickly. Do not wait. We cannot trust them to wait thirty days. Spread the word and make preparations. Now all of you, go to your homes and families. Only the Council, the tower guards, and the rest of the forty may remain here in the council chamber."

The chamber cleared with not a sound but the shuffle of feet. Lamech gestured to Will and his family to stay. Khaliil joined them once the crowd thinned enough.

Soon only Lamech, the council, and a few dozen men and women remained. Lamech gestured, and a handful of guards assumed posts outside the entry to guarantee privacy.

Lamech addressed the council. "The time has come for you to carry out our plan."

Joachim's face paled. "But this plan is madness. We never expected to carry it out."

Another council member spoke simply. "We must protect the orb, Joachim. We have taken oaths."

"But we mustn't act rashly. We can still take the orb farther west."

"Away from the tower? You know we cannot do that."

"But this is foolishness. What we need..."

Lamech interrupted. "What we need is time, Joachim, and here and now, we have run out of it. May I remind you that this is why you were placed in power. You're not elders, none of you. You were chosen because each of you has lived less than two centuries. You and your descendants will guard the orb for as long as it takes, even if it means handing it to the Redeemer, Himself when He establishes His own reign on Earth."

Joachim fell silent and stared down with tense eyes. The other council members looked around the room.

"Then it is decided. How long will final preparations take?"

Another council member turned to speak. "Two families should go ahead. Those who remain behind will need seven days to send our provisions and equipment along."

"Then two men and their wives will go tomorrow at sunset. The rest will gather the provisions and ensure they are delivered. Then they will follow."

Joachim stood. "My wife and I will travel ahead to prepare the distant end."

Lamech contradicted him respectfully. "Your eagerness does you credit, Joachim, but your expertise is unique, and we will need you here to ensure the right provisions are sent. No, Gemaliel and Kadmiel will go."

Joachim's eyes drifted to the side. He tensed his lips and sighed.

Will watched Joachim and whispered to Khaliil. "His intentions may or may not be noble, but I don't like to see any man acting out of fear."

Khaliil stared at Joachim and nodded.

Lamech dismissed the council. Conversations broke out throughout the room as they stood and made their way out. Will turned to Khaliil. "Just where are they going?"

Khaliil gathered Will, Kat, and Joel close and whispered his answer. "The important question is when. We didn't build the tower for security alone. It serves as a conduit for creating a gateway through time."

"Do you mean they could have sent us home any time?"

"No, Will, No. At least, I don't think they could. The other end of the gateway has already been determined."

Joel leaned in. "But what good is it to flee through a gateway and leave the orb behind?"

"Once the orb has opened the gateway, it can be carried through. The gateway will collapse soon after."

A sober thought came to Will. "Will you go through?"

"No, my friend. Forty people have been chosen."

Kat's mouth fell open. "Then you have to head west soon. Tomorrow."

"No. Not until the orb has been taken through. We in the Tower Guard have sworn to remain until then."

Lamech cleared his throat to tactfully announce his approach. "Joel, I regret that this event has poisoned your celebration."

"Thank you for the thought, sir, but it wasn't your fault." Joel's words betrayed no fear.

Lamech addressed Will. "I assume Khaliil has explained things."

Will hesitated, unsure if saying yes would cause trouble for his friend. Khaliil answered for him. "Yes. I have told them the basics."

Lamech nodded and curled his lips up. "Will, now that you know our plan, I believe you will have some questions for me."

"Where and when will they be going?"

Lamech took a deep breath. "We searched for years. It was like shooting an arrow in the dark, but at last, we hit something four thousand five hundred years into the future. From the little we've been able to ascertain, the seas appear to have subsumed much of the earth by then. We found an isolated island far to the south. There the Guardians will protect the orb and will use it to fight any nephilim who may be spawned across the ages."

Will would never show any disrespect to his host and spiritual father, but the question burned in his mind. "Sir, if you have this ability, why have you not sent us home to our own time?"

Lamech sighed with a look of sincere compassion. "I have been most cautious as the steward of my grandfather's orb, and I will not use it lightly. I can never be certain that I wouldn't be making irreparable changes to history. More than that, though, I did not send you through, Will, because your friend Kemuel entreated me not to before he died. He was very convincing."

Will tilted his head. "Kemuel? Kemuel told you not to send us back?"

"He said it was imperative that you remain here, but he would not say more. He implored me to trust his judgment, and once he told me who his father was..."

Will turned his head but kept his narrowed eyes on Lamech. "His father?"

Lamech nodded. "Joachim. Did he not tell you?"

Will's stomach quivered. He leaned back and shook his head with tightened lips. "The same Joachim who convinced the council to destroy the second orb and my ship?"

"You question his motives?"

"I have to consider the possibility that Joachim and Kemuel were conspiring to take the orb all along. If the second orb hadn't been destroyed with the..." Will thought his temples might burst with the realization. "Lord, help us. He didn't intend to stow away. He wanted to take the orb." The implications hit Will more quickly than he could speak. "That's why he programmed the ship to fly without our help. That's why the ship didn't explode. He concocted that story about a self-destruct capability so he could take the ship through time. He failed to take the second orb in the future, so he stole it here and took it back."

"I cannot believe that, Will." He turned to make sure they were alone. "Joachim doesn't even know that Kemuel was his son. Joachim doesn't yet have any children."

Kat put a hand on Will's shoulder. "And don't forget that Joachim brought extra clothing along for us."

Will struggled to reconcile all of the information. He couldn't shake his suspicion. "I can't dismiss the possibility that Joachim has taken the device to his father, Dr. Aelter, in the future."

Lamech looked at Will and softened. "I concede the possibility, but I will not judge hastily. I cannot implicate Joachim for something he has not done, but if what you say is true, you must go to your home to stop him."

Will wanted to feel relief, but something in his soul was restless.

Joel shuffled his feet, his eyebrows drawn together.

"What is it, Son?"

"Dad, if you say we're going, I'll go."

"But?"

"But this is my home. We've buried family here. My friends are here, and I don't want to leave them, especially when they need me."

Kat touched his shoulder. "I'm sure your friends will be leaving."

"Then let's help them escape the city. Let's help the Guardians prepare for their own journey into the future."

The restlessness in Will's soul quieted. "All right. We'll stay until the last possible minute." He turned to Lamech. "Can you send us to our time before taking the Guardians and the orb to theirs?"

Lamech nodded. "Of course. I'll instruct the Council to send you to the time and location of your choosing."

CHAPTER 21

Will and Joel looked down the inside of the tower while Joachim manipulated the orb in the chamber behind them. A bolt of light shot from the orb into the tower and spread into a blue, disk-shaped field several feet below the top landing.

Soon after, Kadmiel's hooded head emerged from the field as if he had surfaced from under water.

Will reached down, took his cold, gloved hand, and hefted him up onto the landing. *Just how far south is this island?*

Kadmiel took a moment to shake a dusting of snow off of his coat. "How much time has passed here?"

Joachim emerged from the chamber. "Six days."

"Great. We've been working for a month at our end, and we're nearly ready. The next time you open the portal, make it three days further ahead." Kadmiel looked at the people lined up around the staircase with bags and baskets of provisions and tools. "Give me one minute after I go back through, then start lowering the provisions." He turned, jumped off the landing, and disappeared through the portal.

Will reached a hook out and drew the metal ring from the ceiling toward him. The counterweight had been disconnected and the slack rope hoisted up and coiled at the top of the stairs next to him. He hefted a bag from the floor, attached the hook, and placed it on the metal ring. Then after a minute had passed, he lowered it through the portal while Joel measured the rope out hand-over-hand. They repeated the operation with the bag Joel was carrying, then handed off the hook, ring, and rope to the next people in line.

Just as they headed down the stairs, a horn sounded outside, followed shortly by another. Joachim shouted from the chamber, "They lied. They lied. They're invading now."

Khaliil's angry voice echoed right after. "Of course they lied."

Will and Joel ran into the chamber and looked outside with Khaliil and Joachim. A dozen plumes of smoke began to rise to the east, north, and everywhere in between. Will crossed the tower and looked over the city. A steady stream of refugees had been fleeing west out of the city for days. So far, they continued unmolested, but after hearing the warning horns, they made greater haste.

Will stepped back out of the chamber to where people were lowering supplies. "Forget the hook and pulley. Drop them in." The man at the top of the stairs froze, a basket of dried fruit clutched in his white-knuckled fists. Will took the basket from him and dropped it into the portal.

A moment later, Gemaliel poked his head through. "What's happening?"

Will leaned over the portal. "Nephilim attack. No time to lose. We'll count to ten before dropping each item. Then Joachim will close and reopen the portal to give you the three days you need before everyone comes through." Will had turned away when something else occurred to him. He turned back toward Gemaliel. "And in those three days, make something soft for everyone to land on. They'll be in a hurry."

Gemaliel nodded and dropped his head back in.

Will turned to Joachim. "We need to get Kat."

Joel hurried down the stairs. "She's in the warehouses below the council chamber. I'll get her."

Will raised his hand to stop Joel. "No. We go together."

Joel stopped and looked up at Will.

Will turned again to Joachim. "Give us time to get back, so we can get to our own time."

Joachim looked at the orb, then at the portal, his eyes wide. His tense breaths burst in and out.

Khaliil stepped forward. "He'll wait."

Will nodded and ran down the stairs after Joel. They sprinted across the field and passed several councilmen and other members of the forty on the way. They ran through the tunnel and around the path down the mountain. By the time they neared the council chamber, nearly the entire city to the east was aflame.`

They had just passed the council chamber when Kat shouted from the armory next door. "Wait. I'm here."

They ran into the armory. Several members of the tower guard rushed out and up the path.

Will shouted ahead to Kat. "Where's Lamech?"

Kat ran back to where she had stockpiled several weapons. "He's leading his people west. I hope he has left the city by now." She handed sheathed longswords to Will and Joel. "Here. We have to give the forty time to escape." They quickly tied the swords around their waists, then Kat helped secure small shields to their left arms. Then she flung quivers of arrows to them and handed them bows before she took a double-loaded crossbow and a rapier for herself.

They ran from the armory. A horde of imps swarmed up from below. They sprinted up the path, through the tunnel, and across the field.

They saw the last members of the forty disappear into the tower just as several dozen *sheddim* climbed over the side of the amphitheater behind the tower. A dozen members of the tower guard stood outside the entrance, their weapons drawn. Will, Kat, and Joel had only made it halfway across the field when the *sheddim* surrounded the base of the tower and drew their weapons.

Will looked up at the tower. "They need more time."

The *sheddim* attacked the tower guard with a cacophony of shouts and clangs of swords and shields. A giant *overlord*, at least seven meters tall, turned and stepped away from the *sheddim* to face Will, Kat, and Joel. He drew two thick, long swords, growled with seething fury, and charged toward them. Kat turned to the side, broadened her stance, aimed her crossbow, and fired. She hit him in the soft spot of the forehead she remembered from the story of Goliath, and the silenced giant fell to the ground. Will and Joel followed her example, drew their bows and dispatched *sheddim* one by one.

Kat let out a fierce yell behind Will. Will spun. A horde of imps crossed the field toward them. Kat fired her crossbow's second arrow at a leading imp. She pierced it through the neck. It clutched its throat desperately and fell to the ground. Will killed a second imp and drew again.

The imps were easily deterred and drew back. They cowered with their arms lifted to shield themselves.

"They're coming over the wall," Joel shouted.

More *sheddim* crested the amphitheater wall. Five of the tower guard lay on the ground. Will and Joel drew their bows and fired arrow after arrow while Kat aimed her empty crossbow back and forth at the cowardly mob of imps to keep them back.

The *sheddim* soon noticed the attack from behind and charged across the field. Will killed two *sheddim,* lowered his bow, reached across his waist, and grasped the hilt of his sword. Then Khaliil shot an arrow from the tower and killed another. The *sheddim* paused to look up at the tower. It gave Will, Joel, and Khaliil time to kill three more. Then Khaliil disappeared into the tower, and the *sheddim* charged again toward Will and his family.

Will, Kat, and Joel drew swords and prepared to engage their attackers. Then with a deafening crack, a bolt of lightning struck from the top of the tower, killed two *sheddim,* and left a smoking scorch mark on the ground. Then a second bolt killed another *sheddih,* then another. The *sheddim* scattered and ran for cover.

Will looked up. Khaliil gestured for them to come. They sprinted between several terrified *sheddim* and joined the surviving guards at the tower entrance. They heard the tower pulley's rapidly punctuated squeak, followed by a thud on the ground. Khaliil's bass voice resounded up the tower to Joachim. "Keep firing."

Khaliil emerged from the tower. "Hurry, my friends. Joachim will send you home and then destroy the tower after he goes through."

They ran in and quickly drew back to avoid the heavy, falling rope that gathered onto the floor in a random pile. They looked up just in time to see Joachim jump into the portal and disappear.

Khaliil bared his teeth and bellowed. "Joachim no! Coward."

Sparks fell down the tower's interior. The portal field turned red. Khaliil's eyes opened wide. "Run!"

They sprinted from the tower right through a bewildered mob of *sheddim,* imps, and *overlords* converging on them. The surviving tower guards followed at Khaliil's command. The *nephilim* were first surprised but rallied quickly to attack when a random bolt of lightning struck from the tower.

Will pointed to the bullpen at the side of the field. "There." More bolts of lightning struck the ground. Some narrowly missed them. While the *nephilim* fled for the tunnel, Will and the others ducked into the bullpen and looked back. The top of the tower glowed orange. A field of blue static crept down the sides of the tower while dozens more bolts of lightning scorched the ground in all directions, incinerated *nephilim,* and blew craters in the amphitheater surface.

Will held Kat and Joel close. They ducked against the wall. *Nephilim* outside screamed in terror as the flurry of lightning bolts became too numerous to avoid. Then Joachim sent a final, massive surge through the portal. Will thought his eardrums would burst from the pressure, and for a moment he could hear nothing. He and the others grimaced and covered their ears. The top of the tower exploded with a ground-shaking crack of thunder. Massive rocks and fragments thudded into the field. The remainder of the tower toppled and crumbled with a deafening roar and a huge burst of gray soot and dust.

Will waited for the thunderous echoes to subside and the dust to settle, then looked outside. One end of the amphitheater was gone, and part of the mountain had slid away. Half-buried boulders and hundreds of dead *nephilim* littered what was left of the field. They left the bullpen and headed for the tunnel. Then Adrok emerged from the entrance, followed by an endless stream of *sheddim*. Will turned and directed Kat, Joel, and the guards up the stairs next to the bullpen. They sprinted to the top and looked over the side. Will shook his head. It was a steep drop hundreds of feet down onto craggy rocks. They moved back down a few steps and stopped.

Khaliil rallied the guards. "Form a line." The seven survivors spread out with Khaliil and pointed their weapons down toward the amphitheater floor. Adrok gloated from the field below, gathered his *sheddim* in perfect, aligned formation, and walked alone toward them.

Khaliil took a deep breath through clenched teeth. He turned his intense gaze left and right to his fellow guards. "You've fought well, men. We gave the forty the time they needed to escape, and our charge is safe. We will die victorious. Now we give praise to our Redeemer Yahweh."

Adrok climbed up the side of the amphitheater and stood a few steps in front of the line of guards. They pointed their weapons at him without fear. His arrogant satisfaction was all too clear. "I come now for what is mine. Give me the woman, and I'll see to it you die quickly."

No one budged. Kat stared daggers at the giant. She whispered to Will, "My kingdom for one more arrow."

Khaliil laughed boisterously. Adrok's nostrils flared. He gestured behind himself and yelled. "Just look at this field full of troops. They're only a small part of the legion I brought with me."

Khaliil stopped laughing. "You may kill us, Son of the Watchers, but Yahweh will deliver us. We will have enjoyed our reward for thousands of years, and you will still be wandering the earth aimlessly as a senseless, hopeless spirit, parched and empty."

Adrok flexed his arms and roared so loudly Will thought his larynx might rupture. The *overlord* gestured for the first ranks of his *sheddim* to attack. "I've ordered them to kill you slowly, humans." He glared at Kat. "You can watch me torture your husband and your son. You'll *beg* me to kill them before I take you to my father's palace." He moved down a few steps to make way for his army and spoke over his shoulder. "Only a miracle can keep me from getting what I want this time."

Just then, a bolt of lightning struck the field from nowhere. Three charred *sheddim* fell to the ground. Adrok stiffened and dropped his jaw. He turned and stared at the smoking corpses. Other bolts of lightning followed with greater frequency. Dozens more smoking *nephilim* corpses toppled. The other *sheddim* scattered. Then an elliptical field formed thirty feet above the amphitheater floor and glowed brighter and brighter. Even Adrok lifted an arm to shield his eyes.

Will and Kat looked at each other and smiled. *Chronos* materialized with deafening crack that reverberated like thunder. It sent a shock wave across the field and knocked the surviving *sheddim* off their feet.

Khaliil wasted no time. He drew Joel and Kat to himself in a firm embrace. Then he hugged Will. "Go, my friend. Take your family home. We'll hold them off while you escape."

Chronos maneuvered over them to the top of the amphitheater.

Joel grabbed Khaliil's arm. "Come with us."

"No, Joel. Let me die here with honor." Khaliil took Joel by the shoulders and looked him in the eye. "Carry on the fight, Joel. Our God has great plans for you."

Adrok gathered the *sheddim* and screamed at the top of his lungs. "Attack."

Hundreds of *sheddim* swarmed up the amphitheater. Kat pulled Joel away and up the stairs. Will nodded gratefully to his friend and ushered his family back to the top.

Chronos stopped and hovered above them while the main hatch opened. Chris popped his head out and lowered the ladder.

Will shouted to Kat, "You first." She jumped onto the ladder and climbed up. The *sheddim* collided with the line of guards below.

Shouts and the clang of swords filled the air. Joel jumped onto the ladder and climbed in. Then Will pulled himself onto the ladder and turned back. *Chronos* rose and pulled Will away from the amphitheater, and he watched the last two guards fall next to Khaliil. Then a *sheddih* ran Khaliil through and pulled his sword out. Khaliil staggered back and fell to the ground. His eyes met Will's, and he grinned with satisfaction. Then he turned his eyes heavenward and drew his last breath.

Will whispered. "Thank you, my friend. Enjoy your reward."

CHAPTER 22

Will climbed in. Kat grabbed her controls, and Kemuel directed Joel to the pair of seats in the back. Will spoke first to Kat. "Take us up. We're going home."

Kat pulled up on the throttle and turned it in her hand to gain altitude.

Chris scratched his cheek. "Umm, would someone tell me what just happened? I hit the self-destruct button Kemuel rigged just like you ordered. I thought the ship was supposed to detonate."

Will looked at the guilty grin on Kemuel's face. "I thought so, too. Kemuel?"

Kemuel shifted in his seat. "I did create a self-destruct capability, but I also rigged the seventeen-year time jump."

Chris gasped. "Seventeen years!"

Will fixed his gaze at Kemuel. "A jump while hovering thirty feet above the ground?"

Kemuel shrugged. "It can be done, but I don't recommend making it a habit."

"Why seventeen years?"

"Because I was told it must be so."

"Who told you?"

Kemuel tensed his lips.

"Is it one of us? Is it Joel?"

208

Chris blinked and shook his head. "Who's Joel?"

Kemuel seemed to measure every word. "I had to walk a fine line to avoid... impacting your decisions. You needed to stay. Joel needed to be born. Things could still go terribly wrong, and then we won't be warned at all, and there'll be nothing to stop the enemy. You must trust that I have everyone's best interest at heart."

Will stared into Kemuel's eyes and let out a frustrated sigh. "I did trust you. Why didn't you tell me Joachim is your father?"

Kemuel looked at the floor. "He and I never really saw eye-to-eye. I didn't even tell him who I was because I didn't want him to know he had authority over me. I didn't tell you, because, honestly, I'm not particularly proud..."

Kemuel stopped abruptly, so Will dropped it. Instead he turned back to the business at hand. "How high do we need to be to jump forward safely?"

Kemuel thought for a moment. "To jump five thousand years, give or take? During this age, there's nothing to collide with, so the lower stratosphere should be more than sufficient. I'll help Chris arrange for us to arrive far enough into space to avoid any satellites."

"Good. Do it."

Kat interjected. "What about the satellites we launched?"

"Leave them. We have their telemetry readings." Will looked at Joel, who was smiling proudly. It occurred to Will that Joel had never seen them working as astronauts. He winked at his son. "Oh, and Chris, I don't believe you've met our son, Joel Elias Stark."

Chris blinked a few times. "Wow."

"Transition to aerodynamic flight."

Chris activated the controls to rotate *Snowman*. "Aye, sir, rotating *Snowman* forward now. Wait a minute. *Our* son?"

Kat laughed. "*Our* son, Chris." She let go of the throttle just long enough to show off the ring Will had given her in deference to the anachronistic tradition they just weren't willing to give up.

Chris looked at her ring and at the gold band on Will's finger. "Wow." Then something else hit him. "Hang on a sec. If we jumped seventeen years, then you should be in your late fifties by now, sir, and Kat, you should be in your, what, late forties? But you both look younger than when we left." He pointed to Will's hair, "Nice locks, by the way, sir."

Will turned his eyes up as if to look at his own hair.

Kemuel interjected for Will. "The antediluvian Earth is a tremendously healthy place, Commander Saif-ad-Deen. No one can be certain how long-term the effects could be."

Will pulled the ship into a steep climb. "Let's go home. Altitude three thousand meters and climbing."

Kemuel stepped to Chris's station to assist with the calculations.

Chris conferred with Kemuel and entered the appropriate settings. After a few moments, he lifted his head to report. "Ready to time jump on your command."

Will nodded. "Strap in, Kemuel. You, too, Joel. Altitude nine thousand meters... ten thousand meters... eleven thousand meters... jump now."

Chris activated the control system, and on the monitors Will saw the charged elliptical field appear outside the ship. Immediately afterward, the earth swung away and took its gravity with it.

Even with the abrupt transition to zero-G, Will felt comfortable enough to turn to Kemuel. "It's much smoother this time."

Kemuel nodded. "I helped Chris refine how to activate the phase inducer. That first jump of yours was terribly uncomfortable."

The earth swung by, much like before. Then a moment later, it swung by again, and the interval between revolutions decreased until their steadily increasing distance from the earth became apparent.

A growl resounded through the ship followed by a loud clang. The time jump's feeling of uncomfortable resistance returned, and it became difficult to move or speak. Then a horrifying shriek pierced the air followed by another clang, and the field outside disappeared just as the earth swung back into view.

Will turned to Kat and unstrapped his harness. "Stay here." He pushed off his chair and floated to the ladder. Chris and Kemuel followed behind. When they reached the compartment with *Snowman,* Chris gasped. A wide gash in the cylinder's side partially exposed the blue and white orb within.

Chris swung around Will to examine the housing and the laser apparatus. "No, no, no."

Kemuel narrowed his eyes, searched around and continued past the next compartment. Will followed and left Chris with the damaged device.

Another deafening shriek ripped through the air behind Will. He spun. A shaking imp with eyes bulging out of its skull held a battle-axe above its head. Its deformed feet grasped the ladder like claws and enabled it to move quickly toward Will. Will took in a tense breath and searched for anything to defend himself with. He found nothing. The imp raised the battle-axe to strike. Will raised his arms to shield his head. Then the imp grunted and froze in place, its eyes wide. The tip of a sword protruded from its abdomen for a moment and disappeared. The imp floated toward Will. Behind it, Joel grasped the ladder with one hand and his sword with the other.

Will thought his chest might burst with pride. He let out a deep sigh and grinned. "Great job, Son."

Kemuel walked his hands along the ladder back into the compartment. "It must have crept on board before we left you and Kat behind." Then he pushed himself over to analyze *Snowman*.

Will stared at the imp corpse and the floating drops of blood for a moment, then turned to Chris and Kemuel. "How bad is it?"

Kemuel spoke first. "Bad. The crystals in the orb's shell that control time travel have been forced out of alignment. We can't get home now."

Chris was still analyzing the rest of the equipment. "We may still be able to use it for flight, though. At least I think we can. The laser system is undamaged, as near as I can tell, as is the opposite side of *Snowman*."

Will rubbed his eyes. *I need options.* "Kemuel, do you think there's any possibility of the Guardians reopening the gateway to the City of Enoch?"

Kemuel didn't look hopeful. "It's possible. Honestly, I can't think of any other course of action available to us."

"How far forward did we travel?"

Chris moved out from behind *Snowman*. "Six hundred thirty-nine years."

Kemuel paled visibly.

Will didn't like that expression on Kemuel's face. "What is it?"

Kemuel swallowed. "Sir, this is the year sixteen hundred fifty-six after creation. That's the year of the catastrophe."

Will sighed. "When it rains, it pours, I suppose."

"You have no idea."

Chris stared at the floor and mumbled. "Then there's no hope."

Will turned away from the others. This was when the burden of command was the heaviest. *Okay, our choices are to die in space or to die on the* surface. He tensed his lips. *I don't think anyone will like that, and I need to offer them hope.*

Lamech's blessing to Joel echoed in his memory, "...especially when there seems to be no hope at all."

A weight lifted from Will's shoulders. He turned to Joel, who was watching him expectantly. "There's always hope because our hope has an object."

Joel grinned. "And His hope does not disappoint."

"We'll set down at the amphitheater to see if we can make contact with the Guardians. Whatever happens, if there *is* hope, Our Lord will lead us to it."

CHAPTER 23

For the first time, they successfully used *Snowman's* hover capability to lower themselves smoothly into the Earth's atmosphere and convert to aerodynamic flight. Will piloted them across the west lands, which were now as untamed as the East had been before. Given the urgency of their situation, they didn't wait to travel under cover of night.

They watched the array of monitors as they approached the City of Enoch. Wilderness had taken over. Only a few surviving structures carved into the mountain remained as evidence the city ever existed.

Will readied to pass off control of *Chronos.* "Transition to hover flight. Kat, see if you can set us down in the amphitheater."

Chris touched his controls. "Hover flight aye, sir."

Kat grasped her controls and circled them around the amphitheater once to reconnoiter. Not a soul was in sight. A scarred cliff gouged the mountain where the tower had once stood, and the sides of the amphitheater were significantly eroded. She landed smoothly in a spot between two half-buried boulders on the field.

They emerged onto the field and inspected the ruins. Will felt more like an archaeologist than an astronaut, except that this place held powerful memories. He looked up where Khaliil and the brave tower guardsmen sacrificed themselves to enable them to escape. *I hope your sacrifice won't be in vain, my friends.*

Will and the others looked over the gouged cliff where the tower and part of the mountain had fallen away. A steep trail had been carved along the cliff to the ground below. No one said a word. Will tensed his lips. *Yeah, I don't see the Guardians coming back here anytime soon.* Chris slouched with a hand on his forehead.

Will decided to see if the council chamber was still intact. As he rounded the ship for the tunnel, he prayed silently. *Father, I trust you, but please give me some way to offer hope to the others.*

Just then, a man peered from the tunnel's shadow and emerged onto the field. Will looked over his shoulder. The others were walking to join him. He stepped toward the stranger and was about to greet him when he spoke first.

"You must be Will Stark?"

Will blinked.

"My father told me about you, but I never expected to see you... or your ship. He said you escaped more than fifty years before I was born. Or at least he hoped you did, since he never saw you again."

Kat, Chris, and Kemuel joined them and listened silently.

Will saw something familiar in the man's features. "You must be Lamech's son. Can you tell me where he is?"

The man's expression softened. "My father died five years ago. He was only seven hundred seventy-seven years old, but God had mercy on him." He looked at the ruins around them. "I don't think my father's heart could have borne any more pain."

Kat stepped forward and spoke with gentle compassion in her voice. "What happened?"

The man looked at her for a moment before speaking. "In the centuries since my birth, the *Nephilim* Empire spanned the globe. They conquered mostly by force. Cities who resisted were destroyed, and many others submitted out of fear, but tragically, most of humanity chose to accept the two hundred as their pantheon of gods, and the *nephilim* as agents of the gods on Earth. The humans who submitted became just as evil as the angels they worshiped. I warned them and warned them to call on Yahweh instead."

He swallowed and looked up. Tears streamed down his face. "Those who remained faithful to Yahweh fell under vicious persecution from *nephilim* and fellow human alike. They were martyred in such great numbers that I don't believe any are left, save for my own family."

Kat flushed. Her tone became edgy. "The *nephilim* will fall under God's judgment."

"Many already have. The *nephilim* produce nothing of value. They simply take what they want. When resources grew scarce, they turned on each other. Clans fought clans, and even the Watchers battled each other. The *se'irim* have been virtually wiped out. Only *overlords* and *sheddim* remain. I hear they're conducting a gathering to plan something even more terrible, but I can't imagine what that could be."

A younger man poked his head from the tunnel. "Father, is everything all right?"

"Yes, Japheth." He turned back to Will and the others. "We've been using the council's warehouses to stockpile provisions. We're taking the last of them now. Do you need food?"

Will shook his head. "No, thank you, sir."

Japheth sounded concerned. "Time is short, Father."

The man smiled to reassure his son. "I know." He turned to address them one last time. "We have much to do." He looked at *Chronos,* and worry crept over his face. "My father told me of your ship's capabilities. You must use it to escape now."

Will looked to one side.

The man looked sympathetic. "I gather there's a problem with that." He glanced with concern at Japheth and looked intently at Will. "The enemy considers this ground to be cursed, which is why we've been safe all this time."

Will realized his quandary. "But you're concerned that someone might have seen us land."

The man nodded. "I'm certain they saw you. The enemy has many, many spies."

Will was grateful to have a clear purpose. "Then we will leave." He threw a look of determination toward each of the others. "We'll draw the enemy's attention away."

The man looked relieved. "Thank you. God bless you, my friends."

He and his son disappeared into the tunnel.

Kemuel turned to Will and Kat and spoke for the first time since they had landed. "You're both descendants of Japheth, in case you didn't know. You know, we might be able to escape with them, but I don't think they'll have enough provisions for four more people."

Will led them back to the ship. "And they have no way to fight off the enemy if they're discovered. Let's go."

A few moments later, *Chronos* rose above the amphitheater.

As they rose, Joel pointed at one of the monitors. "Look. There."

Right where Lamech's house had been, a long wooden structure stretched along the ground. A massive side door lay open in the middle of the structure and served as a ramp to the second of three visible decks inside. Two men and two women led a small herd of cattle up the ramp.

Will couldn't believe he was witnessing such a pivotal event in history. He drank the image in as long as he could.

Chris frowned. "I thought they took two of each animal."

Kemuel shook his head with a sad smile. "People always say that. They also took seven of every clean animal and seven of each bird."

"Clean animals?"

Kemuel's eyes were locked on the ark below. "God will tell them to eat meat when they come out. Do you know it's the length of one-and-one half of your football fields?"

As they continued to rise, they saw a support structure that stretched to each side of the ark, halfway between the side door and one end.

Joel stared at the massive cross on the ground below and leaned over his father's shoulder. "Dad, is that... ?"

"Yes, Joel." Will gazed without focus for a moment. "It's God's plan to save the world."

Kat looked at Will. "Heading?"

Kemuel startled them from behind. He pointed to one side. "Look."

Miles away to the north, an ominously familiar glow streaked across the horizon to the east.

Will's gut wrenched. It was an angel.

Kemuel shouted. "We have to head south, away from him."

"No. That'll lead him right over the ark." He looked at Kat. "Take us west, fast."

Kat leaned them hard and pulled up on the throttle. Joel fell to the deck from his position behind Will. He grunted hard with the abrupt sensations of rising and falling.

Will's tone was urgent. "Get to your seat and strap in, Son. Chris, transition to aerodynamic flight. We need speed."

Chris responded promptly. "Aerodynamic flight aye, sir. Rotating *Snowman*."

Joel struggled to climb back to his seat, then pointed again. "It's too late."

The angel turned and carved a path straight for them.

Will took them to full throttle just as Joel climbed into his seat. The acceleration forced them back hard, and Joel let out a long, labored grunt. They were just approaching Mach 1 when something hit the ship hard from above. Will struggled to keep control of the ship. *Okay, let's see if you can go supersonic.* They flew over what looked like a vast army on the ground. A vast plume of dust rose from the ground a short distance away. Will considered trying to lose the angel by flying through.

Something hit them again, and a deafening voice shook them to the core. "Land your ship now or I'll destroy it." Another jarring impact rocked the ship.

Will saw no choice. He reduced thrust. "Hover flight. Take us down."

Chris and Kat obeyed promptly. Once they slowed to hover-flight and turned, the angel forced the ship to one side. Kat resumed their original course, but the angel pushed them again. She looked at Will.

"Go where he wants. At least the ark is safe." He turned to Chris and Kemuel. "I need that self-destruct capability now, for real this time. Can you rig up a remote trigger?"

Chris held up a small device with a sober expression. "Already done."

Now that Kat was following him, the angel flew ahead and descended onto a desolate plain just in front of the nearest army. A few moments later, they were on the ground near him.

Will looked at Kemuel, who clasped his tense hands together with tense breaths.

The deafening voice shook the ship again. "Out of the ship now."

Will took the device from Chris, opened the hatch, stepped through, and descended to the ground. He immediately recognized Semyaza. *Help us, Father.*

Kat, Chris, Joel, and Kemuel joined him. Will drew Kat and Joel behind him and stared at Semyaza. The metal-clad army marched in lock-step as it approached east of them. Incessant thuds echoed, and the ground trembled with the impact of each step.

This time, Semyaza chose to appear taller. He folded his wings behind him and stared at the crew, his chin thrust out, his eyebrows raised. He glanced toward the city ruins in the distance. "I gather you just met the prophet."

Will furrowed his brow. *So he knows?*

Semyaza's tone was caustic. "In case you're wondering, human, yes, I know about his little engineering project. He's been building it for a hundred twenty years, after all." He snarled. "At least having a hobby finally got him to shut up. He and his family can rot in their little box, for all I care. The Earth is mine, and he can't change that."

Will's body tensed with a flush of heat. "You mean God won't let you destroy them."

Semyaza flushed red and shook. Will thought the angel's head might explode. Just then, the first *nephilim* army reached them. Adrok walked ahead of his legions, approached Semyaza, and bowed.

"Greetings, Father." Still bowed down, he turned his head and stared malevolently at Will.

Will returned the stare. Even as Adrok's army came to a stop, the earth continued to tremble as the second army approached from the northwest.

Semyaza barked at Adrok. "You're supposed to be at the palace for the gathering."

"I know, Father, but the clan of Baraqiel dared to defy your rule. They must pay for their treachery."

"What treachery?"

"They seized the opportunity of your gathering to plunder your treasures in the northern plains. Word reached me a week ago that they slaughtered our garrison at *Sharf al-Harb.*"

Semyaza spun toward the other approaching army. A second angel arrived ahead of them and landed gracefully in front of Semyaza.

Semyaza glared at his counterpart. "Baraqiel."

Baraqiel bowed his head slightly. "My Prince."

Semyaza bared his teeth. "So you dare defy my rule."

Baraqiel spread his hands in a poor attempt to feign innocence. "I don't know what you mean, my Prince. I'm leading my army to your gathering now."

"The gathering is tomorrow, fool. Your army will never make it."

Baraqiel looked over Semyaza's shoulder. "Perhaps not, but then neither will yours."

Semyaza's shout shook the earth. "You bound yourself with a curse to obey me."

Baraqiel stretched his wings up. "But of course, my Prince. I will attend the gathering as you wish." He swung his wings down with a deep rush and leapt into the air. As he rose above the ground, he roared a command to his approaching army. "Slaughter them all!"

Semyaza's nostrils flared. "No, you fool." Baraqiel's army shouted in unison and stampeded toward their position.

Adrok pointed his sword toward the attacking force and shouted. "Attack." His own legions shouted and ran around the ship toward their enemies.

As they dodged the stampede of *nephilim,* Will saw an opportunity and ushered his crew to the ship's ladder.

Will looked around. "Where's Joel?"

Adrok approached with one arm tight around Joel's neck and two *sheddim* in escort, their swords raised.

Semyaza followed and looked on with satisfaction. As he neared the ship, the stampede of *nephilim* gave the angel a wide berth.

Will crouched with clenched fists, ready to die for his son. Kat held her hand out to the *overlord* and shouted desperately. "No."

Adrok gloated in his newfound victory. "Words cannot express how happy this makes me." He looked at Joel and smiled. "I swear, your son has only aged a week since his initiation more than six centuries ago."

Will looked into his son's eyes, which were hard as flint. Joel gritted his teeth and struggled to breathe in the *overlord's* tight grip.

The armies collided some distance away with angry shouts, the clangs of swords and shields, and shrieks of pain.

Adrok stared at Will. "This time I get what is mine, human."

Will wanted to choke the *overlord* with his bare hands. "Let him go."

"Oh no, human, I wouldn't dream of it. I'll also take your ship and..."

Will held up the remote detonator. "You know I'll destroy it first."

"No you won't. I know about your Orb of Enoch now. You'll just use it to disappear into time like you did before." He smiled and lifted Joel off his feet. "But not this time." He spoke mockingly. "I have become quite a prophet myself, and I'm going to predict what will happen next. My father will take me, along with your son, to his palace. You will follow in your ship and place it in the citadel chamber outside the Great Hall. There I will present your ship *and* Enoch's orb to my father as a gift." He looked at Semyaza, who nodded his approval with a wicked grin. Adrok glared again at Will. "If you don't come, I won't bother killing your son before we consume his flesh."

Kat stepped forward. "No."

The *sheddim* moved in front of Adrok and pointed their swords at her throat.

She stopped. "Take me instead."

Joel grunted in Adrok's vice grip. "Mom, no."

Will lightly touched the detonator button with his thumb and searched for another way out. He agonized. *No matter what I do, Father, I'm gonna lose somebody, won't I? What do I do?*

Kat took a deep breath and swallowed. Her voice quivered. "Leave my son. I'll go with you willingly."

Adrok let out a deep, trembling sigh while he looked Kat up and down. He moved forward with Joel still held off the ground with one arm, and stroked her long hair. "Very well, woman." He grabbed her, released Joel, and pushed him hard into Will. Then he pulled Kat with him. "I expect you to arrive tomorrow at midday, human, or I'll make her death very painful."

The *sheddim* kept their weapons raised and followed Adrok to cover his departure.

Joel shouted. "Mom!"

Semyaza took Adrok and Kat in each arm and leapt into the air.

Will's whole body shook. "I'll come for you, Kat."

Her voice was calm as Semyaza carried her away. "I know you will. I love you both."

Will choked down his anger and wasted no time. "Quickly. Let's go." He headed for the ship. Once on board, he leapt into his seat. "Get us off the ground, Chris."

Chris activated an automated subroutine to lift off and transition to aerodynamic flight.

CHAPTER 24

Will sat in his bunk and buried his head in his hands. He had tried to rest, but sleep eluded him. He stood, opened a cabinet, and put on his flight suit for the first time in seventeen years. He couldn't get his mind off of Kat. He stared at her empty bunk and repeated his old mantra to himself with more conviction than ever. *There's no room for failure.* Then he pondered all the *overlords* and *sheddim* who would stand between him and Kat, and the further risk of losing Joel in the process of saving her. *Four men against thousands.* He paced back and forth and struggled to come up with a plan. *Any plan.* He stopped and dropped his head. *It's impossible.* Fury welled up in his chest. He clenched his fists and pounded the wall. He tensed every muscle in his face, wept, and slid his fists down the wall next to his face. Even in his despair he had just enough restraint to keep his tears absolutely silent. He didn't want company,

His soul cried out in agony. *Please, God. Don't let me lose her. I can't lose her, too, and I can't lose my son trying to save her. Please. Please.*

He slid down the wall and fell to the floor. *Father, I don't know what to do. Give me hope... any hope.*

Turbulence shook the ship with a deep rumble, and something slid from the open cabinet. Thin pages fluttered as it fell to the floor. It was his father's Bible. Will picked it up, squatted against the wall, and ran a hand over the cover. He thought he had lost it with the ship all those years ago. Now the book meant more to him than ever. He opened it to one of the dog-eared pages and read the highlighted passage.

Peace I leave with you; my peace I give you. I do not give to you as the world gives. Do not let your hearts be troubled and do not be afraid.

Will wept again, but this flood of tears washed over him and left him calm. He stretched his arm across his eyes and let the sleeve dry them. Then anger gripped his heart again. He slapped the Bible closed and prayed aloud. "I don't want peace. I want my *wife* back."

He dropped the Bible and buried his head in his hands. Then in the corner of his eye, he spotted handwriting inside the Bible's back cover. He furrowed his brow and pulled the Bible up.

Dear Will. I have so much to say. Son, I'm sorry. My last words to you were angry, and I should never have left you like that. You are no failure, Will. You never were. I hope you can forgive me, and I want you to know I'm so very proud of you. You're only twelve, but I can already see what a fine man you're becoming.

The letter blurred, and tears streamed down Will's face. He swallowed, took a deep breath, wiped his eyes with a sleeve, and continued.

Will, you need to know that I've become a Christian. I know that must sound really weird, but it's true. A good friend showed me how important it is, and he has also showed me what the Bible teaches about being a father. I know I haven't been a good father to you, Will, but I promise to do better when I get home—if I get home.

Will, if I don't, never forget that I'm proud of you—I always have been—and that you will never be fatherless. My greatest hope is that you'll follow Jesus as I do now. In your greatest hour of need, let Him guide you into battle, and your victory will be sure. I know you will be a great warrior, Will, but you will always be my beloved son. Your Proud Father.

Will sniffed, set the Bible down gently, and took a deep breath. *Thank you, Lord.* He wiped his face and looked up. *Would you tell Dad I found his message? And would you tell him I am following You? I think it would mean a lot to him.*

Will climbed up onto one knee and lowered his head. *All right, Father God. I trust you, and I will follow you into battle. Lead me. Whether I live or die, give me victory.* He stood, stepped into the ladder chute, and headed for the bridge.

Joel and Kemuel were talking in the galley compartment. When they heard Will, they headed forward after him.

Chris looked up as Will entered the bridge. "I was about to come get you. We'll be there shortly... a little early, too. With any luck, they won't be expecting us yet. The mist will have risen when we arrive. We might be able to use that to our advantage."

Will nodded. Joel and Kemuel arrived and took their seats. Will's eyes followed Joel.

"What is it, Dad?"

Will put a hand on his son's shoulder. He swallowed hard to make sure his words came out. "I hope you know how proud I am of you."

Joel smiled.

Chris gestured for Will to come to his station. "Sir, believe it or not, one of our satellites is still operational."

"After six hundred years? You've gotta be kidding."

"I guess we have Dr. Sekulow's genius to thank for it. I thought you should see this."

Will leaned over to look at an image of the earth on Chris's monitor. A zone of red flashed ominously on one side.

"That's the canyon east of Semyaza's palace."

"Why is it flashing?"

"The satellite is detecting tectonic pressure."

"I thought there were no tectonic plates yet."

"There aren't. That's what makes this so strange."

Will stood where he could see everyone and tugged at his flight suit. "Gentlemen, I won't order you to come to Semyaza's palace. We can set down now and let you off. You need to decide now."

After a moment of silence, Joel spoke first. "Die a coward's death running away? I'd much rather die fighting with you."

Kemuel stood and faced Will. "My fate is with you, Colonel Stark."

Chris shook his head and shrugged. "I'm not going anywhere."

Will let out a sigh of relief. "That's good, because... and I don't think I've ever said this before... I can't do this alone." He looked at Chris. "And I need you to land the ship in hover mode. So far you've only taken off. Can you do it?"

Chris nodded. "Sure. I can't perform combat maneuvers, but I can land her."

Satisfied, Will distributed communication earpieces. "Here. I want us in constant contact." He took his seat, strapped in, and spoke through the comm link. "Transition to hover flight now."

The fog obscured the palace as they approached. Chris activated a computer-enhanced infrared view to give them a clearer image. A massive additional structure surrounded the old walled city. Will stared at it with wide eyes. There was no doubt in his mind that the additional fortress was impenetrable. Within it, thousands of people appeared as tiny, red images, all gathered around what used to be the outer wall. A few hundred *nephilim* showed up bright orange, all headed into the citadel. There, a throng of at least a hundred thousand *nephilim* filled the Great Hall.

Will stared into the monitors ahead. "Deploying landing gear. Hover over the citadel antechamber until it clears."

Chris moved them over the citadel. They watched as the last hundred or so *nephilim* filed through into the Great Hall.

A buzzer sounded at Chris's workstation, and the ship listed to the right. Chris shouted, "Software controls are out."

The ship began to fall. Will pulled himself over to Kat's station and grabbed the controls. "This isn't gonna be pretty." He pushed the cyclic over and pulled up on the throttle to level the ship. Then the ship fell a few dozen feet before Will pulled up harder on the throttle.

Chris looked helpless. "*Snowman* must have shifted out of alignment. We're losing thrust."

Will took them down as quickly and smoothly as he could, but the controls only responded intermittently. The ship listed again, and he pushed hard on the cyclic to compensate. Still tilted a few degrees, they hit the ground hard.

"We're a few degrees off kilter." He studied his instruments. "Looks like the starboard landing gear is bent."

Will rose from his seat. On the onboard monitors dozens of *nephilim* surrounded the ship. Will closed his eyes and sighed. "So much for stealth."

He followed as Chris and Kemuel hurried to inspect the orb. As Chris had feared, it had slipped out of alignment, and the lasers had scorched the mounts around the stones that stimulated thrust.

Chris looked like he might cry. He turned away and threw his arms down. "That's it. *Snowman* is useless now."

Will decided to pray for everyone to hear this time. "Father, we really need Your help right now." Then he noticed the stone at the end of the cylinder glowed brightly.

Kemuel leaned in for a closer look. "Wait a minute."

Will leaned in with him. "I saw it glow like that in the tower."

Kemuel brightened. "When it was in the presence of the other orb."

"But we saw the Guardians take the first one into the future. Could something have gone wrong?"

"Your guess is as good as mine."

"So where is it?"

"Close."

The *nephilim* started to beat on the side of the ship. Will led them back to the bridge and contrived a plan as quickly as he could. He was about to share it when the side hatch opened.

It caught Will completely off guard.

Chris's mouth hung open, his eyes wide. "But that's impossible."

Sheddim streamed onto the bridge and pulled them out one-by-one. Only Joel managed to slip back unnoticed.

Will, Chris, and Kemuel stood outside, their hands behind their heads. The *sheddim* had weapons drawn but didn't seem to know what to do with their prisoners.

A rousing speech echoed from the Great Hall, punctuated by enthusiastic cheers. Will looked up at the open hatch. *We have to draw attention away.* He slowly moved toward the stern of the ship. The hatch quietly closed from the inside.

A *sheddih* noticed and objected. Then a hooded man climbed to the hatch and entered a code into the keypad. An electronic squawk indicated failure. Will strained to see the stranger's face but couldn't see into the hood. The stranger tried the code again unsuccessfully and pounded the hull with his fist.

Will wanted to tackle him and pull off that annoying hood, but he was grateful that Joel managed to override the keypad. He stared at Chris.

Chris winked and whispered. "Kemuel thought this might happen, so I showed Joel a few tricks while you were asleep." Suddenly Chris jumped up, gained a foothold on the ship, and pushed himself onto the wing. He sprinted to the tail and taunted the *nephilim* below. "Come and get me."

Heavily armed, the *nephilim* didn't look like they felt much like climbing. They ran around the tail of the ship and stood below with their weapons drawn. They herded Will and Kemuel along with them.

The hooded man jumped from the ladder to the ground, walked behind the ship to Will, and pulled a pistol from inside his robe. His voice was raspy and menacing. "Open the hatch now."

Chris shouted louder from atop the ship's tail, and the hooded man turned to look.

His hands still behind his head, Will subtly got Kemuel's attention and gestured with his eyes to move as far to one side as the armed *sheddim* would allow.

Chris kept shouting his taunts. "Over here. You're getting warmer. Warmer." Dozens of *sheddim* and a few *overlords* gathered below him.

The hooded man turned back to Will and Kemuel. They moved slowly to the side.

A *sheddih* drew a spear back and prepared to throw it at Chris. Chris's eyes went wide. He hollered and stomped his feet on the hull twice, "Now you're getting really hot."

The ship's computer voice spoke in Will's earpiece. "Test sequence activated."

Something popped, and a whining noise rose quickly in pitch. Chris covered his ears and jumped forward on the hull. Will pulled Kemuel to the ground, and the hooded man dove under the ship's tail just as jet-hot flame burst from the thruster cones and incinerated the crowd behind them. The thruster roar nearly drowned out the *sheddim's* screams. The blast forced the gun from their captor's hand, and it slid across the ground.

In the confusion, Will jumped to his feet, grabbed the gun, and sprinted from the citadel. He tapped his earpiece. "Kemuel, join Chris and get in the side airlock over the wing."

The courtyard was deserted, so he ran straight for the stairs and bolted to the top of the wall. Once there, he removed the magazine from the pistol, checked the ammunition, and found to his surprise that the chamber was clear. *That was naïve of him.* Satisfied, he reinserted the magazine, chambered a round, and looked down the passageway.

He ducked and ran until he reached the boundary where the other passage split off along the front of the citadel. He carefully checked around the corner, ran past, and peeked over the wall into the antechamber.

He cursed under his breath. A *sheddih* forced Chris off the wing to join Kemuel, who again stood with his hands behind his head. The hooded stranger ignored the locked hatch, climbed onto the wing, opened the side airlock instead, and led a pair of *sheddim* inside.

Will sat on the floor, touched his earpiece, and whispered. "Joel, they're coming in."

Joel's whisper came through the earpiece. "Got it." Then he spoke full voice and left his mike hot. "So why don't you pull down that hood and let me see you?"

The stranger's voice was barely audible over the comm link. "Good. You have the second orb, but I see you haven't taken good care of it. Pull it out and bring it." He sounded pleased with himself. "Your arrival is quite fortuitous for me. I just provided the first orb to Semyaza and warned him that the coming catastrophe is quite real. I've also informed him that the earth in the twenty-first century is ripe for conquest. I thought I would have to return to the future with the *nephilim*, but now with your orb, I can escape to the time and place of my own liking. Now open the hatch."

Will stood and peered over the wall. Joel opened the main hatch, lowered the ladder, and carried the broken device down to a company of *sheddim* soldiers while the two *sheddim* with the hooded stranger kept their swords pointed at him. The stranger shouted orders to the company of soldiers. "Hold these two here and await Adrok's orders." He turned to the two *sheddim* accompanying him. "See to it he carries the orb with me into the Great Hall."

Will ducked down and searched in vain for options. He looked at the handgun. *Fifteen bullets against a hundred thousand nephilim.*

He heard Kat's voice down the passageway. He looked in her direction, peered over the wall, and ducked again. Then he steeled his countenance, raised the gun with both hands, and crept toward the ornate balcony chamber he had seen seventeen years before, give or take six centuries.

CHAPTER 25

Will approached the balcony chamber. The *nephilim* speech echoed from the Great Hall.

"Nearly twelve hundred years ago our fathers landed on Mount Hermon and ushered in the Nephilim Empire." The crowd cheered. "We have waged war on the humans the enemy created to bear His image." Another cheer. "The image-bearers who followed the enemy thought they could stand in our way, but we have wiped them off the face of the earth. Now they are gone, and we will soon complete the dream of our fathers to destroy all the enemy's image-bearers and replace them with our kind. Some say our fathers have been cursed and can never return to the heavenlies, but I tell you this is a lie. They still have friends, other Watchers waiting to rise up with them." The speaker shouted at the top of his lungs. "Even now our fathers are gathering on the Holy Mount Taneen Sharr, planning the next stage of our rule. Only a short time longer, and we will achieve paradise on Earth. Then our fathers will march on the heavenlies and take the throne for themselves. Heaven will be theirs! Earth will be ours! Forever!"

The final cheer shook the citadel. Will peered into the balcony chamber. Kat sat gagged and bound to a chair in the center. Dozens of prize weapons were mounted on the wall. He secured the gun in a flight suit pocket, grabbed a knife, and ran to her. After he cut her loose and removed her gag, he knelt in front of her, set the knife down, gently swept her hair back, and held her head in his hands. He stared into her eyes. "Are you okay?"

She nodded, kissed him, and threw her arms around him.

Will held her for a moment, then helped her to her feet, picked up the knife in one hand, pulled the gun from his pocket with the other, and hurried to the balcony railing. He gestured for her to follow. "Someone has Joel."

They looked over the side. The hooded stranger and his *sheddim* escort marched Joel through the throng of *nephilim* to the front of the auditorium.

The *overlord* at the front of the auditorium saw them approach. "Make way for the Gatekeeper." The *nephilim* mob parted. A broad aisle formed for them to walk down.

The *overlord* continued. "The enemy prophesied one-hundred-twenty-years ago today that our world would be destroyed, and I say, let Him destroy it."

This time the crowd was silent.

The *overlord* broadened his stance. "We know of a time where more than seven billion humans wait for us to enslave them, and now, we have the power to do it." He gestured toward the first cylindrical device, which rested on an ornate mount on the altar. "If today's world is to be destroyed, then we will establish our Holy Empire in the future." The applause was thunderous.

The hooded man stepped onto the platform while one of the *sheddim* pulled Joel to one side and restrained him from behind.

The hooded man reached to the first device, placed a hand on it, lifted his other hand, and opened a portal above the altar. Awed silence filled the room as a company of armed nephilim marched up to the altar in lock step and prepared to go through. Each step of the marching army echoed off the walls until a final, louder stomp punctuated their halt.

Will stared into the portal. He could just make out a city skyline. *Whatever we're gonna do, we've gotta act fast.*

He tapped his earpiece. "Joel, I have your mother, and we can see you. Are you okay?"

Joel's voice responded quietly in Will's ear. "So far. Our evil monk has me at the front of the Great Hall."

Will looked along the railing to find access to the platform below. The stairway he had used centuries before was gone. "We know. I'll come for you, Son...."

"Dad, I see the first device. It's right here."

Something yelled from behind. Will spun. Two *sheddim* closed on him fast. He fired two quick shots into their chests. As they fell, a third *sheddih* swung the blunt end of his spear and knocked the gun from Will's hand. Kat dove for the gun. Will jumped forward and plunged his knife into the *sheddih's* heart. He saw Adrok over the *sheddih's* shoulder.

The gun. Get the gun. Will spun toward the pistol. Kat's hand was inches away from it.

Adrok ran for the gun, grabbed it by the barrel, tackled Kat to the floor, and charged for Will. Will crouched and raised his arms. It didn't help. Adrok tackled him hard and landed on top of him. Will slammed to the floor and grunted. Adrok pulled him up by the collar, grabbed a shoulder, spun him, and placed his arm around

Will's neck. Will's feet hung above the floor. He grabbed the *overlord's* leather-clad arm and struggled to breathe.

Kat stood slowly, her hands in the air.

Adrok held the gun in his free hand in front of Will and analyzed it carefully. His oversized finger wouldn't fit through the trigger guard opening, so he placed the end of his finger against the trigger. "Not a very elegant weapon. Where's the honor in killing from such a distance?" He pressed the end of the barrel into Will's head. "I prefer to be very close when I kill."

Despite the pressure Adrok kept on Will's neck he managed two words: "Kat, run."

Adrok shouted bitterly. "Run and I'll kill him now. Now get over here so you can see."

Kat walked slowly to the balcony railing, her hands still raised.

Adrok turned to give Will a view in both directions. He laughed with perverse satisfaction. "This has turned out better than I could have planned, human. Now you can watch your son and your crew die before I kill you and take the woman."

Will struggled to look at the front of the auditorium. The hooded stranger walked in front of the altar, took a dagger from one of the *sheddim,* and pointed it at Joel's neck. His voice rang in Will's earpiece. "Now give me the orb."

The *sheddih* guard pushed a spearhead against Joel's back. Joel slowly handed the damaged cylinder to the stranger.

The company of *nephilim* started to march through the portal in columns of five. A cacophony of march steps, screams, car horns, tires screeching, and gunfire echoed from the portal.

The stranger's voice rang in Will's earpiece again as he pressed the knife into Joel's neck. "Now, my boy..."

Joel's voice seethed with indignation. "I'm not a boy."

"And just who told you that?"

"The man best qualified to. My father."

"Well, boy or not, my orders are to kill you."

Anguish surged into Will's throat. *Please God, not my son.*

Adrok forced Will to look over the back wall of the Great Hall into the antechamber. Chris and Kemuel were on their knees near the ship. Two *nephilim* behind them lifted swords to behead them.

Every adrenalin-charged heartbeat shook Will's whole body. *Father, there has to be something I can do. But what? Father?*

He looked back at Joel, who stared at the hooded stranger with steely courage, the stranger's knife still pressed into his throat. A wave of peace swept over Will. *Father, whatever happens, I trust you. Please deliver my family home to you safely.*

The top of Mount Sharr exploded on the horizon. A meteoric arch of sparks and molten rocks spewed over the canyon. Thunder shook the auditorium. A second blast cracked the floor of the Great Hall across its center. A bright beam of light shone up from the mountain, and bolts of lightning struck from a point in the sky to the peak.

Near the altar, Joel slipped from the *nephilim's* arms, slapped the knife from the hooded man's hands and punched him square in the jaw. The hooded man slumped to the ground.

The altar lurched and knocked everyone on it to the ground. A fissure opened in front of the platform. Several columns of the *nephilim* fell in and screamed in terror. The hooded man crawled away from the fissure. Joel scrambled on all fours along the base of the altar. He ducked around the corner just as the hooded man found the knife and stood.

The ground under the whole citadel shook, and the crack across the auditorium opened into another fissure. Panicked *nephilim* screamed and ran in every direction. Adrok, inexperienced with firearms, lifted the pistol from Will's head.

Will lifted his feet and pushed off the balcony railing. Kat tackled Adrok from behind his legs. Adrok's knees buckled, and he fell to the ground with a grunt. The gun slid across the shaking marble floor. Will freed himself from Adrok's grip and dove for the gun. A crack formed under him. The marble balcony split and stopped him short of the gun. The crack stretched across the floor, and the railing behind Will began to fall.

Will reached back for Kat. She sprinted forward to grab his hand, but the end of the balcony crashed to the amphitheater below. The floor under Kat sloped steeply, and she slid away to the floor below. Will grasped the level floor in front of him with flat palms as his legs hung over the crack. "Kat, get to the ship." He saw the gun in front of him, swung his legs over and struggled to his feet. Adrok kicked it over the edge and pointed his sword at Will.

The metal on stone scraping told Will the gun had slid far from his reach. He ran for the wall, pulled down another sword, and pointed it at Adrok. The earth still shook beneath them as they circled each other. Adrok lunged. Will met the blade with his own and diverted it away while stepping to the side. Adrok moved with his thrust, spun, and swung hard. Will blocked, but the *overlord's* sheer strength knocked him to the floor. He leapt back to his feet just in time for the point of

Adrok's blade to press into his neck. Will froze and held his sword out to his right, unwilling to drop it. The panicked *nephilim* behind Adrok leapt over the widening crack and stampeded from the auditorium. Will glanced at Joel, still crouched at the end of the crumbling altar.

Adrok pushed the sword harder into Will's neck. Will refused to give him the satisfaction of fear.

Adrok smiled arrogantly. "I'm going to enjoy this... human. Now you're going to die alone."

Will glared into Adrok's eyes. "I'm never alone."

A loud crack echoed through the chamber. Adrok's eyes went wide. Then another crack, and Adrok struggled to draw breath. He dropped his sword, grabbed his neck, gasped for air, and fell to his knees. Behind him, Kat perched on a crumbling balcony over the auditorium entrance, the handgun aimed squarely at the *overlord's* back.

Adrok choked out his last threat. "I'll haunt you."

Will grasped his sword with both hands and swung hard. Adrok's head toppled and rolled away. His body fell limp to the floor.

Will shouted to Kat and pointed. "You get to the ship. I'll get Joel."

She looked at Joel and at the stampede below. She nodded to Will and disappeared just before her balcony crashed to the floor.

Will ran along what was left of the balcony and stopped where it overlooked the platform. He looked at the end of the altar but couldn't see his son. "Joel, can you hear me?"

Cracks of gunfire echoed from outside the Great Hall in the antechamber.

Joel jumped onto the altar from behind. "Right here, Dad." He snatched the first device from its mount. The portal closed instantly. He dove to one side to avoid an *overlord* running toward him, and the altar cracked in two. It sent the *overlord* tumbling into the opening. Joel jumped to the platform below.

Will shouted and gestured down. "Joel, climb the tapestry up to here."

Joel looked up at Will and ran toward him. Before he reached the wall, the end of the platform crumbled, fell, and opened a wide gap between them. He kept the device clutched tightly against his chest and looked for a way around. The fissure in front of the platform was impassable. Two *overlords* crossed the platform from behind him.

Will reached down, grabbed one of the long tapestries, ran farther along the balcony, and streamed the cloth through his grasp. Then he stepped over the balcony railing, pulled the tapestry taught like a rope, and pushed off. He swung down with his feet raised, kicked the *overlords* into the fissure, and dropped onto the platform. He kept a tight hold onto the cloth. "Grab this, swing over to the wall, and climb up."

Joel handed Will the device and grasped the cloth. The balcony above them crumbled and collapsed, and the top end of the cloth fell loose below them. Joel let it fall into the fissure as it deepened around them.

The platform cracked again, and the end where they stood listed toward the crevasse that had opened below. They jumped across the crack back toward the center just as the end collapsed.

The platform on each side had fallen away. They were stranded. On another isolated section at the far end of the platform, the hooded man watched the destruction around him, the damaged device still clutched in his arms. He glared at Will and Joel in the distance for a moment before he raised his hand and opened a smaller portal with the damaged orb. He walked through, and a few moments later, the portal disappeared behind him.

Will shook with adrenalin and scrutinized the device in his hands. *There has to be a way to use this to escape, but how?* He put one arm around Joel and pulled him to his chest. Together they looked into the chasm below as the citadel crumbled around them.

Then a deafening roar filled the chamber. *Chronos* rose above the antechamber and hovered into the Great Hall. Flying without *Snowman,* its thrusters created a storm of debris that spun in its turbulent wake.

Will and Joel shouted together. Joel raised a fist into the air.

Kat's welcome voice rang in their earpieces. "Need a lift?"

Kemuel lowered the ladder from the open hatch as Kat carefully maneuvered the ship next to them. Joel grabbed the ladder and reached up to allow Kemuel to pull him in quickly. Will jumped onto the ladder just as the platform below fell away. He carefully handed the device up to Kemuel before he pulled himself in.

Will turned to close the hatch. The amphitheater below crumbled and fell into the broad, endless crevasse. The seismic rumble gave way to a deep, growing roar.

Will slammed the hatch shut, leapt into his seat, and strapped in. "Kat, fly west fast. Chris, install the device now. Joel, Kemuel, strap yourselves in."

Kat turned the ship, leaned it forward, and pulled hard up and away while Chris struggled back with the device. In the monitors around them, they watched the citadel and the rest of the city fall into the growing, bottomless canyon as humans and *nephilim* ran in vain for safety.

Will activated a nearby control. "Retracting landing gear." A shrill beep announced failure. He tried again to no avail. "I was afraid of this. Our starboard landing gear won't retract. It must have been too severely damaged when we landed hard in the citadel."

An intermittent telemetry alarm sounded. They turned to the monitor display of the satellite's view of the earth. A flashing zone of red revealed that the crevasse had stretched thousands of kilometers north and south.

Kemuel's voice shook. "The earth's crust is cracking, and it's about to release the pressurized water underneath. Mount Sharr's about to become part of the Pacific Basin."

Will turned to Kat. "We need more speed. Level us off for aerodynamic flight. Chris, brace for acceleration."

Chris responded in their earpieces. "Aye, sir."

Kat pulled back on the cyclic to level the ship, and Will engaged the main thrusters. The force pushed them hard into their seats. The turbulence from the lowered landing gear shook the ship violently with the increased speed.

Will shouted over the din. "We can't go supersonic or launch into space with the landing gear down. See what you can do."

Kat nodded, released her harness, and ran aft. She hollered to Kemuel on the way by. "You're with me."

Kemuel unstrapped his harness as the intermittent telemetry alarm changed to a loud, sustained beep. "Here it comes."

In the monitor view behind, the entire horizon erupted in a cataclysmic explosion of water and rock. The wall of water and mountain-sized projectiles soared into space. Massive boulders hurtled overhead and crashed around the ship.

Will craned his neck back and forth to see the barrage of rocks in the monitors around him and pulled the ship in abrupt, hard turns to avoid them.

He heard thumps and grunts from Kat, Chris, and Kemuel. He could only imagine what they were going through in the back. Joel clutched the arms of his seat and grunted with each high-G turn.

The storm of boulders subsided, and Will held their course until they were out of immediate danger. He studied the monitors and breathed a sigh of relief. Joel was breathing hard and looked ready to throw up. Will couldn't blame him.

Will watched the tall, endless wall of water in the distance behind them and furrowed his brow. It appeared to be subsiding. Another telemetry alarm drew his attention to the satellite view. A long, gaping hole from north to south had been blown out of the earth, and as the exploding water below that region depleted, the earth's crust on each side collapsed.

Will turned from the satellite display to the reverse view. The explosion of water and rock stopped, and the entire horizon plummeted out of view. It pulled the earth's surface, and everything on it, into the chasm like cloth pulled off a table.

Will magnified the view. Buildings, trees, *nephilim,* and people swept helplessly into the chasm. Another telemetry alarm sounded with a flashing label, "Infrared sensor warning." It didn't take Will long to figure out the earth's collapsing crust pierced the mantle. The horizon exploded with lava, black smoke, and steam, followed by another surge from the subterranean sea. Now instead of rocketing into space, a deluge swept over the sinking crust as it collapsed into the fissure.

A mass of mud and debris swept across the earth behind the ship, high above them. Will saw it in the monitor and gasped. He pulled up hard to increase their altitude, and the deluge swept below. It buried everyone and everything in its path. Will heaved another deep sigh. "Chris, Kat, what's our status?"

"Chris here. I've installed the orb, but I still need to align it."

"Kat here. No luck yet." Her comm stayed active as she shouted. "Kemuel, find the mining supplies and bring me the det cord, fast."

Kemuel's voice came through a moment later. "Here it is."

Will steadily increased their altitude. "Kemuel, should we wait until we get to the opposite side of the earth before we launch into space?"

Kemuel grunted from whatever he was struggling to do in the back. "Not a good idea. The Atlantic Basin will be opening next."

The telemetry alarm drew Will's attention to the satellite view again. The Earth's broken crust slid across what remained of the subterranean sea below from both sides of the fissure and collapsed into the chasm that had been blown away, even as the water rushed over the surface. The resulting tension pulled the crust apart on the opposite side of the earth, ripped another fissure from north to south, and released the pressure below.

Another wall of water and debris erupted from the earth and blew a hypersonic explosion of mountain-sized meteors into space. Will turned to Joel, who stared at the satellite display in awe.

Kat yelled in Will's earpiece. "Fire in the hole."

A loud boom rocked the ship. The turbulence subsided. Indicators went green to confirm the landing gear compartment had successfully sealed shut.

A few moments later, Kat and Kemuel returned to their seats on the bridge and secured their harnesses.

Kat turned to Will. "We no longer have our starboard landing gear, but the hull is sealed for launch."

Will nodded, increased throttle, and pulled up. "Chris, get it done fast."

Chris came back in Will's earpiece. "Sir, I'm almost there. I just need a few more…"

Kemuel interrupted. "Don't wait, sir. Get us up through the vapor canopy ASAP."

The urgency hit Will like a ton of bricks. *The floodgates of the heavens.* Another telemetry alarm sounded.

They watched the satellite view while Kemuel translated the imagery. "Much of the water that blasted into space is following a high-arc trajectory and returning to the earth frozen. The shower of ice and snow is condensing the layer of vapor above the atmosphere."

Joel pointed to one of the outside monitor displays. "Look."

Will turned. A sheet of torrential rain was closing in on them fast. He banked away from it and increased to full throttle. The ship roared, trembled, pushed them hard into their seats, and raced for space. Will stared at the monitors. They couldn't outrun the approaching deluge, but he gained precious time by turning away. Kat, Joel, and Kemuel clutched their armrests with wide eyes, but no one said a word.

Several minutes later, they collided with a wall of water from above and lurched forward hard in their harnesses. The engines growled against the resistance until they broke free, but another wall of water followed and hit them again. The roar of the engines and the impact of water on hull were deafening.

Kat held the arms of her seat to steady herself. She shouted over the din. "Is there any way to ride this out until it passes?"

Kemuel shook his head. "It'll be like this for forty days."

Will held them in their climb. *Please God, give us enough momentum.*

The displays around them filled with gray. Impact after impact struck the ship as they crashed through successive walls of falling water. A terse computer voice barely pierced through the noise, "Warning, maintain escape velocity." Will's gut tensed.

After what felt like an eternity the impacts diminished in intensity and they rose above the falling deluge into the condensing vapor above. They all cheered.

The view in the external monitors cleared, and for the first time they got a clear image of the moon. Thousands of meteors rocketed toward its pristine surface.

Labels and arrows flashed on the satellite display as the Earth's image continued to morph. Kemuel tried to explain. "The subterranean ocean in the region below Mount Sharr is depleting as the crust rolls over it and falls into the volcanic chasm. As the water below runs out, the crust is striking the mantle below and grinding to a halt."

Joel watched the display intently. "So the entire surface will fall in and become submerged?"

"Not exactly." Kemuel pointed. "See, the crust behind is still pushing along over the water that remains beneath it even as the deluge sweeps above it. It'll pile up like a train derailment."

"What's a train?"

Kemuel tightened his lips. "Later. The pileup will drive up the continental shelves and the mountain ranges."

Joel remained fixated on the display, and Will remembered that his son had only a vague idea what the future Earth would look like.

An alarm voice rang through the bridge. "Fuel level critical."

Will touched his earpiece. "Chris, what's your status?"

"We have basic time jump capability."

"What about thrust?"

"Not yet."

The computer voice interrupted. "Collision warning. Fifteen seconds to impact."

Will stared in the display at a spinning, mountain-sized meteor careening toward them. There was no way to avoid it. "Chris, we need to time-jump now."

"Ten seconds to impact."

Chris responded with frustration. "I'm not ready. We can only go one year."

"Five seconds to impact."

Kat grabbed the arms of her chair. Will tightened his grasp on the yoke. "Do it now, now, now."

Chris activated the laser system below, and the earth swung away.

CHAPTER 26

A few moments later, the earth swung back into view. Everything went quiet.

The satellite image darkened and lit up again, and a message flashed across the bottom: *Telemetry download initiated.*

They finally had a moment to survey the monitors in peace. Hundreds of long-tailed comets dotted the space around the earth.

Kemuel pointed. "Debris from the explosions will orbit the sun and fall back to Earth as meteorites for thousands of years. Now you know why there are so many icy comets and so much space dust in the solar system."

Kat looked thoughtful. "And the asteroids?"

"You've seen a Crookes Radiometer, right? A light mill?"

"Those glass globes with four, diamond-shaped fan blades inside, black on one side and white on the other?" Kat tilted her head as she thought. "The black sides of the blades absorb more light energy, causing them to spin."

"Exactly. The sun's energy exerts force on asteroids the same way. Those that aren't spinning or traveling too fast or too slow will settle into orbit and form what you know as the asteroid belt."

Kat blinked. "So they all used to be part of the Earth. Wow."

Joel pointed to the planet below. "Is that Earth?"

Will smiled. "Yes, Joel. That's the earth your mother and I know."

White cloud systems had formed, and familiar continents were emerging. Bodies of water were still unusually large as the runoff continued, and the polar icecaps were massively oversized.

Kemuel continued from his seat in the back. "The atmospheric pressure diminished by half in the cataclysm, causing a planet-wide drop in temperature. It's the same principle used in an air conditioner. Combined with the falling ice and snow, it led to what you call the Ice Age, but it will warm consistently over the coming millennia."

Chris emerged onto the bridge with a broad grin. "I've aligned the device. We have full capability, including thrust." He looked directly at Will. "I locked the compartment this time, just in case. I don't want another imp destroying this orb, too."

The telemetry alarm sounded again. A white-orange explosion burst in the external monitors to one side and lit up the horizon. The telemetry alarm silenced, and the satellite image faded instantly to black.

Chris checked readings at his console. "I think we just lost the satellite to a meteor collision. It's a miracle it survived the catastrophe for this long."

The computer voice shouted again. "Collision warning."

Will analyzed the radar image, then looked at the external monitors. Hundreds of red streaks pierced the earth's atmosphere. They started in the far distance but appeared to strike the atmosphere closer and closer to their position.

"Chris, we need to time jump again."

Chris gestured for Kemuel to join him.

The computer voice continued its warnings. "Impact in forty seconds."

Joel looked puzzled. "Is it really so bad?"

Kat turned to answer him. "Those meteorites will pierce right through us."

"Impact in thirty-five seconds."

Kemuel spoke to Chris. "No, no. Stop scraping across time like that. It takes too long. Use my configuration to open a portal."

"Impact in thirty seconds."

Chris entered calculations feverishly while Kemuel pointed and shouted observations.

Will turned to them. "Gentlemen?"

"Impact in twenty-five seconds."

Chris slapped a button on his console. The elliptical field formed around the ship.

"Impact in twenty seconds."

Energy shot from the elliptical field into a point of space and formed a small sphere that quickly expanded and formed a blue portal.

Kemuel shouted to Will. "You need to take us through."

Will engaged the throttle to activate the orb's thrust. It pushed the ship toward the portal.

Their speakers rang with static. A barely audible voice came through. "Time jump... seconds..."

The active radar alarm competed for attention. "Impact in fifteen seconds."

Chris looked at his console as communication links lit up. His face brightened with hope. "Ivory Tower, do you copy?"

Jamie's voice barely pierced through the static. "*Chronos One, this is Ivory Tower. Say that again?*"

"Impact in ten seconds."

A panel next to Chris burst open in a shower of sparks, and their forward thrust stopped. Chris looked back and forth at his readings. "No, no, no. We've lost the entire laser control system. *Snowman* is useless."

The portal began to shrink. Kat gasped.

Will slammed his controls back to conventional thrust and threw the throttle forward. The engines roared to life and pushed them hard into their seats.

"Impact in five seconds."

The computer voice announced a new problem. "Fuel depleted." The thrust again stopped, and the engines went silent.

The ship continued to drift toward the shrinking portal. Its nose penetrated it just as a meteorite struck the hull. A blinding flash of light filled the monitors and windows. The portal engulfed them and collapsed. Will and the others raised their arms to shield their eyes. Then the monitors and windows went dark and normal space reappeared.

Kemuel heaved a sigh. "We made it through."

Chris took in a tense breath. "Uhh, sir, somehow we gained a *lot* of momentum going through the portal, and..."

The computer voice interrupted, "Hull breach. Collision warning."

Kat pointed, "There's another ship."

Will shouted into his mike. "Unidentified ship, this is *Chronos One*. Collision warning. We have no power."

The speakers emitted static.

Chris announced from his station. "They're transmitting simultaneously on the same frequency. We're jamming each other."

The computer shouted again. "*Hull breach. Collision in ten seconds.... nine... eight...*" The other ship grew closer and closer.

Will let go of the yoke and shook his fists. "Unidentified ship, emergency, if you don't make evasive maneuvers..."

"*...six... five...*"

An ellipsoid of energy surrounded the other ship.

Will's eyes went wide. "It's us."

"*...four... three...*"

Kat grasped the arms of her chair. "It's gonna be close."

"*...two... one...*"

The other ship streaked away. Will breathed out a silent *whew* and wiped a bead of sweat from his brow. Then he stared at the earth. It grew steadily ahead of them.

He tried to alter their course, but his controls didn't respond. "Ivory Tower, this is *Chronos One*. We have no control."

Chris shouted from his station. "The meteorite collision pierced the hull. We're bleeding air. We've got less than an hour."

Will turned to face him. "It won't take us that long to reenter the earth's atmosphere. We need to change vector and orientation for reentry, but we're dead in the water. What can you give me?"

Chris ripped the fried panel open and analyzed the contents. "I don't know, sir. I'm at a loss."

Jamie's voice came back through the speakers. "*Chronos One*, this is Ivory Tower. What happened? How did you gain speed so quickly?"

Will stared at the earth ahead. "Our mission is complete, Ivory Tower." He looked back and forth. Flashes of red appeared in the windows and monitors. "We're entering the earth's atmosphere."

"*Chronos One,* you need to alter course five degrees and change orientation. Did you say you have no control?"

"Roger, Ivory Tower. We're working on that. Prepare for radio silence during reentry."

Will looked back toward Chris, who pored through a mass of fried wires and scratched his head. Kemuel dropped a hand from one ear, released his harness, and pushed himself into the ladder-way. Will could think of nothing to do but pray. *Father, I trust you, but did you bring us all this way just to burn up on reentry? We need another miracle.*

An alarm sounded at Chris's workstation. He abandoned the burnt circuit panel and stared at the display, incredulous. "That's impossible." Then the alarm silenced. Chris stared at his workstation without a word.

Will expected a report but got none. "What was it?"

"The airlock."

Something collided from below and heaved the ship up at least four Gs as the flashes of red grew brighter in the windows. Will tensed his gut and legs so his blood wouldn't rush from his head, but without benefit of a G-suit, he was losing the battle. He saw spots, and his vision started to tunnel. Then after about thirty seconds, the force stopped.

Will blinked, squinted, and shook his head. The spots faded, and his vision returned. He struggled to make sense of the readouts in front of him. The ship rumbled with turbulence, and the red flashes continued outside the window. He looked at the others. Joel had passed out cold. Chris had been caught off guard and slumped over his workstation. He moaned faintly. Only Kat remained fully conscious.

Will spoke to her as if asking a question. "The course change and reorientation are complete. We're reentering normally."

Kat shrugged as if to say, "Don't ask me."

A blue glow slowly replaced the orange flashes, and the increased wind resistance drove the ship's nose down. Soon, Will was able to pull them into unpowered aerodynamic flight, and their full sensation of gravity returned.

Jamie's worried voice echoed through the speakers. "*Chronos One,* this is Ivory Tower, do you copy?"

Will was already planning for their next challenge. "Ivory Tower, this is *Chronos One.* We read you five-by-five."

Dozens of exuberant cheers filled the background. Jamie's voice trembled with emotion. "Welcome back, *Chronos One.* Umm, we've analyzed your reentry vector, and you'll need to engage powered flight to reach the landing site."

Will checked his controls again. "Negative, Ivory Tower. I'm calling a flight emergency. We have no fuel, no... alternate thrust, and no landing gear. Only glide control surfaces."

A moment of silence followed. "Roger, *Chronos One.* Stand by."

Chris moaned again and sat up at his station.

"*Chronos One,* You've overshot Edwards, White Sands, and Houston. You'll need to land at Whiteman. We'll have them scramble emergency teams."

"Roger, Ivory Tower."

Chris had one hand on his head. "Did they say we're landing in Missouri?"

Kat stared at the useless landing gear control. "More like crash landing."

Chris blinked hard and resumed work at his station. "I'll bet when they included Whiteman Air Force Base on the list of shuttle landing sites they never expected it to be used."

Joel moaned and struggled to raise his head. Kat looked at him for a moment and then at Chris. "You're not kidding." She turned to Will. "Let's hope our landing isn't too spectacular. You know, as far as the world knows, we just took off yesterday."

Chris pecked in a few last keystrokes at his workstation. "Landing vector and coordinates are laid in for you, sir." He turned to Kat. "That's why we were supposed to return ninety days in the future. This will be tough for them to explain."

Soon they passed south of the remote bomber base in rural Missouri. Will leaned them into a long, soaring one hundred eighty degree turn and leveled them off in line with the runway. Chris trained an external view monitor on the flight line below and increased magnification. The tarmac came to life with dozens of emergency and support vehicles. A fire crew worked in the middle of the runway.

Will activated the flaps without success. He tried again and shook his head, his jaw tensed. "Flaps aren't deploying. I suppose we're lucky to have control surfaces. We're going in hot."

The runway grew visible in the distance in the unmagnified monitors. They could just see emergency crews clear away from a spot some distance down.

The controls grew sluggish, and the ship lumbered awkwardly back and forth. Will struggled to keep them centered on the runway. "Chris, what's happening?"

"We're losing power to the control surfaces."

Will spoke under his breath. *"Father God, please get us home."*

They approached ground, and the runway sped by below. Will nosed up as much as possible to reduce speed. Just before touchdown, he leveled the craft to make sure their path down the runway was a smooth skid instead of a destructive, deadly tumble.

Proximity to the ground gave them the clearest evidence of their breakneck speed. The speeding pavement beneath them was a grey-black blur.

Will grasped the yoke with tense knuckles. *I don't think I've ever touched down at this velocity.* His dying spacecraft pierced through the air and finally struck ground. Instead of the familiar yelp of rubber, the deafening screech of metal on concrete assaulted their ears and announced the touchdown. In their rear-view monitors, a shower of sparks erupted from the bottom of the fuselage and streamed behind like the plume of water jetting from a speedboat. The ship skidded and began to yaw left. Will held his breath. If they spun, they'd almost certainly flip and tumble, and there wasn't a chance they'd survive that at this speed. He slammed his right foot down on the rudder control with all his might. It had little effect.

Kat pounded a large button with her fist to deploy a parachute from the ship's tail. They watched it open on the monitor. It caught both air and the stream of sparks from the hull, but it worked. The ship yawed back to the right, nose forward, and the parachute helped them decelerate.

The hot friction of metal on concrete roared throughout the ship in a deafening, dying scream. The taut parachute, assaulted by the shower of bright orange sparks, began to melt and shake back and forth. The burn holes grew and rendered it less and less effective.

Will saw what the fire crew had been working on in the runway and announced it to the others. "Foam."

The ship plowed into the wall of foam and forced them hard into their harnesses. Bursts of white exploded up and covered the windows and monitor views. They emerged from the other side, their speed barely retarded. Will grimaced.

The parachute disintegrated into a useless trail of rope and melted canvas, and the screaming ship again yawed to the left, slid off the runway onto the grass, and gashed a wide, brown strip of dirt and mud into the earth. A panel below burst open with a shower of sparks, and the sphere of monitors went dark. The narrow windows became their only view outside.

Will held on as they lurched on the uneven soil, and he knew their course had devolved into a dangerous spin. Their speed finally diminished, and the roar subsided. Sliding backwards, *Chronos One* caught her tail on the ground, shuddered to a sudden halt, and forced Will and the others back into their seats hard. The ship's nose lifted several feet off the ground, hovered for just a moment, and fell back with a hollow boom. A ruptured hydraulic system burst in an abrupt and subsiding hiss, and *Chronos* heaved her final sigh, finally at rest, her nose pointed toward their point of touchdown several kilometers back. Will looked through the scratched windscreen at the trail of destruction they had left behind. A fleet of emergency vehicles approached in the distance with lights flashing.

After a moment, Will remembered to breathe again. He took in a deep breath, pried his fists off the yoke, and released his harness. He stood and surveyed his crew. Kat and Chris were silent and still. Joel clenched the armrests of his seat and trembled, his face pale. Will knelt and placed his hands on Joel's shoulders. Kat released her own harness, rose from her seat, and knelt next to Will.

Joel looked into Will's eyes, drew in a labored breath, and forced it out. "Dad?"

Will released Joel's harness for him. "Yes, son?"

"I don't think I like flying."

Chris burst out laughing. Kat laughed and wiped a tear.

Will pulled Joel to his chest and threw his arms around him. Then he reached to Kat, pulled her into the embrace, kissed both their cheeks, and held them tight. He prayed aloud with tight, moist eyes. "Thank you, Father. Thank you. Thank you." They stayed there silent for a long moment.

Chris burst the bubble. "What, don't I rate a hug?"

Will laughed, removed his hand from Joel's back just long enough to wipe his eyes, then furrowed his brow and looked down the ladder chute. "Where's Kemuel?"

Chris frowned and hurried aft. Within a few seconds, he shouted back. "He's not here."

Will didn't want to let go of his family. "What about the device?"

"The compartment was sealed. It's still there."

Kat's visible relief melted into concern. She pulled away from Will just enough to look into his eyes. "Everything we've seen will be classified, won't it?"

Will knew she was right. "Time travel has to be kept a secret. Besides, many people won't want the rest of the truth to get out. Heck, most people won't even want to hear the truth."

Kat pointed toward the hatch. "If we walk out there right now, the world will see how different we look, and they won't be able to suppress the truth."

"And they'll know about Joel. Are you ready for him to live in the limelight?"

Chris stepped onto the bridge. "Sir, *Snowman* is secure, so the choice is yours. What do you want to do?"

Kat added, "Yeah, how are we gonna control this situation?"

Will mustered half a grin. "We won't. We'll trust God." He held onto his wife and son and looked up. He had so much to thank God for.

Epilogue

They watched Kemuel sit down, exhausted.

The first man spoke with folded arms and an icy stare. "You were supposed to bring the second device."

Kemuel massaged his temples. "I know. I couldn't get to it at the end. Time was too short."

The second man's rebuke was clear but gentle. "Don't be so hard on him, Kadmiel. He's been through a lot." He looked compassionately out the window. "They'll have a tough time, you know."

Kadmiel softened, sighed and looked at his counterpart. "How so, Gemaliel?"

"They know the truth, and the world will hate them for it."

"Regardless, they can't be trusted with the second device. Now that we have confirmed its existence, we must take it."

Kemuel leaned forward. "It won't be easy. The Americans are very good at security."

Gemaliel smiled. "Good, we have a friend in America."

"Now we have more."

They gazed together out the window at the earth below.

wwwwwwwwww

He stepped from the shop with a blue-and-white globe in one hand and suitcase full of cash in the other. He looked back inside where the proprietor caressed the gold and precious stones that remained undamaged on the orb's empty, ruptured shell. The storeowner looked up and smiled broadly. "*Obrigado.*"

The man responded in perfect Portuguese. "*Aproveite!*"

After donning a handsome, gray suit and hat from another shop, he found his way to the ticket office. He smiled and passed a wad of bills through the hole in the window and watched the grinning agent pocket the extra cash then pass a ticket back through.

As he stepped through the door onto the field, a second man entered, breathless. "Excuse me, where is this ship going?" The agent looked annoyed.

The man shook his head and caught his breath. "Never mind. Will this be enough?" He passed a similar wad of cash through. The agent replied with a smile and the last ticket.

He hurried through the door. The first man was walking across the field toward the mooring tower. The second man followed and kept a wary eye on the first, except for the moment he threw a look of unhidden disdain at the swastikas on the tail of the *Graf Zeppelin* above.

The End

CPSIA information can be obtained
at www.ICGtesting.com
Printed in the USA
BVHW07s1234300718
523023BV00002B/85/P